LOOKING FOR GROUP

ALEXIS HALL

RIPTIDE
PUBLISHING

Riptide Publishing
PO Box 1537
Burnsville, NC 28714
www.riptidepublishing.com

Looking for Group
Copyright © 2016 by Alexis Hall

Cover art: Simoné, dreamarian.com
Editor: Sarah Lyons
Layout: L.C. Chase, lcchase.com/design.htm

ISBN: 978-1-62649-446-6

First edition
August, 2016

Also available in ebook:
ISBN: 978-1-62649-445-9

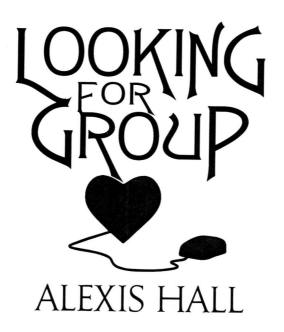

ALEXIS HALL

To all the friends I haven't met.

He makes a Secondary World which your mind can enter. Inside it, what he relates is "true": it accords with the laws of that world. You therefore believe it, while you are, as it were, inside.
— J.R.R. Tolkein, "On Fairy Stories"

Don't look so smug! I know what you're thinking, but Tempest Keep was merely a setback. Did you honestly believe I would trust the future to some blind, half–night elf mongrel?
— Kael'thas Sunstrider

TABLE OF CONTENTS

CHAPTER 1

<Same Crit Different Day> is Recruiting

SCDD is a tight-knit raiding guild (heroic and normal difficulty), currently looking for a main tank to join our mature, dedicated, and frankly fabulous team. Founded in 2011 by a group of friends with no fecking clue how to run a Heroes of Legend guild, but definite ideas about the right way to treat people—fairly, without harassment, and with equal opportunity to participate—SCDD roared past the traditional guild life expectancy of six months and has been getting awesomer ever since.

As a guild, we want . . .

> to have fun ffs
> to have a friendly community where everyone is treated
>   with respect and fairness
> to be damn good at what we do
> to maintain our server-wide reputation for kindness,
>   courtesy, and good old-fashioned arse kicking.

We promise . . .

- to organise and fill raids in an equitable and timely manner
- to recruit people, not specs, while also being sensible about guild and raid balance
- to have fair, transparent loot policies.

In return, we expect . . .

- **a team-based approach to the game:** When you have to make a choice, think of how it benefits the team, not only when it comes to loot and items, but also when it comes to your actions and attitude.

- **a mature approach to the guild:** Communicate, be honest, and be excellent to one another.
- **your best damn behaviour:** We're here to succeed and to have fun, not to put up with rudeness, bigotry, or other asshattery. This is not about political correctness gone mad. This is not about nobody having a sense of humour. This is not about censorship. This reflects the fact that our guild encompasses a diverse range of people, and being a dick isn't big, cool, or clever. And if you want to call me a carebear for that, then I don't give a damn.

Application: Orcarella (Dread Knight tank)
Name (optional): Drew
Tell us a bit about yourself: Just an ordinary guy, 19 yo, currently doing game art design (lol) at uni. I like doing ordinary shit, hanging out with mates, playing games, whatever.
Character Name: Orcarella
Character Race / Class: Orc, Dread Knight
Primary Spec: Vengeance (Tanking)
Secondary Spec: Dishonour (DPS / PVP)
Which professions do you have: Metal Working & Gem Crafting
What was your previous guild (if relevant) and why did you leave: K, look, everybody knows I was the main tank for Annihilation (server first guild) for like three years, and last night we downed heroic Vilicus in Crown of Thorns, for about the hundredth time, and the axe finally dropped—the TANKING axe—which is the last piece of 345 gear I've been freakin waiting for, for like ever, and so I roll on it and so does the freakin healer. The freakin healer. For his freakin offspec. And I'm like dude wtf and the guild leader is all like, oh yeah, we're trying to gear him up as a tank. And I'm not a loot whore but I think I should have been AT LEAST INFORMED, y'know.

Anyway, we both rolled, and he won the axe and I lost my shit, and I quit. But it's not about the axe. I mean it is about the axe, because that was my axe, but it was more than the axe. It's not like I mind gearing up guildies, but I was the MT, and I've been with that guild, every single raid night, for three years. And it was like it meant nothing. They wouldn't even give me a goddamn axe to make me better at doing the thing they have me around to do.

And then I realised I was losing my shit over an axe. A pixel axe. But seriously the thing never drops. I've run heroic CoT since the patch hit, waiting and yearning for that axe, and that's the first time I've ever seen it drop. The ranger bow drops every freakin time. It's like every ranger in the guild has one to wield and one to stick up his arse. But is there a tanking axe for Ella, is there bollocks.

And that was when I realised I must have stopped having fun in this game a long time ago. Because why else would I be like completely BROKEN over an axe. Enough to throw away three years of raiding. But Annihilation threw me away too. Over the same nothingy axe.

Tell us a bit about your raiding experience: Just look me up on the armoury. Been raiding with Anni since the first expansion.

How did you hear about <Same Crit Different Day>: I've seen you guys around and I checked the rankings and you seem to know what you're doing.

Why do you want to be in this guild: Just looking to have fun in the game again. I guess I want to be more casual, but at the same time I don't want to waste my time fannying around with a bunch of clueless noobs.

How would we benefit from recruiting you: Best tank on the server. Check my gearscore.

Do you know anyone in the guild: N

What aspects of the game are you most interested in: Raiding, PVP

Do you have a microphone, and are you able to connect to Mumble: Y

Have you read the guild rules and actually thought about them for more than two seconds: Y

Are you going to be racist, sexist, homophobic, or otherwise bigoted, offensive, or dickish in the name of lulz: N
Anything else you want to tell us? N

[Officer][Ialdir]: You know, if he had that axe, he'd be the best geared tank on the server ;)
[Officer][Heurodis]: I pugged w/ this guy once. he was an arrogant tosser like the rest of Anni
[Officer][Ialdir]: Yeah but you say that about everyone you pug with.
[Officer][Heurodis]: No I dont. sometimes I say they're shite
[Officer][Morag]: Not worried about his skillz, just his attitude.
[Officer][Heurodis]: What do you expect??? Hes 19
[Officer][Solace]: Um, I'm 19
[Officer][Ialdir]: Omg, /gkick Solace
[Officer][Morag]: Guild policy is 16+ so let's make this about his app not his age
[Officer][Ialdir]: I say we give him a chance. Unless he's an epic dick, we'd be mad to turn down a good tank
[Officer][Morag]: He pretty much admitted he ragequit his last guild over loot drama. I'm not sure that's a good sign
[Officer][Heurodis]: FWIW if I lost a good drop to someone's offspec Id be pretty fucking pissed. Specially if it was the healer.
[Officer][Solace]: Healers are people too.
[Officer][Ialdir]: Bjorn's healerist.
[Officer][Heurodis]: Hey, some of my best friends are healers

[Officer][Ialdir]: I rolled a healer once. I was young. I was just playing around.
[Officer][Solace]: And it was just a phase you were going through
[Officer][Heurodis]: lol
[Officer][Ialdir]: lol
[Officer][Morag]: Can we actually make a decision? I'm getting my nails done in 20.
[Officer][Ialdir]: scroll up, already said yes
[Officer][Heurodis]: yeah go on then.
[Officer][Morag]: Sol?
[Officer][Solace]: His app was okay, he obviously knows what he's doing, I say we take him.
[Officer][Morag]: You've talked me round. Let's take him. We can always kick him again if he's an arsewipe. Lemme whisper him.
To [Orcarella]: Hi Ella, got a moment to talk?
[Orcarella] whispers: sec
To [Orcarella]: kk
[Orcarella] whispers: Soz, was just pugging BL. Healer kept dying on Tolvus the Arachnomancer cos he kept standing on the webs
To [Orcarella]: If the healer dies, its the tanks fault :P
[Orcarella] whispers: you can't taunt fire
To [Orcarella]: lol anyhoo, still up for joining SCDD?
[Orcarella] whispers: y
/ginv Orcarella
Orcarella has joined the guild.
The Guild Message of the day is now: Welcome to our newest member, Orcarella. If you have questions, just axe.
[Guild][Morag]: Hi Ella

[Guild][Ialdir]: Yo
[Guild][Mordant]: Welcome
[Guild][Orcarella]: Hey all, thanks for the inv
[Guild][Dave]: Not another dread knight
[Guild][Morag]: This one's different, he's actually got a tank spec.
[Guild][Dave]: Hey I said id go vengeance if we needed it
[Guild][Heurodis]: Yeah but you were blatantly lying
[Guild][Dave]: DPS4EVA!!!1111
[Guild][Jargogle]: Didn't you used to run with Anni?
[Guild][Orcarella]: I um kinda ragequit
[Guild][Orcarella]: I think I just wasn't enjoying that sort of raiding anymore
[Guild][Orcarella]: and it was making me into somebody I didn't like
[Guild][Heurodis]: thats where you're going wrong. I try to be someone other people don't like
[Guild][Jargogle]: so you're slumming with us now?
[Guild][Solace]: I don't think that's fair, Magda.
[Guild][Jargogle]: I'm just asking the question
[Guild][Orcarella]: no, its cool. I looked into it and you guys are the most progressed casual guild on the server
[Guild][Ialdir]: wow we're flattered.
[Guild][Heurodis]: we should put that on the website
The Guild Message of the day is now: Welcome to the most progressed casual guild on the server!!

[Guild][Orcarella]: I think i'll just STFU
[Guild][Solace]: We're just teasing you. It's
how we show we care.
[Guild][Orcarella]: cool, anybody up for a
random heroic?
[Guild][Heurodis]: I'm maxed out for the day,
and it's not even noon. Bow before Bjorn,
king of grinding
[Guild][Orcarella]: *bows*
[Guild][Morag]: Don't. It only encourages
him.
**The Guild Message of the day is now: Welcome
to the most progressed casual guild on the
server!! New guild rule: don't encourage
Bjorn.**
[Guild][Morag]: Anyhoo, gtg, my nails need me
[Guild][Solace]: I'm up for that hc
[Guild][Ialdir]: Me too

Drew grabbed a Dr Pepper from the minifridge he technically
wasn't supposed to have in his room, sent a couple of invites to his new
guildies, and fired up the random dungeon finder.

[Group][Ialdir]: Please not Steamworks,
please not steamworks

A loading screen popped up. Drew recognised it straightaway
as the Steamworks Furnace. And then he found himself standing in
a long grey-brown hallway, metal rivets in the walls and a pair of equally
grey-brown, metal-riveted golems waiting patiently to be pwned.

A severe-looking high elf with long golden hair drawn into a
topknot appeared in the corridor. He was tricked out in ornate brown
and green leather with gold scroll work, tangles of briars running
down his arms and across his huge shoulder pads. Almost a complete
set of Tier 14. Nice. And he was wielding that damn bow from Vilicus.

[Group][Ialdir]: FML

An orcish assassin wearing a cobbled-together set of black leathers from the last patch spawned next.

```
[Group][Ialdir]: Yo
[Group][Orcarella]: hey
```

The assassin, obviously staying true to his mysterious profession, said nothing.

Next in was a dark elf chick with deep-brown skin and shock-white hair. She was striking and pretty, in a video game avatar kind of way. Drew liked to think he'd grown out of his fancying-imaginary-elves phase, but Solace had obviously put a lot of work into her look. She was wearing a full set of Tier 8, which, after a quick inspect, Drew was relieved to see was in the cosmetic slot, not the stat slot.

```
[Group][Orcarella]: Nice wings
[Group][Solace]: Thanks
[Group][Ialdir]: It took us weeks to farm
them
[Group][Solace]: A well-dressed priest is a
happy priest
```

She did a twirl, all white and gold and stirring feathers. Drew was really glad that the fancying-imaginary-elves phase was way behind him.

After a moment, he selected Solace and typed /whistle into his chat window, and Orcarella signalled her approval.

Then a human elementalist appeared and threw huge ball of fire at the golems. The assassin logged out instantly. Drew leapt into action.

```
[Group][Orcarella]: wwwwwwwws1111
```

He stared in dismay as his carefully executed keyboard commands, that had been intended to send Ella dashing forward to grab aggro on the mobs, instead popped up as a stream of gibberish in chat, making him look like a total noob in front of his new guildies.

Nice work, Drew. Hit return next time.

The golems were lumbering forward, heading straight for the elementalist, who was wearing nothing for armour and still cheerfully spamming fireballs like it was Guy Fawkes Night. Drew sighed, threw a Circle of Corruption under the monsters, and charged forward to draw their aggro. He hammered the keyboard, alternating threat-building strikes between the two golems. He was pleased to see a protective little halo surrounding his character, which meant Solace had her head in the game.

Arrows whistled past him, cutting into the golems' health. They were followed by a small owl Drew was pretty sure came from the high elf starting area. Even without the extra DPS, the golems went down pretty quickly.

```
[Group][Orcarella]: Don't pull without the
tank
```

Another fireball whooshed by and called the attention of two more golems and a purple-robed machine priest.

```
[Guild][Orcarella]: ffs
```

It was time for this guy to learn a life lesson.

Drew pulled his character back and typed */sit*. Next to him, Solace and Ialdir started dancing together. Typical of the game's animation, Solace writhed slinkily while Ialdir flailed around like a complete prat who was being electrocuted. Drew had typed */dance* on this character exactly once and instantly regretted it, but it was nowhere near as bad as the male high elves.

The elementalist was still throwing fire while two robots and a loony cultist beat on him with hammers. The moment he died, Drew threw down his CoC and leaped into the fray. This group fell over slightly more slowly, but not by much, cultist first, then robots.

Drew was starting to feel he'd made the right choice. The other two clearly knew what they were doing, and he was almost having fun, despite the failamentalist.

```
[Group][Burnzurfais]: ffs
[Group][Orcarella]: Don't pull for me
[Group][Burnzurfais]: y no healz
[Group][Solace]: Because you pulled without
the tank
[Group][Burnzurfais]: u suk
```

Solace resurrected the tragically fallen Burnzurfais. Somehow, even the guy's avatar looked sulky.

```
[Group][Burnzurfais]: buff me
[Guild][Ialdir]: Guys, I think we've found a
potential new recruit.
[Guild][Solace]: He's a real prince.
[Guild][Orcarella]: lol
```

They took down the next pack with no problems, and then the corridor opened out into a wide, circular ring. In the middle, streams of lava converged and flowed into the furnace beneath. The first time Drew had seen it, he'd thought it was pretty majestic. The twelfth time, he'd just wished the whole place was smaller. This was well more than the twelfth time.

There were three bands of golems and cultists patrolling the rim. Once, he'd hit on the cunning notion of knocking them all over the edge with his Ruthless Surge, but they'd gathered at the bottom and come slowly back up, bringing the entire dungeon with them. He'd found it kind of hilarious, but his guildies at the time had been furious.

To give Burnzurfais due credit, he somehow managed to avoid throwing fire at them until Drew had put down his circle and charged into the first group. It was all going pretty smoothly until three extra burning robots lumbered over from the other side of the room.

Drew gave the guy the benefit of the doubt. Maybe he'd just had a tabbing accident. *Happens to the best of us.* He strafed awkwardly over to intercept, just in time to see the elementalist hurl a fireball at the final group and then wrap himself in a cloud of mist, leaving them to run straight for Solace.

Shit had just got serious.

Circle of Corruption was still on cooldown, and he only had two taunts. He dashed across the room, just as Ialdir trapped a cultist with a bolas. But that left seven mobs still standing, and he was pretty sure some of them were healers and some of the others were firing rockets more or less at random.

At that moment, one of the golems lost interest in Orcarella and started pounding on Ialdir, while Burnzurfais went back to spamming the one spell he knew how to cast, standing in a puddle of flaming oil that was quickly eating his health bar.

```
[Group][Solace]: Don't stand in fire
[Group][Burnzurfais]: healz
[Group][Burnzurfais]: healz!!!!11
```

He died.

```
[Group][Burnzurfais]: y no healz
```

Drew's taunt came off cooldown, and he yanked the golem away from Ialdir just in time for the bolas to drop and the final cultist to take it personally. Out of the corner of his eye, Drew saw Solace's health draining like pasta in a colander. Nipping between oil spills, she ran towards him, throwing HoTs, and he darted forward to meet her, unleashing Hail of Vengeance on everything around them. For a moment, he couldn't see their avatars for giant robots and particle effects, as if they were standing together at the centre of a storm.

They took out a couple more golems before the damage and the chaos got too much for them and Ialdir took the wrong end of a rocket blast.

```
[Group][Ialdir]: You can do it guys, only
four left!!
```

Drew was sweating slightly as he mashed his rotation. It wouldn't really be his fault if they wiped, but he was the best geared tank on the server and he didn't want to be dragged down by some mouth-breathing pillock with an RP-inappropriate name.

Also Solace was kind of depending on him. And the healer wasn't dying on his watch.

His health dipped, and he threw up Wall of Blades as one more cultist keeled over.

```
[Group][Ialdir]: *waves pompoms*
```

Solace's mana wasn't looking great and, in his Vengeance spec, Drew's damage output was pretty low. This was the point where all the graphics and all the sound effects and all the story just went away, and it became a game of blue bars and red bars and which of them hit zero first.

Another golem down. Two left, both on half health.

Then one.

```
[Group][Solace]: oom
```

Drew's health ticked away. Ten percent. Five percent. His vampiric aura was giving him a slow trickle of healing, but it was nowhere near enough. The golem was dying too, but not quite as quickly.

And, at last, Orcarella collapsed to the floor and the golem, a last sliver of red clinging mockingly to the bottom of its health bar, turned to Solace.

Drew hated this bit. Not his fault but, damn, it felt like it.

```
[Group][Orcarella]: Sorry guys
[Group][Burnzurfais]: fucking noobs
```

Solace was kiting for all she was worth, but she had no health and no mana and she probably wouldn't last another five seconds. The golem slammed its fist down. Then there was a rush of purple light and Solace was standing over the machine's broken body.

```
[Group][Solace]: omg i cant believe that
worked
[Group][Ialdir]: GJ guys
[Group][Orcarella]: wtf was that
```

[Group][Solace]: Dark elf racial.
[Lifesteal]. Hee. I've never used it before.
[Group][Ialdir]: That used to be really OP
back in the day.
[Group][Solace]: Back when all this was grass
[Group][Solace]: When you had to farm for
mats uphill both ways in the snow
[Group][Ialdir]: And you had to respect your
elders
[Group][Burnzurfais]: rez
[Group][Solace]: Sec, need to mana up. Just
sipping on my [Fermented Cave Mould]. Mmmm.
[Group][Ialdir]: Better than the [Brackish
Sump Water] you were drinking in the last
expansion.
[Group][Solace]: Game developers hate
spellcasters.
[Group][Burnzurfais]: rez

Drew stared at his crumpled corpse, which was lying at a slightly awkward angle on the floor, his axe clipping through the foot of a fallen golem. Solace drifted between the bodies of her slain companions, swaying gracefully as she worked the magic that would call their spirits back from the netherworld. Magic that, as one of the Heroes of Legend, she would have learned long before she learned to ride a horse.

A window popped up on screen.

**Solace is trying to resurrect you: accept /
decline.**
[Group][Orcarella]: Thx
[Group][Burnzurfais]: rez

Solace moved to Ialdir and did her thing again.

[Group][Burnzurfais]: rez

Another window popped up.

```
Burnzurfais has initiated a vote-kick against
[Solace] Reason []. Yes/No.
The vote to kick Solace has failed.
[Group][Burnzurfais]: rez
[Group][Orcarella]: dude, why did you just
try to vote-kick the healer
[Group][Burnzurfais]: no healz
[Group][Ialdir]: if the tank dies, it's the
healer's fault, if the healer dies it's
the tank's fault . . .
[Group][Ialdir]: IF THE DPS DIES ITS BECAUSE
YOU PULLED A BUNCH OF MOBS THEN STOOD IN FIRE
[Group][Burnzurfais]: too slow
[Group][Solace]: Why, are you late for the
opera?
[Group][Burnzurfais]: i cud solo this on my
main
```

With what seemed to Drew like an air of visible reluctance, Solace resurrected Burnzurfais. Then she jogged to the centre of the room, where the streams of lava met and plunged down into the furnace below. She teetered on the edge for a moment, her silver wings shining in the red glow from the final boss waiting in the depths.

```
[Guild][Solace]: Woah, that nearly went
really badly wrong
[Guild][Dave]: Wut
[Guild][Solace]: I nearly fell down the
middle of the furnace
[Group][Burnzurfais]: go
[Guild][Dave]: I did that once
[Guild][Dave]: Had num lock on
```

Ialdir and his pet owl, which seemed to be called Small Mangy Owl, went to the ledge and sat down next to Solace.

[Guild][Heurodis]: Once I jumped down because
i was trying to show there was an invisible
wall and you couldnt fall off it
[Guild][Solace]: I know. I was there
[Guild][Heurodis]: I was getting mixed up
with the oubliette in FK back in vanilla
[Guild][Jargogle]: Oh, have you been playing
since vanilla, Bjorn? I didn't know because
you never mention it.
[Group][Burnzurfais]: gogogo
[Group][Solace]: I never get tired of this
view

It had been a while since Drew had even bothered looking at it.
He sent Ella to join the others and tilted his mouse so he could see
right down into the fiery chasm.

[Yell][The Forge Master]: MORE STEEL, MORE
FIRE, MORE SERVANTS FOR THE GREAT MACHINE!
[Group][Burnzurfais]: gogogo
[Group][Ialdir]: you'd think he'd have enough
servants by now
[Group][Solace]: I love how it's the Great
Machine. Like, how good is this machine?
Pretty great.
[Yell][Ialdir]: MORE STEEL, MORE FIRE, MORE
SERVANTS FOR THE ADEQUATE MACHINE
[Group][Orcarella]: lol
[Group][Solace]: Well you wouldn't want to
worship a machine with self-esteem issues
[Group][Burnzurfais]: what the fuk is wrong
with u fukin noobs
[Group][Solace]: Just taking time to smell
the lava
[Group][Burnzurfais]: ffs
[Group][Orcarella]: Ok, lets just finish this.
If we skip Gabraxis and Irontongue and go

```
straight to Pyrite we'll be done in about
20 mins.
[Group][Burnzurfais]: kk
[Guild][Solace]: But I like doing the
optionals. I don't feel I've had a good day
unless I've been impaled by Irontongue's
mighty shaft.
```

Ialdir ran around in circles, very nearly falling into the furnace.

```
[Yell][Ialdir]: IMPALED!!!
```

Drew's Dr Pepper was suddenly all over his keyboard.

```
[Group][Orcarella]: shit, sec
```

He cleaned up after himself, still grinning and not sure why this wasn't the worst dungeon run he'd been on in months. Then he settled back down, marshalled his merry band, and led them deeper into the furnace. The next few packs of mobs went down fairly smoothly. Burnzurfais was still bad at avoiding damage and worse at keeping quiet about it, but he'd stopped pulling and hadn't actually died again, so it seemed like they were making progress.

The party turned left into the rough-hewn cavern where Pyrite stood around waiting obligingly for adventurers to come and kill him. The entrance was swarming with tiny golden rocklings. Drew knew from experience that they exploded when they died. When the patch had first come out, you'd had to take them down one at a time so the damage didn't spike too much, but a tier and a half later, Orcarella had enough health to eat it twice over.

```
[Group][Orcarella]: r
[Group][Ialdir]: r
[Group][Solace]: r
```

He waited a second or two for Burnzurfais, who bounced about impatiently but didn't actually say anything in chat. Then he slapped down his Circle of Corruption and charged. The little rocks swarmed round, glittering and glinting as Ialdir's exploding arrows landed neatly amongst them.

Suddenly, Burnzurfais was standing right on top of Ella, lightning coruscating around his body. It was the one time Drew had seen him cast a spell that wasn't Fireball or Shroud of Mist.

The rocklings dropped dead with the precision of a synchronised swimming team, unleashing a massive chained explosion. Ella's health plummeted, stabilised, and then began to climb steadily.

Drew remembered to breathe.

Out of the corner of his eye, he saw a halo of golden light appear around Burnzurfais, which probably explained why he lasted three whole seconds before keeling over.

```
[Group][Burnzurfais]: ffs
[Guild][Ialdir]: is Mike around?
[Guild][Ignatius]: he's making me a sammich
[Guild][Ialdir]: is there any reason for a
fire ele to use that pb aoe lightning thingy
[Guild][Ignatius]: I'll ask
[Guild][Ialdir]: thanks Helen
```

Solace was standing over the perennially incapacitated Burnzurfais, slowly bringing him back to life.

```
[Guild][Heurodis]: there isnt
[Guild][Heurodis]: fire aoe rotation should be
fb to proc rof, then conflag til everythings
dead
[Guild][Ialdir]: do you even play an
elementalist
[Guild][Heurodis]: i had one back in RotU
before they got nerfed
[Group][Burnzurfais]: heal me
[Guild][Ignatius]: Mike says Eye of the Storm
is mostly a threat generator for the tanking
tree
```

```
[Guild][Ignatius]: fire normally waits until
Reign of Fire is up, then spams conflagration
[Group][Burnzurfais]: heal me
[Guild][Heurodis]: :D
[Guild][Jargogle]: I thought it was against
the rules to encourage Bjorn.
```
Ignatius has now been demoted to Guild Peon
```
[Guild][Ignatius]: hey, I was out the room,
doing you a favour, Jacob
```
Ignatius has now been promoted to Guild Mascot
```
[Group][Orcarella]: mb before boss?
[Group][Solace]: please
```

Solace curled up on the floor and began sipping what was probably a delicious mug of [Fermented Cave Mould].

```
[Group][Burnzurfais]: heal me
[Group][Ialdir]: Dude, you're an
elementalist.
[Group][Ialdir]: not only do you have your
own healing spells
[Group][Ialdir]: you can make your own food
for free
[Group][Burnzurfais]: is healers job to heal
[Group][Burnzurfais]: stupid ffn noob healer
```

Drew gave up, right-clicked Burnzurfais, and initiated a vote-kick.

Burnzurfais vanished.

```
[Group][Solace]: Thank you
[Group][Solace]: Sadly, I can't heal dickhead
[Group][Orcarella]: Want me to requeue?
[Group][Ialdir]: I think I'm done with
randoms for today
[Group][Solace]: We can three man
```

[Group][Solace]: And now Mr Likestodie has gone we can go back and down Irontongue too
[Group][Orcarella]: God do we have to?

Solace shuffled up so close to Orcarella that the sleeves of her robe were clipping through the dread knight's spiky armour, and performed a winsome little animation.

[Group][Solace]: Please?
[Group][Solace]: Please?
[Group][Solace]: Please?
[Group][Solace]: I'll heal you real good baby.

Drew was glad he was sitting on the other side of a chunky orc in a skull-shaped helmet because he thought he might be blushing.

[Yell][The Forge Master]: MORE STEEL, MORE FIRE, MORE SERVANTS FOR THE GREAT MACHINE!
[Group][Orcarella]: Well, since you put it that way.
[Group][Solace]: Yay

Solace boinged happily around the cavern, just out of reach of the towering rock giant.

[Group][Ialdir]: If you pull, we're letting you die
[Group][Solace]: gogogogogogogoggogogo
[Group][Orcarella]: sure we can do this?
[Group][Ialdir]: course we can, we're the most progressed casual guild on the server
[Group][Solace]: I've 3-manned this with Morag and Bjorn a bunch of times
[Group][Orcarella]: you must kick a lot of randoms
[Group][Solace]: No, no, we fly in the door

```
[Group][Ialdir]: Omg retro
[Group][Orcarella]: Um why
[Group][Solace]: It's fun
[Group][Ialdir]: Omg crazy
[Group][Ialdir]: Having fun in the game
[Group][Orcarella]: right, lets do this
[Group][Orcarella]: Ill turn him to face the
back wall
[Group][Orcarella]: Ialdir you're on
rocklings
[Group][Solace]: Let me switch to Glory
[Group][Solace]: It's got slightly better DPS
[Group][Ialdir]: You know what else is really
good DPS
[Group][Solace]: Bjorn
[Group][Ialdir]: *cries*
```

Drew carefully put what was left of his Dr Pepper out of harm's way. He caught a glimpse of the time on his minimap and realised they'd been in the instance for over half an hour. Normally, he could blitz this place in twenty minutes, and it still felt like forever.

And, shit, he was meant to be meeting his mates for the £5.95 lunch deal in the Slug and Lettuce down the road. Well, it was only the pub, he could be late. They'd take the piss, but, hey, what were friends for?

He checked his buffs, made sure Solace had mana, and ran straight for Pyrite's crotch, dropping CoC somewhere under his big toe. He strafed round, and Pyrite wheeled after him, waving huge rocky fists and paying no attention to the arrows thunking into his gold-encrusted arse. It was a pretty straightforward fight most of the time, and Ella had nothing to do except swing her maces at the boss's knees and occasionally get slammed on the head.

Now that Drew thought about it, tanking wasn't exactly a dignified role a lot of the time. He basically spent his evenings staring at a series of monstrous packages and being chewed on by irate minions. Unless it all went wrong, and then he was running around like a headless chicken right up to the point where he dropped dead.

But things were a bit more tense with only three. Every so often, Pyrite would stop and encase a member of the party in something called Fool's Gold, and they had to be broken out by the DPS. Since Ialdir was the only one there who could do anything remotely approaching damage and Drew had to keep the boss against the wall in case his cone attack squished the whole party, sometimes it was up to Solace to smash Ialdir out of a rocky prison. Which was bad for Ella's health and Drew's nerves.

But the most progressed casual guild on the server triumphed in the end, and Pyrite slowly collapsed into a pile of rubble, dropping a pair of bracers that would have been useful a tier ago and a set of spiked knuckles nobody had ever wanted.

```
[Group][Ialdir]: GJ team
```

Solace ran past him, jumped into the giant's body, and vanished.

```
[Group][Solace]: Weeeee
[Group][Ialdir]: That looks so wrong
[Group][Solace]: You don't know what I'm
doing in here
[Group][Ialdir]: Please exit the boss corpse
in a calm and orderly fashion
[Group][Orcarella]: Does she always do that
[Group][Ialdir]: Not always
```

Pyrite's remains vanished to reveal Solace doing her slinky dance. At his keyboard, Drew sighed and shook his head, but he was smiling.

```
[Yell][The Forge Master]: MORE STEEL, MORE
FIRE, MORE SERVANTS FOR THE GREAT MACHINE!
[Group][Solace]: Still no rockling
[Group][Solace]: *cries*
[Group][Orcarella]: ?
[Group][Ialdir]: Pyrite has a really low
chance to drop a [Baby Pyrite Rockling] and
Solace has wanted it forever
```

```
[Group][Solace]: It's the same model as the
[Diminutive Ruby Golem] which is sooooo cute
[Group][Solace]: But nobody makes them
anymore because it's so fiddly to unlock the
recipe
[Group][Orcarella]: how come
[Group][Ialdir]: It drops from a hidden boss
in Magmarion's Caverns. You need to do the
whole raid in a special order
[Group][Ialdir]: And then activate the
[Bejewelled Music Box] you got from the
attunement quest
[Group][Ialdir]: And you can't get the box
anymore, so you can't summon the boss, so you
can't find the plans
[Group][Solace]: *cries*
[Group][Solace]: And I'm this close to
getting the Heavy Petting achievement
[Group][Orcarella]: i've never really seen
the point of the pet thing
[Group][Solace]: They're cute. That's kind of
their whole deal.
```

Next thing Drew knew, Solace was standing next to a [Tiny Angry Shrubbery] and Ialdir had pulled out a [Miniature Giant Space Hamster]. Honestly, he still didn't see the appeal.

```
[Group][Orcarella]: Right. Irontongue?
[Group][Solace]: Yay
```

Once Solace had finished hugging Orcarella, they backtracked through Pyrite's cavern, up the spiralling corridor, across the top ring, and up the staircase that led to Irontongue's aerie.

They stepped out onto a plateau at the top of a twisted iron spire. A great metal serpent, winged and clawed and studded with rusted rivets and slowly turning gears, lay coiled around a dull black pillar.

[Yell][IRONTONGUE]: WHO DARES DISTURB THE
SLUMBER OF THE WORLD MACHINE?
[Group][Orcarella]: wow i haven't done this
guy in six months
[Group][Orcarella]: can't remember the tacs
[Group][Ialdir]: fairly straight forward
[Group][Ialdir]: main things are impale and
scalding rage
[Group][Ialdir]: impale is when he stabs
someone on his tail and hovers in the air
putting shit on the floor
[Group][Ialdir]: don't stand in the shit
[Group][Ialdir]: scalding rage is whole area
aoe
[Group][Ialdir]: he'll fly up and cover the
platform in grey stuff so we all need to get
behind a pillar
[Group][Orcarella]: cool
[Group][Ialdir]: plus standard dragon stuff
[Group][Ialdir]: you can get tail-swiped off
the platform so like don't
[Group][Orcarella]: kk going in

Orcarella raised her maces, shouted a battle cry, and charged.

[Yell][IRONTONGUE]: PITIFUL CREATURES OF
FLESH! YOU SHALL NOT DISTURB THE HOLY WORK!

Drew started his rotation, barely able to see what was happening
with his screen full of dragon face. But he wasn't dying and Irontongue's
health was dropping at a good rate so everything seemed to be going
according to plan.

[Group][Ialdir]: shit
[Group][Orcarella]: ?
[Group][Ialdir]: Small Mangy Owl just got
punted off the platform

```
[Group][Solace]: omg noob
[Group][Ialdir]: hes an owl
[Group][Ialdir]: shud be able to fly
```

Suddenly Irontongue reared back and thrust its pelvis vigorously in Orcarella's direction. And the next thing Drew knew, he was hoist aloft on the creature's tail.

```
[Yell][Irontongue]: IMPALED!!!
[Yell][Solace]: IMPALED!!!
[Yell][Ialdir]: IMPALED!!!
[Group][Ialdir]: ooh on a first date
[Group][Orcarella]: *sigh*
[Group][Orcarella]: do you two have that
macroed
[Group][Solace]: :D
[Group][Ialdir]: :D
```

There was nothing Drew could do while he was up there except make his own macro and enjoy the view, and actually the view was pretty good. The aerie was a tangled mess of steel and ash, bits of broken stone and fallen pillars littering a battered iron floor. He could even see a little bit of the Great Fissure below, shattered islands and rivers of lava. It was almost enough to make him forget what a pain the zone had been to level in.

At last Irontongue flung Orcarella to the floor, and Drew threw off a taunt to reestablish threat. He'd just got back into his rotation when Irontongue swooped into the air again.

```
[Yell][IRONTONGUE]: BOIL ALIVE!
```

Solace and Ialdir were already fleeing to the central pillar, and Drew pegged it after them, not wanting to be the noob who ate dragon breath.

```
[Group][Ialdir]: sw
```

Ella, Solace, and Ialdir grouped up neatly on the southwest corner of the pillar while clouds of scalding vapour billowed around them.

[Group] [Solace]: group hug

When the steam cleared, Ella dived out from behind the pillar to meet the oncoming dragon, and Solace and Ialdir scattered to the opposite edge of the platform, clinging tight to Irontongue's sides to avoid the tail-swipe. The boss was creeping towards fifty-percent health when it pulled back from Ella and soared into the air.

[YELL] [IRONTONGUE]: BOIL ALIVE!
[Group] [Ialdir]: n

They snuggled up on the north side of the pillar this time, and let Irontongue spew his scalding rage over the empty platform.

[Group] [Solace]: no impale :(:(:(
[Group] [Ialdir]: i'm sure you'll get it soon
[Group] [Orcarella]: lol

Then it was back to a screenful of dragon face, Orcarella pounding mercilessly against the dragon's iron scales with her twin maces. Things settled into a rhythm. Ialdir got impaled, then Ella again. They hid from another couple of scalding rages, and Irontongue's health ticked steadily down. They'd got it to about four percent when the dragon suddenly wheeled away from Ella and lashed its tail towards Solace.

[Yell] [Irontongue]: IMPALED!!!
[Yell] [Ialdir]: IMPALED!!!
[Yell] [Orcarella]: IMPALED!!!
[Group] [Solace]: yay

Drew strafed around the platform, dodging superheated oil, and lobbed his one ranged attack, a slightly feeble DoT called Traitor's Curse, at the dragon.

```
[Group][Solace]: Look ma, no hands
```

On the other side of the platform, Ialdir sprayed volley after volley of glittering arrows into Irontongue's underbelly.

```
[Group][Solace]: I can see my house from here
```

For want of anything better to do, Drew renewed Traitor's Curse, and only then noticed that Ialdir had stopped firing.

```
[Group][Ialdir]: hold dps
```

Just then, Traitor's Curse, which had been ticking away barely tickling the dragon, critically hit, shaving the last few points off Irontongue's health. He dropped out of the sky like an enormous block of inert metal, whistling straight past the platform, taking Solace with him.

There was a brief silence and then Solace's portrait greyed out.

Solace was killed by Solace: fall damage (0)
Solace has died.
```
[Group][Solace]: . . .
```

Before Drew could say anything a little gold box popped up in front of him.

Achievement unlocked: Rage Against the
Machine
[Defeat Irontongue in Steamworks Furnace on
Heroic Difficulty with no member of the group
taking damage from Scalding Rage.]
```
[Guild][Ignatius]: grats
[Guild][Sindarella]: grats
[Guild][Dave]: gz
[Guild][Heurodis]: gratz
[Guild][Jargogle]: grats
```

```
[Guild][Solace]: He doesn't deserve your
grats
[Guild][Solace]: He just killed me
[Guild][Solace]: He shot Irontongue while I
was impaled
[Yell][The Forge Master]: MORE STEEL, MORE
FIRE, MORE SERVANTS FOR THE GREAT MACHINE!
[Guild][Ignatius]: lol
[Guild][Heurodis]: lol
```
Orcarella has now been demoted to Guild Peon
```
[Guild][Orcarella]: I'm really sorry
[Guild][Solace]: Hee hee
[Guild][Solace]: You so owe me now
[Guild][Solace]: I'm going to make you my
pocket tank
[Guild][Solace]: And you have to do ALL the
optional bosses
[Guild][Solace]: ALL the time
[Guild][Orcarella]: i'm okay with that
```

They ran back to the entrance to meet Solace, who seemed genuinely fine about what had happened. Drew drifted between confusion and relief—a mistake like that would not have been well-received in Annihilation. But, then, if he'd been running with Anni, they wouldn't have been faffing about with optional bosses anyway.

Thankfully, the rest of the run went off without a hitch. They battled their way through the trash and down into the depths of the furnace, taking a short detour into the temple complex to deal with Arch Priest Garaxis, a skinny human in an outrageous robe who worshipped the Hand of Zoth-Arun and was the final boss of the previous raid tier. People had been smashing the Hand to pieces for a good six months, but Drew guessed the Arch Priest hadn't got that memo. They beat heavily on him with pointy objects, and he fell over, dropping his [Mantle of Hydraulic Communion].

```
[Group][Solace]: omg need
```

Drew did a quick inspect. Solace's shoulders were way better, and the mantle was healer gear so it couldn't have been for her offspec.

```
[Group][Orcarella]: ?
[Group][Solace]: Have you seen how awesome
these look?
[Group][Solace]: I'm working on a steampunk set
```

She put them on. Her angel wings disappeared, replaced by a disproportionately huge pair of shoulder pads filled with a mesh of wires and rotating gears.

Then she bounced up and down while Ialdir applauded and Drew grinned at the monitor like an idiot.

```
[Group][Solace]: Hmm
[Group][Solace]: I'd better switch back
[Group][Solace]: Thinking I'm giving off a
bit of a mixed message fashion-wise
```

They pressed on through the Furnace, knocked over the Smelter and the Smith without too much trouble, and finally came face-to-face with the Forge Master.

```
[Yell][The Forge Master]: INTRUDERS! AUTOMATA
TO ME! DEFEND THE FORGE!
[Group][Ialdir]: I always kind of feel sorry
for this guy
[Group][Ialdir]: he's just trying to do his
job and a bunch of complete jerks bust in and
start brokking his shit up
[Group][Solace]: What's this guy's deal
anyway?
[Group][Ialdir]: did you sleep through the
last patch or something?
[Group][Solace]: I was distracted by all the
shiny things
```

[Group][Solace]: plus I'm not a massive lore nerd
[Group][Ialdir]: :P
[Group][Orcarella]: lol
[Group][Ialdir]: so it turns out the whole world of Heroes of Legend is actually built on this giant ancient machine god thing
[Group][Ialdir]: and when Raziel returned from the Underworld he opened this fissure
[Group][Ialdir]: that unleashed a bunch of crap
[Group][Ialdir]: so all this stuff is like prototypes for the stuff in the world
[Group][Ialdir]: like Irontongue's a prototype dragon and this dude's a prototype giant
[Group][Solace]: oh right
[Group][Ialdir]: aren't you glad you know a massive lore nerd now
[Group][Solace]: *hugs*
[Group][Orcarella]: whatever this guy is i'm killing him and taking his stuff

They killed that guy and took his stuff. Well, the stuff wasn't very good, so they ripped it apart for the raw materials. Then Drew said a hasty good-bye to his new guild, logged off, and rushed out to meet his mates in the pub.

CHAPTER 2

Drew's mates were a bunch of fairly typical randoms who had come together and stuck together over the course of their first year. Sanee and Tinuviel were both on his course. He'd bonded with Sanee over *Dark Souls*, which Sanee thought represented the epitome of ludonarrative coherence and Drew quite enjoyed. Tinuviel was exactly like you'd expect someone to be if they'd grown up with the sorts of parents who named their kid Tinuviel.

Apparently her mother was a graphic artist and her dad was some kind of Oxford don, and she was here at De Montfort pursuing her bliss. Which was the sort of thing she actually said. That just left Andy, from Drew's ultimate Frisbee team, and Stephanie, known as Steff (or Smidge if Sanee was talking to her) who was here on a nursing and midwifery course. She and Sanee had been inseparable since fresher's week. They were very slightly unspeakable, and right now rubbing noses and sharing a basket of curly fries.

"Sorry I'm late, guys." Drew grabbed a stool from a nearby table and squished in between Sanee and Tinuviel. "Instance overran."

Sanee pulled away from Steff and made the loser sign.

"You know only losers do that, right?" asked Drew.

"A loser is well-placed to recognise loseriness in others. You need to play some proper games, man. Not ones where you kill the same stupid wizard every week for six months."

Drew rolled his eyes. "It's about mastering the fight. You don't go up to Man United and say, 'Why are you playing Liverpool again, you played them last season?'"

"Dude, it's a game, not a spare. A game should be a self-contained experience that does what it needs to do without wasting your fucking time."

"What, you mean like *Dishonored*?"

"Okay, what was wrong with *Dishonored*? And if you say it was too short, I'll punch you."

"You see." Steff grinned at them. "Video games do make you violent."

"Too short, too easy, Blink, Dark Vision, Shadow Kill: game over." Drew stole one of their fries. "Also, it's from like 2012."

Sanee had that outraged look, meaning a serious lecture was on the way. "Dude, so not the point. *Dishonoured* is totally a designer's game. What it does is create a space and give the player total freedom to interact with that space. If the player decides to take the easy option, then the player doesn't get to whinge about the game being too easy. And it's still relevant today because nothing has done that since."

"So what you're saying," said Drew, "is that the designers didn't bother to balance their gameplay properly and that's somehow my problem. The game has to provide the challenge, not the player. Don't give me an 'I win' button and then have a go at me for pressing it."

Tinuviel waved her burger in the air, scattering iceberg lettuce and bits of tomato over the table. "What I thought was really interesting about *Dishonored* was its embrace of found narrative. Mission objectives are delivered through dialogue, but story is inherent in the world and emerges with the player's visual engagement with the environment. So where I look and what I see creates the story for me. But where you look and what you see creates the story for you."

Drew suspected Andy had a bit of a thing for Tinuviel because he'd been listening with a kind of rapt look. "Oh wow," he breathed, "that's really fascinating."

"Yeah, I know. Isn't it?" She smiled. "It's similar to what I find so compelling about *Twine*, the way story is constructed not just through words but through text."

Drew and Sanee sighed in stereo. But where Drew would have let it go, Sanee, well, didn't. He took a deep breath. "In the twenty-first century, making a text-only game is like shooting a film in black and white. The only reason to do it is to make things look artsier."

"Oh my God." Drew pulled back as much as he could, given the space. "They're having the Interactive Fiction discussion. Everyone take cover."

Steff clung to Sanee. "Don't kill my Squidge."

"I love you, Smidge." Sanee snuggled into her.

And Andy made gag face. "No, please, kill him. Put us out of our misery."

"I'm going to take the paragon option," said Tinuviel serenely.

Drew couldn't resist. "Renegade interrupt." He threw a chip at her.

She ate the chip. "The most important thing to remember about *Twine* is that it makes game design accessible to anyone, no matter who they are or where they come from."

"If," interrupted Sanee, "they've got a computer, an internet connection, and free time to spend faffing around with indie games."

"That's still the lowest barrier to entry out there. It's free, it takes seconds to download, it's visual and very straightforward, and you can start using it immediately."

This was an old argument and never went anywhere or ended well, so Drew sort of tuned out. He wasn't a big fan of IF—he'd once told Tinuviel he thought it was basically reading, and that hadn't ended well either.

With no burger in sight, his mind drifted back to his new guild. Anni had been a big part of his life for three years, and it was amazing how quickly it had gone away. Except maybe it wasn't really because the whole thing was built on pixels. After he'd gquit, he'd thought some of his ex-guildies might have whispered him or messaged him or something, but nobody had. And it was stupid to be so upset, because it was just a video game. It wasn't like it was real life or they were real friends.

His real friends were squabbling about minority voices in interactive media. At least, two of them were. Andy was watching awkwardly, and Steff was stuffing chips in Sanee's mouth in an effort to keep him quiet.

"So," said Drew, as a harassed-looking waiter plonked his food down in front of him, "how did you guys find *Dragon Age: Inquisition*?"

Sanee rolled his eyes. "I skipped it because the only press release I could remember was about how the sex would be mature and tasteful. Which I thought was a pile of Molyneux."

"Actually—" Tinuviel leaned across the table "—I was pleasantly surprised by that. It seems like BioWare finally realised that the best way to represent sex in a video game is not to have stiffly animated underwear sequences. But I agree it sounded like Molyneux at the time."

Steff made a confused noise. "Sorry, what's a Molyneux?"

"Molyneux," explained Sanee, "noun, a promise made for an upcoming video game which you can't keep and which no one would be able to recognise even if you did."

Drew spoke round a mouthful of burger. "Like trees that grow in real time in *Fable 1*. Or the game teaching you the meaning of love in *Fable 2*."

"Ooh," said Tinuviel. "Wasn't *Fable 3* supposed to know what the weather was like where you were, and set the weather in game to match?"

Andy smiled hopefully at Tinuviel. "I hear *Fable 4* will come with a special headset and the weather in the game will be controlled by your brain."

From then on ideas flew thick and fast around the table.

"In *Fable 5*, if you get married in the game, you get married in real life. To Peter Molyneux."

"In *Fable 6*, the game will be able to sense if you're not enjoying it and will ask you what's wrong."

"*Fable 7* will cure cancer."

"*Fable 8* is Luke's father."

"*Fable 9* killed Dumbledore."

"*Fable 10* will be *Half-Life 3*."

"So," asked Steff, when they'd finished laughing, eating, and insulting an innocent game designer, "what are we doing this afternoon?"

Drew was having fun, but part of him really wanted to get back to *Heroes of Legend*. It was kind of important to make a good impression on a new guild, and a little part of him was hoping Solace would still be online. But if he ditched his real-life friends for an MMO, they'd never let him hear the end of it.

"Well, I don't know, Smidge. How about what we do every Saturday afternoon. Go back to ours and play board games." Sanee grinned at them. "We've just got Space Alert."

Tinuviel clapped her hands. "Brilliant, I played that with my parents at Christmas. We had one game where my dad went the wrong way really early on and spent the rest of the game walking into a wall, trying to launch missiles."

Drew finished the rest of his pint. "Sorry, your dad did what? What game is this?"

"Space Alert." She thought for a moment. "It's like RoboRally on a timer in space with sound effects."

"Oh, why didn't you say? I'm in."

One game of Space Alert led to another, and then another, and eventually—when they'd all got bored about being blown up by space amoeba—into pizza. Then they ended up watching *Drive Angry*, which Sanee had bought for £2.99 in the HMV closing-down sale.

"Well," said Drew, when they finished, "that wasn't the worst movie I've ever seen."

Andy had claimed the beanbag in the corner. "It wasn't even the worst Nicolas Cage movie I've ever seen."

Which inspired a long and heated discussion about what the worst Nicolas Cage movie was, and how the badness of a Nicolas Cage movie could be rated because, as Sanee pointed out, sometimes Cage at his worst was Cage at his best.

With one thing and another, it was after midnight by the time Drew rocked back to his room. He should probably have gone to bed so he could get up at a reasonable time tomorrow and do some work on his project, but he wasn't feeling that tired and he wanted to get in a couple of dungeons before the weekly badge limits rolled over. He logged into his bank alt and checked his auctions, about half of which had sold and about half of which had come back to him because some git was flooding the market with cut-price gems. If he was really lucky, one of the other gem crafters would buy them out and repost, but he couldn't be arsed to do it himself. He hopped onto Ella.

```
[Guild][Orcarella]: Hi
[Guild][Morag]: wb
[Guild][Solace]: Evening
[Guild][Heurodis]: yo
[Guild][Morag]: how's it going?
```

[Guild][Orcarella]: good, just been hanging out
[Guild][Heurodis]: we just knocked over bloodrose
[Guild][Orcarella]: anything good drop
[Guild][Heurodis]: maidens ring from BR
[Guild][Morag]: everybody lol *sigh*
[Guild][Heurodis]: woeful gauntlets from CoT
[Guild][Heurodis]: and the net from Vilicus
[Guild][Caius]: *does happy dance*
[Guild][Caius]: I'm a proud Retiarius from a long-line of orcish warriors and I've been fighting with a dildo in my off-hand since Rimefrost
[Guild][Orcarella]: myrmi used to be my main but I never went ret
[Guild][Orcarella]: anybody up for a dungeon
[Guild][Heurodis]: still maxed
[Guild][Heurodis]: ask me again in 2hrs17
[Guild][Morag]: I'd come but I'm knackered and my offspecs a bit crap
[Guild][Caius]: I should have gone to bed half an hour ago but I've been running around Vala'Threk waving my net in people's faces
[Guild][Orcarella]: Sol?
[Guild][Solace]: Sorry, I'm not in the mood to pug
[Guild][Solace]: I'm fishing
[Guild][Caius]: nn
Caius has gone offline.
[Guild][Orcarella]: isn't it easier to buy fish on the AH
[Guild][Heurodis]: lol
[Guild][Morag]: lol
[Guild][Orcarella]: what am i missing
[Guild][Morag]: Solace is basically the only person in this entire game who actually likes fishing

```
[Guild][Solace]: It's peaceful
[Guild][Solace]: I'm sitting on a rock in
Alarion, and the sea is a sort of rich purply
blue and I'm trying to catch the moon
[Guild][Heurodis]: is that a new achi :P
[Guild][Solace]: The sun'll come up in an hour
or two and everything will be gold and red
[Guild][Orcarella]: you're seriously going to
sit there till 2 am to see the sunrise in a
computer game
[Guild][Solace]: you were going to stay up
till two in the morning doing fights you're
not interested in with people you don't like
[Guild][Morag]: zing baby
[Guild][Solace]: if you haven't seen the sun
rise over Alarion you haven't played this
game
[Guild][Orcarella]: don't think I've even
been to Alarion. isn't it like vanilla
endgame?
[Guild][Heurodis]: it was a lvl 48-50 zone
before entry level raiding Wyrmsbreath Lair
[Guild][Heurodis]: since RotU everyone just
goes straight to Jormenheim
[Guild][Solace]: it's a really beautiful zone
[Guild][Solace]: it's like this fallen
kingdom full of ruins and ghosts and drifting
leaves
[Guild][Heurodis]: dude, that's Raziel's
kingdom from like Legend 1.
[Guild][Solace]: you should come and see it
```

Drew stared at the screen for a moment, wondering what to do. It wasn't the sort of invitation he'd ever received before, and if he had, he wouldn't have taken it seriously. But they obviously did things differently in this guild, and he didn't want to look like some kind of elitist jerk. Besides, it was probably a bit late to be running dungeons, and as they said, when in Rome, go fishing in Alarion.

```
[Guild][Orcarella]: omw
[Guild][Solace]: Really?!
[Guild][Orcarella]: y
Solace has invited you to join a group: y/n
Solace is now group leader
[Group][Solace]: Hi
```

Drew had a moment of panic. He really wasn't sure what the etiquette was here. Normally, when he was in group it was for a reason and there was some kind of script, usually along the lines of *mana up, protect the flag, buff me, you two take blacksmith, anyone know tacs*. But he wasn't sure what to say when the plan was sit on a rock and fish.

```
[Group][Orcarella]: Hi
```

Shit. That was not a good opening. Traditional, but not good.

```
[Group][Orcarella]: how are you?
[Group][Solace]: I'm feeling quite virtuous
actually
[Group][Solace]: I went over all my lecture
notes on the Lorentz transformation
[Group][Orcarella]: you're at uni?
[Group][Solace]: Yes, physics
[Group][Orcarella]: Me too. not physics
though lol
[Group][Solace]: What are you reading?
[Group][Orcarella]: Latest Scott Lynch. You?
[Group][Solace]: Um . . . I kind of meant
what are you studying
```

Drew felt like a knob.

```
[Group][Orcarella]: oh right, game art design
lol
[Group][Solace]: Cool
```

Drew still felt like a knob. And he suddenly realised he had no idea how to get to Alarion. He called up the map, something he hadn't done basically since he'd started raiding, and squinted at it, mousing over the different zones to try and figure where the hell this place actually was. To his embarrassment, it turned out to be due south of Orcarella's home city, the orcish stronghold of Vala'Threk. His bindstone was set to the City of Stars, that being the closest major hub to Crown of Thorns, where he spent ninety percent of his game time, so he was going to have to travel the old-fashioned way.

He got on his dreadsteed and galloped through the shining streets of the City of Stars and up the spiral ramp that led to the skyship tower that would take him to the eastern continent. As usual, one was just leaving as he arrived, so he parked himself on the platform to wait, another thing he hadn't done since he started raiding.

[Group][Solace]: I've been meaning to pick up Republic of Thieves
[Group][Orcarella]: i only read the other two last year
[Group][Solace]: Any good?
[Group][Orcarella]: not as good as the first one, better than the second
[Group][Solace]: I thought the first one was a bit all hail my awesome main character
[Group][Orcarella]: yeah but he was actually awesome
[Group][Solace]: That's the problem. He was clearly supposed to be
[Group][Orcarella]: I like Jean best anyway
[Group][Solace]: Me too. He'd be a great friend to have.
[Group][Solace]: I'd rather hang out with him.
[Group][Orcarella]: wwwwwwwwwwwwwwwwww
[Group][Solace]: wwwwwwwwwwwwwwwwwww to you too
[Group][Orcarella]: lol no
[Group][Orcarella]: nearly missed my airship

Drew cantered back and forth impatiently over the deck of the ship as it glided towards the transition that would trigger the loading screen. And then went and stuffed his horse into the prow like Kate Winslet in *Titanic*.

It was a deep black night for the Heroes of Legend, the skybox lavishly dusted with stars.

Then the familiar loading screen popped up: it showed a scantily clad human with a staff, a dwarf with a huge hammer and even huger beard, a kobold with tiny goggles, and a severe-looking orc warrior. Drew felt a strange rush of nostalgia for his first experiences of the game when he'd looked at those figures and thought, *Wow, I want to play one of those*, instead of *Wow, I wish this zone would hurry up and load, and yes I know a Tempest employee will never ask for my password.*

He got off the skyship at Vala'Threk and paused on the dock to give actual serious consideration to which flying mount he'd show up on.

Part of him was embarrassed to even be thinking about it.

Still, in the end, he settled on El'ir Reborn, the black and purple phoenix that you got for doing the top-tier raiding achievements at the end of Rise of the Underworld. A random level five orcish elementalist cheered him as his mount unfurled its shadowy wings.

He soared into the air and flew south for Alarion.

He passed over a range of black, pointy mountains and the landscape changed abruptly from bare tundra to red-brown forests as he crossed over into the new zone.

You have discovered Invader's Pass.

He pulled up the area map to look for Solace, who was a little purple dot a short way out to sea. Wheeling his mount round, he headed diagonally across the zone. Beneath him, the ghosts of ancient armies battled in the ruins of a once great city, while a fifty-third level kobold scampered in circles, picking flowers for potion crafting.

He found Solace sitting alone on a piece of broken temple jutting up from the sea. He landed his phoenix, which engulfed the whole thing, including Solace, in a whirl of shadows and feathers.

```
[Group][Solace]: Is that El'ir Reborn or are
you just pleased to see me?
[Group][Orcarella]: lol
```

He dismounted and stood precariously on the edge of the ruin. Solace was wearing an off-the-shoulder white dress that Drew was pretty sure came from the Valentine's event, and a battered brown hat. She was fishing with a huge, jewel-plated fishing rod.

Drew */pointed* in its general direction.

```
[Group][Orcarella]: nice rod
[Group][Solace]: It's what you do with it
that counts
[Group][Orcarella]: lol
```

Drew */sat* next to Solace, and, for some reason, found himself spinning the camera round so he could see what they looked like.

Which turned out to be kind of ridiculous.

Solace was curled demurely on the floor with her knees together, and Ella was hulked next to her in full Tier 14 raiding kit. The skull helmet was especially atmospheric. He opened his inventory and cleared his headslot. It didn't really help matters. She was now sitting there with tusks and a gigantic mohawk. He was beginning to feel like the gawky one in a chick flick.

And he'd run out of rod jokes.

And he needed something to say.

And this was like the worst date ever, except it wasn't really, it was just two strangers on computers, looking at an elf and an orc sitting on a rock.

```
[Group][Orcarella]: so here I am
```

Shit, was that crap.

```
[Group][Orcarella]: it was a bit of a trip
[Group][Solace]: I kind of miss the
travelling
```

[Group][Solace]: It made the world feel
worldy
[Group][Orcarella]: but it used to take like
7m from the city of ash to the stone forest
[Group][Solace]: Yeah but you felt like you'd
gone somewhere
[Group][Orcarella]: when I started playing I
could normally only play for an hour or so a
night with homework and clubs and shit
[Group][Orcarella]: so those 7 minutes came
out of my playing time
[Group][Solace]: I didn't think of it like
that
[Group][Solace]: I didn't really do any clubs
so I had plenty of time
[Group][Solace]: And, tbh, sometimes I read a
book on the longer flights
[Group][Orcarella]: you know if you're
looking for ways to entertain yourself when
playing a game
[Group][Orcarella]: I think the game's gone
wrong
[Group][Solace]: Hee hee
[Group][Solace]: I used to have this really
crap computer, so I got used to reading on
loading screens
[Group][Solace]: I spent so much time waiting
for The Witcher to load, I managed to read
the whole book it was based on
[Group][Orcarella]: lol

Solace reeled in her line and cast again, right where the moon
reflected on the sea.

[Group][Orcarella]: let me know if you catch it
[Group][Solace]: Hee hee

```
[Group][Orcarella]: So what else are you into
apart from HoL
[Group][Solace]: I'm pretty boring really
[Group][Solace]: I read, I study, I run, I
sometimes play other games
[Group][Solace]: Mainly I play HoL. All my
friends are here.
[Group][Orcarella]: what about your mates at
uni
[Group][Solace]: I'm friendly with my
coursemates
[Group][Solace]: I just don't really like to
do the things they like to do
[Group][Solace]: It was the same at school
[Group][Orcarella]: dont you get lonely
[Group][Solace]: I used to before I met Morag
and Ialdir
```

Drew wasn't sure what to say. He'd always known lots of people and had plenty going on, so it was hard to imagine having no real-life friends. He wished he wasn't trapped behind his keyboard, because he felt this rush of protectiveness towards this shy little elf in her pretty dress and silly hat. He typed various things and they all sounded wrong or stupid or patronising, so in the end he fell back on the old standard.

```
[Group][Orcarella]: :(
```

It didn't really say what he wanted it to. But at least it wouldn't say anything he didn't.

```
[Group][Solace]: No :(
[Group][Solace]: It wasn't a big deal, and
I'm a lot happier now
[Group][Solace]: Nobody was nasty or
anything, just nobody really got me
[Group][Solace]: I sometimes think I'm maybe
hard to get
```

```
[Group][Orcarella]: you don't seem hard to
get to me
[Group][Orcarella]: omg that came out wrong
[Group][Solace]: hee hee
[Group][Solace]: How about you?
[Group][Orcarella]: I'm pretty boring
[Group][Orcarella]: I'm on a UF team
[Group][Solace]: A what team?
[Group][Orcarella]: Ultimate Frisbee
[Group][Solace]: How's that different to
regular Frisbee
[Group][Orcarella]: its a bit like American
football and a bit like netball but
[Group][Orcarella]: with a Frisbee
[Group][Solace]: lol
[Group][Orcarella]: mainly I'm just kind of a
nerd. I read fantasy novels and play games
[Group][Orcarella]: i used to play the guitar
[Group][Orcarella]: it was supposed to be my
cool thing
[Group][Solace]: What happened?
[Group][Orcarella]: I just kind of stopped
[Group][Orcarella]: I guess I've given up
trying to have a cool thing
[Group][Solace]: I've never had a cool thing
[Group][Solace]: I've always done things I
liked
[Group][Orcarella]: Thats pretty cool
[Group][Solace]: Oh I see what you did there
[Group][Solace]: Thank you
```

Shit. He'd run out of steam, but he didn't want to stop talking. He had to remind himself he'd only met Solace twelve hours ago, but there was a strange intimacy to sitting here together, and just chatting like this. Most of his friendships were structured around doing things and going places, and that was fine, but he couldn't remember the last time anyone had just been interested in who he was and where he was coming from.

```
[Group][Orcarella]: You were right. Its nice
here.
[Group][Solace]: :D
[Group][Solace]: I know this is silly but it
feels like my place
[Group][Orcarella]: Yeah, its just you, me, a
bunch of mobs, and a kobold herbalist
[Group][Solace]: Don't spoil it :P
[Group][Solace]: Oh look, the sun
```

Drew brought his camera back into alignment, and turned east. A sheen of light gathered at the far horizon, gilding the edges of the ocean, setting fire to the sky, and rushing over the ruins of Raziel's kingdom in shades of crimson, purple, and gold.

```
[Group][Orcarella]: nice
[Group][Solace]: Yes
[Group][Orcarella]: its kinda weird nobody
ever sees this anymore
[Group][Solace]: Yeah
[Group][Orcarella]: seems like a waste
[Group][Orcarella]: its good stuff
[Group][Orcarella]: looks good
[Group][Orcarella]: i like it
[Group][Solace]: There's some nice quests
here too. It's all spooky lore type stories,
and you help ghosts find peace and stuff
[Group][Solace]: It's also where you first
meet High Theurgist Venric
[Group][Orcarella]: oh i hate him
[Group][Solace]: He's pretty cool when you
first meet him. He's all betrayed and lost his
faith and things
[Group][Orcarella]: and now he won't shut up
```

```
[Group][Orcarella]: it's like you can't walk
into CoT without him whining about his ex-gf
before you're allowed to kill anything
[Group][Solace]: Ahaha
[Group][Solace]: He's probably going to be
really important in the next patch as well
[Group][Orcarella]: if he kill steals us on
Raziel I'm going to be so pissed
[Group][Solace]: :D :D :D
[Group][Orcarella]: Shit its like 2 in the
morning
[Group][Solace]: I had a nice time
[Group][Orcarella]: me too
[Group][Solace]: Night night
[Group][Orcarella]: Gn
[Group][Orcarella]: Aren't you going to bed
as well
[Group][Solace]: I'm going to fish for a bit
longer and then head off
[Group][Orcarella]: kk
[Group][Orcarella]: sleep well
[Group][Solace]: you too
```

Drew gazed blearily at the screen. He really did have to go bed, and he'd just said goodnight about twelve times, but he felt oddly reluctant to log off, like if he did, he'd break something fragile.

After dithering for an embarrassingly long time, he typed /*hug*.

And was weirdly touched when Solace /*hugged* him back.

Then he shut down the game, followed by his computer, and went to bed, slightly confused.

CHAPTER

A couple of nights later, Drew joined his first official raid as a member of <Same Crit Different Day>. He arrived in good time to set up Mumble, repair his armour, make sure he had plenty of buff food and potions, and was standing outside CoT just in time to see Anni gathering across the way.

They ignored him.

Morag showed up next on a flying Halloween goat. She was a dwarven champion, with long red braids and the guild tabard discreetly covering her otherwise quite skimpy armour. She waved and invited him into a raid group.

```
Heurodis has joined the raid.
Ialdir has joined the raid.
Solace has joined the raid.
Jargogle has joined the raid.
Prospero has joined the raid.
Caius has joined the raid.
Ignatius has joined the raid.
Dave has joined the raid.
[Raid][Morag]: Come on guys, get your arses
to Briarsdeep
[Raid][Morag]: -50DKP for anybody not here in
the next 5mins
[Raid][Dave]: But we don't use DKP
[Raid][Morag]: But when we start, you'll be
at -50
```

Drew's ears filled up with chimes as people started logging into Mumble.

"Uh, hi," he tried.

"Hi, Ella, Morag here." She had a youngish-sounding voice, with a faint brummie accent.

"Yo." Somehow, Bjorn/Heurodis sounded exactly the same on Mumble as he did in chat, laconically Scandinavian.

Drew spent the first few minutes just listening, trying to fit voices to names to character names. Ialdir/Jacob turned out to be a softly-spoken American expat, Jargogle/Magda a straight-talking German woman, Dave a Scouse teenager, and the rest sort of blurred into a background of in-jokes and disconnected chatter. He listened for Solace but couldn't pick her out.

At last they were all assembled, on their various flying creatures, under the thorny archway that was the portal to the raid instance.

```
[Raid][Morag]: Anyone not on Mumble?
```

"Everybody in," came Morag's voice, and they all piled through the portal into the Crown of Thorns.

The loading screen was Lady Bloodrose herself, wearing, it seemed, basically nothing but flowers. And then Orcarella was standing at the entrance to a vast spiral maze of thorns and blood-red roses. For some reason, various handy shopkeepers and armour smiths had set up camp here. Drew wasn't sure, but he thought it was meant to be some kind of forward base.

High Theurgist Venric was standing amongst them, emoting and making speeches.

```
[High Theurgist Venric] says: Brothers, I
have anticipated this day with a heavy heart
for ten long years, the day when finally
the monster that is all that remains of my
beloved Anthariel falls to righteous steel
and holy fire.
```

"She dumped you, man," groaned Bjorn. "Get over it."

"Hey." That was Ialdir. "She dumped him for his best friend, then ran away with his best friend halfway across the world, where they turned evil, unleashed a magical curse that destroyed his homeland, and *then* he had to cast them both down into the underworld, where they remained in prison, going slowly mad, for the next five hundred years. You can see why he's bummed."

[Raid][Solace]: Awww, he just needs a hug.

Drew obligingly ran over to the high theurgist and hugged him.

[Solace] whispers: Hee

Solace ran over too, as did Prospero, Ialdir, and Ignatius.

[Raid][Ialdir]: Group hug!
[Raid][Heurodis]: he doesnt need a hug
[Raid][Heurodis]: he needs to shut up and let us raid

"Speaking of." Morag. "Let's get this show on the road. Buff up while I talk to HTV."

[Raid][Solace]: fish on the floor
[Raid][Ignatius]: yay fish
[Raid][Dave]: nom nom

The whole raid sat unceremoniously on the floor stuffing their faces with mystically fortifying fish while Morag jogged up to the high theurgist and triggered the starting event.

High Theurgist Venric strode to the centre of the chamber and carried on declaiming, while the raid group carried on eating fish and ignoring him.

[High Theurgist Venric] says: Brothers, within this labyrinth lurk many vile and

```
terrifying creatures. I and my men will
remain here and guard the portal so that none
may break free into the outside world.
```

"Oh, thanks for having our back, man." Bjorn.

The high theurgist turned away from them and raised his arms, mystical light gathering between his hands. The curtain of thorns that obscured the way into the maze parted.

```
[Yell][High Theurgist Venric]: Anthariel, I
do this for love of the woman you were!
[Yell][Lady Bloodrose]: Your compassion has
always been your weakness. Face me, and die!
```

"See," said Morag. "This is why I don't do men. Well, that and not fancying them. So, anyway, welcome Drew aboard the good ship Same Crit Different Day. We won't go for a full clear tonight. We'll do up to Vilicus and then probably call it. I'll be your raid leader this evening. In the event of an emergency, exits are here, here, and here. Bjorn is loot master because I can't be arsed and he gets off on the power."

A wild cackling laugh echoed over Mumble.

"Rules are pretty simple. Need if you need, mainspec or spec you're running in before offspec, unless special circumstances apply, but in practice, that's nobody tonight. Drew's MT, I'll be your OT, ranged deeps Ialdir, Heurodis, and Ignatius. Melee deeps Jargogle, Caius, and Dave. Our lovely healing team are Solace and Prospero."

```
[Raid][Solace]: I'll be on MT, OT, and raid
in that prio.
[Raid][Prospero]: And my prio is raid, OT,
and MT.
```

"Otherwise," Morag continued, "let's have fun, kill some things, and take their stuff."

A ragged cheer went up from the fish-eaters, and they hustled through the recently opened barrier into the main dungeon.

The first boss was waiting for them on the other side. Kelebos: a vast, three-headed hound, covered in shaggy black fur tipped with fire all the way to its lashing, serpentine tail.

Thankfully, it was a dog, so it didn't have much to say to them.

"You know the drill. Spread out to avoid chaining damage from tail. Drew, we swap on ten stacks of Chew Toy. Everybody run out of Howl, and DPS the heads when someone gets grabbed. Are we good?"

A readycheck popped up on Drew's screen. He was, indeed, ready.

"Take it away, Drew."

Ella pulled out her maces and jogged the surprisingly large distance up to Kelebos's central mouth.

```
[Yell][Lady Bloodrose]: Welcome to my bower,
foolish heroes.
```

Drew dumped CoC under the dog and began building threat. This was a pretty straightforward fight for a tank. As long as he didn't let the debuff stack too high or forget to run out of the Howl, there wasn't much that could go wrong. His screen, as usual, was full of teeth and eyes and particle effects, but Kelebos's health was going down and Ella wasn't dead, so everything seemed to be fine.

Suddenly, the dog turned and bounded across the room, snatching up a couple of raid members before coming back to Ella.

"And I'm in the mouth." Ialdir.

"Me too." Drew didn't recognise this voice. "Solace on heals. Everyone be extra specially careful not to do anything stupid."

That must have been Prospero.

"Prio left head." Morag. "Get the healer back in the game."

Drew popped Unholy Resolve to boost his health while Solace was overextended.

```
[Raid][Ialdir]: Hey, I can do leatherworking
in here
[Raid][Prospero]: Can you make me a
[Gargantuan Corpse-Hide Satchel]?
[Raid][Ialdir]: Yeah sure
```

Out of the corner of his eye, Drew saw the left head suddenly engulfed in an insane swirl of golden fire and flickering shadow from the ranged DPS. A kobold streaked past him and started hammering daggers into its ear. Then the creature's jaws dropped open and its head reeled back in pain.

"Healing Service now resumed." Prospero.

"All on right." Morag. "Ten seconds to Howl."

"Eight stacks," said Drew.

Ialdir was finally shaken loose of the right head, just as the beast rocked back on its haunches and let out a bone-chilling wail. The raid scattered.

Ialdir made a frustrated noise down Mumble. "Sorry, guys, didn't have time."

"You noob, Jacob."

"This is why we don't let Bjorn raid lead," said Morag. "Keep Jacob's health up if you can. Everybody in, I'm picking up. Faster on the DPS next time, please, I don't want anyone else caught by the Howl."

Drew hung back as Morag pounded past him, roaring dwarfy defiance. Kelebos swung slowly to start chewing on her, and Drew switched out of Aspect of Vengeance and into Aspect of Cruelty to lower his threat and boost his otherwise negligible DPS. Then he nipped round and started whacking away at the beast's flanks. The guild seemed to know this fight pretty well, but he'd have been worried if they hadn't, what with it being the first boss of the instance.

Everything went smoothly through the next couple of changes. The heads snatched people up and they were DPSed out, nobody else got hit by the Howl, and he and Morag switched seamlessly at eight or nine stacks of Chew Toy.

Performance-wise there wasn't much difference between this lot and Annihilation. They weren't quite as tooled up, so DPS was lower all round, except Bjorn, who was riding the top of the meters like a kobold on a motorcycle. Healing was pretty smooth, and it was always a good sign when a guild could two-heal. Mumble was a bit livelier, and people seemed to be genuinely comfortable with each other.

Suddenly, Bjorn made a faintly disturbing noise over Mumble, something partway between a purr and a roar.

"Bjorn," asked Ialdir, "did you just come?"

"Unholy Glee with Necrosis and five stacks of Mortified Flesh. Twenty-eight K Darkfire crit and sixteen K Inflame Afflictions. Yeah, baby. Oh yeah."

"Oh dear," came Morag's voice. "Bjorn's crit his pants."

Bjorn made the noise again. "All your DPS are belong to—" Kelebos leaped across the room and snatched Heurodis up in his jaws. "Ah, you shitting little . . . My DoTs. I had no fucking DoTs."

Ialdir gave a whoop of laughter. "More DoTs! Throw more DoTs."

"Get me down, get me down!"

A rather sullen voice said, "I'm in a mouth as well."

Morag: "Prio Dave."

"What the fuck, what the fuck, you crazy dwarf lady."

"We're at seven percent, we need burst."

A second or two later, Dave was disgorged onto the floor and started tearing into Kelebos with an implausibly large double-headed axe.

"Me now," howled Bjorn. "Me now!"

Ialdir whistled, the sound coming sharp and tinny in Drew's earphones. "My, my, I seem to be top of the meters."

"Noooooooooo!"

"Okay," said Morag. "Three percent. Prio the body and bring it home. Full burn."

"Nooooooooooooooooo! You're doing this on purpose. It's conspiracy against the Great Nation of Bjorn."

"The Great Nation of Bjorn should get a better ambassador."

Drew was laughing as Kelebos whimpered and slumped over, finally spilling Heurodis out of its lolling mouth.

"Right, no loot, no loot for any of you."

The raid broke into cheers and random dancing, and despite Bjorn's protestations, there was in fact loot and it was in fact distributed. Solace broke free of the crowds and jumped into the corpse again. After a moment's hesitation, Drew sent Ella over to join her. He zoomed right in so he could see Solace dancing and the inside of the wire frame.

```
[Solace] whispers: So what's a nice orc like
you doing in a corpse like this?
```

Drew tried to think of something witty and flirty to say, but failed dismally.

```
To [Solace]: i just wanted to see what it
looked like
[Solace] whispers: As you can see, it's
a spacious, well-appointed cadaver, with
excellent views of not very much really
```

Shit shit shit. Solace was cute. But Solace was also an imaginary elf on the internet, and it was probably creepy to like her this much.

"Does anybody mind if I skin the boss?" asked Ialdir.

Nobody objected, so Ialdir whipped out a skinning knife and reduced the great hound Kelebos to three scraps of [Uncured Corpse Hide] and a [Patch of Mouldering Leather].

"Well done, guys," said Morag. "That was pretty clean. I know we've done this a lot and we overgear it, but a bit more focus next time early on. If we DPS the heads right, there's no way anyone should get hit by the Howl."

"Yeah, good job, guys," added Bjorn. "Jacob, your DPS was nearly as good as mine. I'd feel threatened if I wasn't so awesome. Really nice work on the transitions there, tanks. And quality work from the healing team, as ever."

Drew shifted a bit in his chair. He knew he was a good tank, and he'd done a good job, but in Anni he'd only ever been told when he screwed up, and he wasn't sure how to handle having someone say he'd done well. Especially if it was Bjorn.

They pressed on through the maze and a few packs of trash mobs to Thornheart. He was kind of an evil, corrupted Ent rip-off and basically just a gear check. There was lots of nasty spike damage on the tank and a hard enrage timer, but nothing a halfway decent guild couldn't handle this late in the expansion. It was Drew's least favourite fight because he had literally nothing to do except stand in one place and mash his rotation.

Also, back when he ran with Anni, there'd been an enormous amount of pressure to get your gearscore up to spec and everyone yelling at everyone else for letting the guild down. The healers always thought the tanks were too squishy, the tanks always thought the healers weren't gemmed right, and every DPSer thought none of the others were pulling their weight. And then, after that phase, came months of people doing stupid crap like trying to swap in alts to gear up or do it with only one healer and blaming Drew when he couldn't stay alive through the Arboreal Frenzy.

There was none of that this time, so it was just a straight tank and spank. And Dave sounded almost happy when the [Bracers of Blackened Oak] dropped.

"Hey guys, can I stone back to Ash to get these gemmed?"

There was a pause. Then Morag said no in a slightly incredulous voice.

"But I'll do better DPS."

"I'm not going to keep nine people standing around with their thumbs up their arses while you go shopping for bling."

"Um," offered Drew, "I think I've got some rubies in my backpack."

```
[Raid][Ignatius]: And I guess I can chant
them for you.
[Raid][Dave]: woot
```

"All right," said Morag. "Take five. But only five. Rebuff, eat fish, but nobody go make coffee, and if you need the loo, you hold it until Arachnia."

Drew flicked open his professions menu, carved a [Puissant Cataclysmic Ruby] for Dave and handed it over.

```
[Raid][Dave]: thx
```

Something had been bugging Drew for a while. "I know I'm new, and this might not be the best time to ask, but why are you called Dave?"

```
[Raid][Dave]: lol
[Raid][Ialdir]: lol
[Raid][Prospero]: lol
```

"When I rolled my DK, all the names I could think of were taken, so I typed it in for a joke, and then it went through and the cutscene was really long, so I thought I'd just go with it."

Bjorn: "If you want, I can report you so you can get a forced name change."

"But then I'd have to think of a new one and I'd be right back where I started."

"You make me a sad Viking, David."

Morag called the raid to order, and Drew was slightly surprised that they had genuinely only taken five minutes. Everything they'd said about casual guilds back in Anni had made him think that a five-minute raid break would turn into a ten-minute toilet break which would turn into half an hour of amateurish faffing.

The maze darkened around them as they pushed through thorns and cobwebs into the realm of Arachnia the Spider Queen. They passed under an archway onto a wide circle of webbing, and Drew dashed into the centre to pick up the vast tide of enemies that he knew were about to drop onto them.

[Yell][Arachnia the Spider Queen]: FEAST, MY CHILDREN AND BRING ME THEIR WITHERED CORPSES.

Tiny spiders began raining from the ceiling, but Drew had Circle of Corruption ready to go.

"I've never understood that." Dave sounded oddly meditative. "Cos if they feast on us, there won't be any corpses for them to bring to her."

A long sigh gusted over Mumble. Drew was pretty sure it was Bjorn. "Spiders, Dave, feed by injecting their prey with digestive fluids, which reduce their victim's innards to the consistency of soup. Then they suck out the soup, leaving only a desiccated husk."

They AoE-ed the spiderlings in a maelstrom of fire, shadow, holy light, flashing blades, and raining arrows.

"The first time we did this," said Ialdir, "Jargogle was scouting and the event triggered right on her head. I've never seen a kobold die so fast."

[Raid][Jargogle]: Thank you for bringing that up
[Raid][Jargogle]: Perhaps we should talk instead about the time you pushed the big red button in the Mechanarium
[Raid][Jargogle]: The big red button that says Do Not Push

"I wanted to know what it did."

[Raid][Jargogle]: What it did was cause you to die horribly in a gigantic explosion
[Raid][Jargogle]: Good times

When the last wave of spiders was vanquished, Arachnia herself began to descend slowly from the ceiling. She was a bloated red-and-black spider-demon thing, all dripping mandibles and pulsing eyes. Drew had spent a good amount of time this expansion with his face in her underbelly and it wasn't pleasant down there.

"Everybody back," called out Morag. "No pulling the boss until we're ready."

The valiant adventurers sprinted back and formed up again in the archway.

"You know the drill," Morag went on. "DPS the adds, don't stand on webs, if you get Royal Venom run away from the raid. When she goes up to the ceiling, we have to get the Sentinels down before she comes back or it'll be an almighty clusterfuck. Drew, I'll mark them up, and we'll take one each. You get star, I'll have the weird purple one that looks like a dildo."

Drew nodded, even though nobody could see him. "Got it."

"Prio star, then dildo. Ranged, you can attack the boss while she's in the air, but if I see a single potshot before the Sentinels go down, I'm sending you into the naughty corner."

[Raid][Ignatius]: Anything but the naughty corner!

This was where Drew would find out if he'd signed up with a bunch of noobs or not. They'd done okay up to now, but Arachnia could be tricky if the raid didn't pull together. When everyone was ready, Ella ran forward, maces whirling, and Arachnia plopped down on top of her.

```
[Yell][Arachnia the Spider Queen]: Come in to
my parlour, little flies.
[Yell][Morag]: That is a rubbish taunt!!!
```

Drew settled into the rhythm of the fight. There was much less cross talk than the last two bosses, because with flying webs and adds coming in and poison chaining through the raid, there was a lot going on and lot to keep track of. Drew focused on the job in front of him, letting instinct and muscle memory take over. He sort of liked this bit of the game. It was that sense you got when you were doing something you were good at and doing it well and not even having to think about it. And sharing that feeling with a group of people who were in the same zone. Mumble was busy with voices, but Drew had stopped worrying about who was who. Right now, it was all about information processing. His eyes and ears were full of data, and long experience had taught him how to filter it.

It was touch and go a couple of times, and Prospero got swarmed by spiderlings when the boss was at about five percent health, leading to a mad DPS race against Ella's dwindling health and Solace's dwindling mana pool. Drew's heart was racing as he blew as many cooldowns as he could and pounded his rotation like he was actually hammering a giant spider goddess. When she dropped, there was stunned silence and then an eardrum-exploding roar across Mumble. He thought he heard Bjorn actually singing.

"Fucking well done team." Morag.

"We are awe-*some*." Bjorn, still in singsong mode.

Ialdir seemed to be breathing for the first time in ten minutes. "Oh man, when Prosp went down, I was like new pants for table five."

"Um," said Prospero, "I'm still kind of dead over here."

Morag hustled over the many spider corpses and shattered egg bits to Prospero's body and began to channel the divine energies that would bring him back from the dead. On the other side of the room, Ignatius was doing the same for Caius.

```
[Raid][Prospero]: Quality healing, Sol
[Raid][Solace]: *blushes* Thanks. Ella's easy
to heal
[Raid][Jargogle]: Well he is the best geared
tank on the server
[Raid][Orcarella]: :P
```

"Can't believe we didn't wipe." Someone? Caius or Prospero?

"Yeah," agreed Morag. "It's gone smoother, but the important thing is we kept it together."

"And we had some really terrible luck." Drew was pretty sure that was Ialdir—as the only American in the raid, he was easy to recognise. "That egg sac on the first Sentinel phase really sucked."

"And somebody chained poison through the melee," said Bjorn in his stern voice. "I've checked the logs and you know who you are, but there's no point naming names, and it wouldn't have happened if you'd all been properly positioned."

Jargogle's stern voice was way sterner than Bjorn's. "Now listen here, young man. It's all very well for you and your fire-flinging friends, but when four of you attack a tiny egg sac you stand close together."

"Okay, guys," interrupted Morag. "It was a difficult situation but there's things we can learn from this. Melee, you do need to pay more attention to the venom, and Bjorn, you have to stop talking like a primary school teacher."

"All right, message received. Now anybody who wants loot put their hand up."

There was nothing Ella needed from Arachnia, so Drew opened a window and got himself another glass of Dr Pepper. Anni had basically got that fight down a few months ago and anyone who chained poison through anything would have been reamed out by the raid leader. On the other hand, as Morag had said, they'd pulled through pretty impressively, and it had actually been fun in a slightly knuckle-whitening way.

One of the problems with raiding was that, after a while, it began to be a chore rather than a challenge. These fights had become so routine to him, they'd stopped being interesting. But learning to work with a whole new team made them come alive again.

Morag jumped up and down for attention. "Okay guys, it's half nine. We can call it here if you like, but we've got plenty of time to take a couple of cracks at Vilicus. We probably won't get him down this evening, but we might as well get some practice in."

"I'm game," said Ialdir, "but I need to help Stefan put the kids to bed."

Bjorn sneered down Mumble. "This is so typical of you, Jacob. Having a family and a life and priorities outside raiding. Such a liability."

```
[Raid][Ialdir]: brb
[Raid][Morag]: Okay everyone, back in 20
minutes. Or else.
[Raid][Caius]: Grabbing a cuppa
[Raid][Prospero]: Two sugars for me
[Raid][Dave]: bio break
[Morag] whispers: Doing okay?
To [Morag]: yeah, having fun
[Morag] whispers: It's really good to have
you along
To [Morag]: thx
```

Drew took a sip of his Dr Pepper. He wasn't used to being checked in on. It was, well, it was nice. Normally he'd have spent this time browsing the forums and reading tanking blogs to keep up on the latest strats, but he didn't want to miss any chat, so he found himself glancing round the raid group to see what everyone else was doing.

Solace had run up one of the sheets of webbing and was balanced precariously at the top, her wings shimmering in the deep blue-green light. Ella ran up to join her.

```
To [Solace]: hi
[Solace] whispers: we have to stop meeting
like this
To [Solace]: you mean at the top of
arachnia's web in the middle of CoT?
[Solace] whispers: hee
```

```
To [Solace]: enjoying the view?
[Solace] whispers: I suddenly realised I'd
never been up here
```

Drew zoomed in and out and spun his camera around. He'd never been up here either. Now he came to look at it, someone had put a lot of love into this place. Arachnia's chamber was a tall dome like the inside of a pepperpot, the walls crisscrossed with webbing as intricate as old lace. Cocooned bodies were strung in spirals from floor to ceiling.

```
To [Solace]: omg, there's a dead kobold up
there.
To [Solace]: look at its little feet poking out
```

Drew put his head in his hands. That had been about as suave as one of the suave options in *Alpha Protocol*. Here he was, with a cute girl at the top of an enormous spiderweb, talking about dead kobolds.

```
[Solace] whispers: Ohmigod, kobold feets!
[Solace] whispers: Is it wrong I find that
cute?
To [Solace]: probably
[Solace] whispers: hee
```

At dead-on twenty minutes, Morag called the raid together and they climbed out of Arachnia's domain and into the Halls of the Torturer.

```
[Yell][Tortured Victim]: AHHHH! NO! MAKE IT
STOP!
[Yell][Vilicus]: Be grateful. To live is to
suffer. To suffer is to live.
```

They passed beneath another archway of thorns and roses into a fairly generic tower of crumbling stone, and fought their way through Vilicus's twisted, tortured guards.

"You know what I don't get?" mused Dave.

Magda: "I keep thinking I do, but there always turns out to be something else."

"What I don't get," Dave continued, unperturbed, "is what this big stone tower is doing in the middle of a hedge maze."

Ialdir: "No, no, this is really cool."

```
[Raid][Prospero]: Oh God, you've started him
[Raid][Ignatius]: Run awaaaaaaaay!
```

"About two-thirds of the way into Legend II," Ialdir—or Jacob, Drew still wasn't sure which he preferred to be called—began, "Raziel goes to speak to this man named Vilicus, who studied the secrets of immortality with the dark elves. And this is basically the tower he hangs out in."

"Yes," added Bjorn, "if you played the original games, which you wouldn't because you were a foetus, there's lots of things you'd recognise."

"Yeah, but why is it in a maze." Dave still didn't sound convinced.

Ialdir sighed. "Because Vilicus betrayed Raziel, which meant the Ritual of Torment Raziel was using to try and save his homeland went wrong, and they all got sucked down into the underworld."

"Oh right. But why is it in a maze?"

"Because," growled Bjorn, "it will allow us to get phat loots. Now shut up and hit things."

They shut up and hit things, and finally arrived at Vilicus's torture chamber. It was a vast, circular room with grooves cut into the bloodstained floor, chains hanging from the walls and ceiling, and gruesome, improbable-looking torture devices scattered around like socks on laundry day.

Vilicus himself was a tall, dark-haired man in a blood-red robe. Drew knew that up close his face was a horrible patchwork of scars.

```
[Yell][Vilicus]: Immortality is found through
pain. Come, friends, and I will make you
immortal.
```

Morag sighed. "Okay, so Vilicus is a three-phase fight. I don't know how you did it in Anni, Drew, but we normally three-heal this one. We only need one tank, so I'm going to go Endurance. Everyone give me a tick while I switch specs and change into my healing pants."

Anni'd had Vilicus on farm for the last couple of months. They'd taken to using this really cheesy strat where they'd had one healer, one tank, and everyone else on DPS to grab the damage buff and burn him down as fast as possible. Unfortunately, you could only get away with that if you were already ridiculously overgeared. Drew had sort of forgotten how to do the fight properly and, in a way, was looking forward to trying, because while it was a total pig, it was also one of the most interesting fights in the dungeon.

Morag had swapped her platemail for slightly different-looking platemail and a slightly gentler-looking sword. "Right. So, in phase one, Drew, can you tank him in a circle so Tainted Blood doesn't spread too far? Melee DPS, seriously don't stand in the shit. If you get Curse of Blood, run the fuck away. If you get Curse of Flesh stand the fuck still and let everyone stack on you. If someone gets Curse of Bone, all deeps on them, and get them out again. Phase two, same, but don't stand in blades. Phase three, all that stuff, but we need to get him down before we get too many Tormented Spirits. Bjorn and Jargogle, you're our top DPS, so run to the torture equipment and grab Glory Through Pain ASAP."

"I'll hop on the rack," said Bjorn. "You get in the iron maiden."

"If either of them go down, then prio is: Ignatius, Caius, Dave, Ialdir."

[Raid][Ialdir]: :(

Bjorn snorted. "Dude, that's what you get for playing a pet class."

[Raid][Solace]: Morag's on Ella, but if you could help out with Glory Through Pain, that'd be great.
[Raid][Solace]: I'll prio Bjorn and Magda, and prop up the raid.

```
[Raid][Prospero]: And I'll heal every-
fucking-body.
[Raid][Solace]: I'll play it by ear, but if
the damage from Glory gets too high I'll be
purging at about 40%
```

Once everyone had readychecked, Ella ran into the room, punched Vilicus in the knee, and then started moving him in a tight circle. As the Torturer took damage, his blood began pooling on the floor, and Drew edged him out to make room for the melee. Mumble was loud again, and slightly frantic.

"No, no, run away!"

"Not that way!"

"This way!"

"I said *towards*, dipshits!"

Drew's health dipped alarmingly, so he threw up Unholy Resolve. Hopefully it'd be off cooldown again by the time the next phase started. He flicked a glance at the raid's healthbars. They weren't looking good, most of them hovering at about the forty-percent mark.

Suddenly there was a massive, fleshy explosion, and Prospero and Heurodis both went grey.

```
[Yell][Vilicus]: DELICIOUS AGONY!
[Raid][Prospero]: ded
```

"Where the fuck were the melee?" roared Bjorn. "What the fuck? When someone gets Curse of Flesh, you stack on them, you don't just stand there mashing your rotation like little noobs."

Morag: "Keep it together, we're not wiping this yet."

```
[Raid][Heurodis]: you look at your boss mods
you see who has the debuffs you go where you
are meant to go its not difficult.
```

"You can rant after the fight, Bjorn."

"I'm just going to sit here and weep."

Things didn't go too badly in the second phase. People stayed out of the blades and handled the curses more or less okay. There was still a lot of raid damage and Caius went down just on the transition to phase three.

```
[Raid][Caius]: Bugger
[Raid][Heurodis]: weeping
```

Phase three was a DPS race. These indestructible ghosts kept spawning, and the trick was to kill the boss before there were too many to handle. Glory Through Pain gave a really big damage buff but at the cost of a really nasty DoT, and with a healer and two DPS down, there was no way the balance was going to work.

"Okay," said Morag. "Hail Mary strat. All DPS get Glory. We'll see if we can keep you alive."

They couldn't keep them alive.

Ialdir—pet-based noob that he was—was first to go, followed by Ignatius, then Solace, then Jargogle. Which left Morag and Ella and Dave desperately flailing at Vilicus while a rising tide of anguished spectres came forth to devour them.

"Aaaand that's a wipe," said Morag as the spirits overwhelmed her.

Next thing Drew knew, Ella was a pile of crumpled limbs and armour of the floor. He released and respawned outside the entrance to Crown of Thorns, next to Dave and Morag, whose ghosts were flying back to the instance. He swooped after them and gave four hundred gold to the nice man with the anvil who was waiting just inside to beat his armour back into shape.

Then he hit num lock and steered Ella through the winding empty halls of CoT, past Kelebos's gate and Thornheart's grove, up Arachnia's web and down Vilicus's tower. The guild was eating fish outside the torture chamber.

Mumble was kind of quiet, and Drew wondered how this would go. Wiping was part of raiding, but people tended to take it badly, especially the first wipe of the night.

Morag: "Well, not the worst effort."

A spluttering noise down Mumble.

"I know you've got stuff to say, Bjorn, and you can say it, as long as you use your inside voice."

"Sorry, I'm just in an angry space because we should not be making these mistakes. I'm not blaming anybody, but people should not be dying from Flesh Curse. Especially not if they're me. Prospero got cursed, only the ranged stacked."

```
[Raid][Solace]: Sorry, I was slow. There was
a lot of damage coming in so I couldn't stop
healing.
```

"If people were where they were meant to be, they wouldn't need healing."

```
[Raid][Jargogle]: Once again, Bjorn, this is
harder when you are in melee. You have to run
around the tainted blood.
[Raid][Jargogle]: And that means you get
everywhere more slowly.
[Raid][Jargogle]: And before you say
anything, my sprint was on cooldown.
```

"Okay." Morag. "Let's have the ranged in a bit closer to make it easier for melee to cover the distance."

Drew wasn't sure if he should say anything. The part of him that had spent three years with Anni was frustrated, just out of habit really. The deal had always been that when something like this happened, there was a rousing chorus of "we shouldn't be wiping on this" before everybody's performance got put under a microscope. The system worked well enough to get server firsts, and while he was pretty sure it wasn't right here, he wasn't sure the softly-softly approach was going to work either. The truth was, the melee should have been sharper and that was that. But everyone was acting like it was the whole raid's responsibility.

Then Drew heard himself say, "I'll try to position him better as well. I'm a bit rusty."

Where had that come from?

He braced himself to be called a noob or told to stop making excuses.

"Cool," said Morag. "Right. We're going again. Ranged stay closer, and everybody stay alert. We're taking too much avoidable damage."

The raid finished their fish and their buffing and got into position. A readycheck popped up.

Drew was still a bit dazed, but he clicked Okay.

"Three, two, one, pull."

And Ella once again hefted her maces and threw herself into battle against the vile torturer Vilicus.

```
[Yell][Vilicus]: Immortality is found through
pain. Come, friends, and I will make you
immortal.
```

Things seemed to go more smoothly this time. People's health bars were a lot, well, healthier, and everybody made it to phase three alive.

"To the rack!" cried Bjorn gleefully as Heurodis broke free of the raid to go and interact with a random piece of dungeon furniture. "Now, I will show you the meaning of imba!"

Jargogle sprinted back from the other side of the room, little daggers whirring through the air like one of those kitchen appliances you get advertised on late-night TV.

"Less boast, more DPS."

Drew kept an anxious eye on Vilicus's hit points, which seemed to be going more slowly than they had last time.

Ghosts gathered at the edges of the room and started drifting inexorably inwards.

"Uhh," he said awkwardly. "I think we're going to need to push a bit harder."

Vilicus's health crept down but still too slowly, and gradually people started getting chewed on by ghosts.

```
[Raid][Solace]: Too much raid damage
```

With Vilicus on a comfortable ten percent, the whole thing turned into a gigantic clusterfuck. Ghosts were everywhere, people were exploding, and Vilicus was still oozing toxic blood all over the place.

Morag made a noise of frustration. "Aaand that's a wipe again."

Five minutes and another hefty repair bill later, the guild were sat back on the floor outside the torture chamber, eating fish and contemplating their failure.

Morag was the first to speak. "Okay, better in some ways, worse in others. Really good job on the first two phases, but we just didn't have enough DPS on three."

"Uhh, can I say something?" asked Drew. Raid leaders could be touchy about too many people weighing in on strats. But he did actually have more experience than these guys.

"Go for it."

He took a deep breath, hoping this wouldn't come out sounding too dickish. "So, I think the trick is to be really, like, super careful in the first two phases so everyone goes into three with full health and mana. There's no point taking chances cos there's no timer. But in three, it's like a race against the ghosts, so you've kind of got to be a bit more . . . y'know."

There was silence on Mumble.

It occurred to Drew that *y'know* wasn't very specific.

"Like not reckless, but people are going to take damage and some people are gonna die, but if you're doing it right it doesn't matter."

"So." Bjorn. "You're saying we need to kill ourselves more."

"Well . . . yeah . . . I mean . . . no. But you've gotta be more willing to, like, take damage to do damage."

"We *have* done this boss before."

"Put your dick away, Bjorn." Morag. "Drew's part of the guild, he can suggest tacs just like anyone else. And I think that's a pretty good idea actually. So, Caius and Ignatius, you get Glory too."

"Just stay away from my rack."

[Raid][Ialdir]: Trust me. Nobody's interested in your rack.
[Raid][Caius]: I'll take the spiky thing at the back
[Raid][Ignatius]: And I'll take the bench thing with the blade above it

"Ready to go again?" asked Morag.

They were ready.

And in went Ella, charging valiantly forward as if doing this exact same thing hadn't just got her killed. Twice.

```
[Yell][Vilicus]: Immortality is found through
pain. Come, friends, and I will make you
immortal.
```

The first two phases went slowly but near perfectly. Raid damage was as low as you could expect with curses firing all over the place, and nobody stood in blood or on knives.

"Steady."

"Good job."

"Phase three coming up."

As phase three hit, Jargogle, Heurodis, Ignatius, and Caius ran to their assigned torture devices and buffed up. There was a lot more damage coming in now, and Drew paced out his cooldowns to take as much pressure off Morag as he could. But, on the plus side, Vilicus was also taking a lot more damage.

"You still need to stack, guys."

"More heals on Bjorn."

"Got him."

"Jargogle's boned."

"Could you possibly rephrase that?"

"Out."

"Losing Helen."

```
[Yell][Vilicus]: DELICIOUS AGONY!
```

"Shit."

"Sorry."

"Focus on Bjorn."

"Dave, get Glory."

"Booyah!"

"Keep it up."

```
[Yell][Vilicus]: DELICIOUS AGONY!
```

"Dave's down."

"Maaaan, I just got the buff."

"Flesh, flesh!"

"Full burn."

```
[Yell][Vilicus]: DELICIOUS AGONY!
[Raid][Ialdir]: I'm out
[Yell][Vilicus]: DELICIOUS AGONY!
[Raid][Solace]: Me too
[Raid][Solace]: 3%. You can do it guys
```

Between dodging ghosts, managing his cooldowns, and trying to output as much DPS as humanly possible, Drew was barely remembering to breathe.

He'd forgotten how completely mad this fight could be.

It was awesome.

Vilicus's health was a tiny red sliver in the bottom of the bar.

And so was Ella's.

Come on, come on, come on.

```
[Yell][Vilicus]: I HAVE . . . TRANSCENDED!
```

And with that, Vilicus sank to his knees and snuffed it, taking his ghosts and his poisonous blood trail with him.

Drew practically collapsed as well.

And Mumble went wild.

"Get in there!"

"Omigod!"

"Holy fuck, we did it!"

"I really didn't think we were going to make that."

"*Check out my DPS!*"

"Can I get a rez, please?"

"Well done, guys, that was awesome."

Slowly, people began to calm down and wander round the torture chamber, bringing their friends back to life.

"And now," announced Bjorn, "the loots."

Drew had pretty much forgotten about loot this run. He had nearly everything he needed from CoT anyway, and the guild seemed to have quite a relaxed attitude to the whole thing, which took the pressure off gearing.

"So, let's see what Uncle Bjorn has in his magic bag. We have a lovely ranger wep, with a beautiful thorns and blood motif. The Tormenter's Bow."

```
[Raid][Heurodis]: [The Tormenter's Bow]
```

"Does anybody not already have The Tormenter's Bow?"

```
[Raid][Dave]: Ill have it for my os
[Raid][Ialdir]: I'll have it for my
mantelpiece
[Raid][Heurodis]: disenchanting. if you need
any purple mats apply to the bank
```

"And, finally, our last prize this evening, boasting an attractive hardwood handle and a blade which I feel I should point out is extremely historically implausible: The Inexorable Axe."

```
[Raid][Heurodis]: [The Inexorable Axe]
```

Drew jerked suddenly alert.
Holy shit.
Holy, holy shit.
His axe.
Bjorn's voice seemed to be coming from far away. "Roll MS if you need it."
Drew scrabbled urgently at his keyboard.

```
Heurodis rolls a 52
Ialdir rolls a 34
Orcarella rolls a 2
Dave rolls a 98
Ignatius rolls a 41
```

```
Solace rolls a 57
Jargogle rolls a 84
Prospero rolls a 65
Morag rolls a 14
Caius rolls a 71
[Raid][Orcarella]: . . .
```

"Looks like it's going to Dave. Well done, Dave. Round of applause for Dave."

```
[Raid][Orcarella]: . . .
```

Mumble exploded again. Drew had never heard so many adults giggling at once.

Honestly, it was kind of a mixed feeling. On the one hand, nine relative strangers were laughing at something he was not only upset about, but still felt quite embarrassed at being upset about. On the other hand . . . it was also weirdly nice. You had to know something about someone to be able to take the piss out of them. And, in a funny way, you had to care.

He was glad he was safely on the other side of a screen, because he was probably grinning like a dork.

You have received [The Inexorable Axe]
```
[Raid][Orcarella]: thx guys
```

He opened his inventory and stared lovingly at his new weapon for a moment before equipping it.

Bjorn kind of had a point. The blade was completely implausible.

It looked like a scythe stuck on a cartwheel stuck on a stick. But it was best in slot for Vengeance.

Orcarella ran around in circles excitedly and a few guildies cheered as she passed.

```
[Raid][Solace]: Hey, you know what this
means?
[Raid][Orcarella]: ?
```

```
[Raid][Solace]: You're officially the best
geared tank on the server
[Raid][Orcarella]: lol
[Raid][Jargogle]: Haha
[Raid][Dave]: lol
[Raid][Ialdir]: Grats dude
```

"Okay," said Morag. "We're calling it here. We'll finish off on Wednesday, so sign up on the forums if you haven't already. That was a really good run, guys."

People said their goodnights and began leaving the raid group.

```
[Guild][Ialdir]: Awesome night
[Guild][Ialdir]: But I need to go to bed
before my husband divorces me
[Guild][Solace]: Night night
[Guild][Sindarella]: nn
[Guild][Heurodis]: anyone for a hc?
```

Drew checked the clock on his minimap. It was just eleven, so there'd be time, but he wasn't completely sure he wanted to.

```
[Guild][Dave]: mums turning the internet off
[Guild][Dave]: :(
[Guild][Dave]: :(
[Guild][Sindarella]: me and Helen can come
[Guild][Sindarella]: I can storm tank it lol
[Guild][Ignatius]: I'm not healing you in
storm
[Guild][Heurodis]: lol
```

Drew realised he was alone in an empty torture chamber. He wondered if Solace would come with them if he went on the heroic, but maybe she'd gone fishing, and by the time he was done, she might have logged off.

He stared for a while at the guild roster, and the little line that read, *Solace: Online.*

Would it be weird to just ask her if she wanted to hang out? What if it was weird? What if she said no?

```
To [Solace]: you fishing?
[Solace] whispers: Yes
[Solace] whispers: It helps me wind down
after a raid
```

There was the text-based equivalent of an awkward silence.

```
[Solace] whispers: You can come join me if
you like
[Solace] whispers: you don't have to
[Solace] whispers: if you dont want to
To [Solace]: omw
[Solace] whispers: :)
```
Solace has invited you to join a group: y/n
Solace is now group leader.

Drew activated his bindstone, then hopped a skyship across continents and flew south to Alarion. He flapped over the ruins looking for Solace, and found her on the same bit of fallen temple. She was sitting on the edge in her battered fishing hat, her line arcing into the purple-blue water.

Ella took off her helmet and plopped down next to her.

```
[Group][Orcarella]: good run tonight
[Group][Solace]: Yeah, it was fun
[Group][Solace]: Nice work on Vilicus
[Group][Orcarella]: you too
[Group][Solace]: I died
[Group][Orcarella]: yeah but heroically
[Group][Solace]: Heroically hit by a ghost
while trying to get off a Greater Heal
[Group][Orcarella]: well you died so others
might live and stuff
```

[Group][Solace]: First rule of healing is healer heal thyself
[Group][Solace]: We pretend to be all nurturing but actually we're just trying to keep lots of warm bodies between us and the enemy
[Group][Orcarella]: like emperor Palpatine

There was a long—for lack of a better term—silence, and Drew wondered if he'd blown it. Dead kobold, fine. Comparing her to Darth Sidious, not so much.

[Group][Solace]: Sorry, I'm trying to make a Star Wars joke but the Emperor has no decent lines.
[Group][Orcarella]: I find your lack of healz disturbing
[Group][Solace]: That's Vader.
[Group][Orcarella]: wow you've put way more thought into this than I have
[Group][Solace]: *blush*
[Group][Orcarella]: no its cool
[Group][Orcarella]: you're right, I can't remember any of his lines
[Group][Orcarella]: except like you know
[Group][Orcarella]: DIEDIEDIE
[Group][Solace]: For a guy called Darth Sidious he's kind of
[Group][Solace]: . . .
[Group][Solace]: not very insidious
[Group][Orcarella]: lol
[Group][Orcarella]: i hadn't even noticed that
[Group][Orcarella]: you know what I find weird about star wars
[Group][Solace]: I'd love to hear what you find weird about Star Wars

[Group][Orcarella]: i have to go google this because it's so weird
[Group][Orcarella]: brb
[Group][Solace]: kk
[Group][Orcarella]: okay so this epic saga of love and war and space and good and evil and stuff opens with:
[Group][Orcarella]: The taxation of trade routes to outlying star systems is in dispute.
[Group][Solace]: lololol
[Group][Solace]: Hey, I played a republic in Crusader Kings II. [Group][Solace]: Trade embargos are hardcore.
[Group][Orcarella]: You play CKII?
[Group][Solace]: I may have the body of a weak and feeble Dark Elf
[Group][Solace]: But I have the heart and stomach of a king, and a King of England
[Group][Orcarella]: don't you mean a concrete elephant
[Group][Solace]: And he likes Blackadder too
[Group][Solace]: Be still my beating heart

Drew flustered at his keyboard, typed about five responses and deleted them all. Then panicked because it looked like he'd panicked.

[Group][Orcarella]: lol
[Group][Orcarella]: but seriously you're into strategy games
[Group][Solace]: CKII isn't really a strategy game
[Group][Solace]: It's an RPG with a big map
[Group][Orcarella]: i never got into it
[Group][Orcarella]: too easy
[Group][Orcarella]: i took over Europe on my third playthrough

Shit. Now he sounded like he was boasting.

[Group][Orcarella]: sorry i just sounded like a dick
[Group][Orcarella]: i just like figuring out games
[Group][Solace]: No, I get that
[Group][Solace]: But sometimes it's nice to experience stuff
[Group][Orcarella]: i'm not very good at that
[Group][Orcarella]: i like to know what my goals are
[Group][Orcarella]: so I know when I'm doing well
[Group][Orcarella]: I guess it's why I like raiding
[Group][Solace]: You're really good at it
[Group][Orcarella]: thx
[Group][Orcarella]: but it kind of stopped being fun
[Group][Orcarella]: i mean until I joined you guys
[Group][Solace]: The most fun I've had in CKII was when I've been losing
[Group][Solace]: There was this one time I got usurped by my evil uncle and banished to a tiny corner of Sicily
[Group][Solace]: Where I sat plotting my revenge for 18 years
[Group][Solace]: And another time my entire dynasty died out because my only heir was a pious homosexual who hung out in Jerusalem with a poet
[Group][Orcarella]: lol
[Group][Orcarella]: you should have had him assassinated
[Group][Solace]: O.O

```
[Group][Orcarella]: sorry that sounds really
homophobic
[Group][Orcarella]: i just meant because it
was game mechanically suboptimal
[Group][Solace]: *snerk*
[Group][Solace]: Some people are game
mechanically suboptimal. Get over it.
[Group][Orcarella]: :(
[Group][Solace]: I might get that on a
T-shirt.
[Group][Orcarella]: :)
```

There was another silence-equivalent. Drew really wanted to move the conversation on, but he wasn't sure what to say.

He stared at Ella and Solace sitting on their rock. The moon was full and silver. And it suddenly occurred to him that he was using this game, for which he paid a monthly subscription, as a glorified chat client.

But he was having such a nice time he didn't mind. It was a bit stressful because he was used to having something specific to talk about in most of his social interactions. With the guild, it was raiding. With Andy, it was Frisbee. With his parents, it was did he have socks and was he eating properly. With his coursemates, it was gaming and the course. There'd been this one time when Sanee and Steff had got into a big argument, and Sanee had sat in Drew's room crying for hours, but that had been weird and a bit uncomfortable, and they'd never mentioned it afterwards.

But with Solace, it was just sort of . . . being with someone you like being with. And that felt . . . nice. And seemed kind of important somehow. Which made him wonder if it was important to her as well. And then he wondered if she was wondering the same thing. So maybe he should tell her, so she would know. But he wasn't sure how to put it, in case it came out wrong, and sounded all intense and creepy.

```
[Group][Orcarella]: I like the way you play
games
```

[Group][Orcarella]: you seem to get a lot out of them

[Group][Solace]: You don't think it's weird?

[Group][Orcarella]: well maybe a bit at first

[Group][Orcarella]: but what's weirder? playing a game because you like it or playing a game because you feel you have to?

[Group][Solace]: Is that how you feel?

[Group][Orcarella]: sometimes

[Group][Solace]: :(

[Group][Solace]: *hugs*

[Group][Orcarella]: but i enjoyed tonight

[Group][Orcarella]: reminded me how it used to be

[Group][Orcarella]: and i liked running that heroic with you

[Group][Orcarella]: and this is nice too

[Group][Solace]: Yes, it really is

[Group][Solace]: Um

[Group][Solace]: If you wanted, we could maybe roll some alts

[Group][Solace]: Go all the way back to the beginning and say good-bye to the old world before they nuke it in the next expansion

[Group][Orcarella]: they're really doing that?

[Group][Solace]: I saw something on MMO Champion this morning

[Group][Solace]: It's going to be called Genesis and crazy machine gods are going to rise up and try to remake the world

[Group][Orcarella]: what? again??

[Group][Orcarella]: i thought we stopped that shit two patches ago

[Group][Solace]: No, that was foreshadowing

[Group][Orcarella]: lol

```
[Group][Orcarella]: so what're we going to
roll?
[Group][Solace]: Something new? For both of us
[Group][Orcarella]: my old main's a human
[Group][Solace]: And I'm not playing a high
elf on principle
[Group][Solace]: They betrayed my people man
[Group][Orcarella]: kk, that leaves kobolds
medusas or dorfs
[Group][Solace]: Also I kind of want to be hot
[Group][Orcarella]: so no kobolds then?
[Group][Solace]: How about medusas?
[Group][Solace]: I've never seen the starting
area
[Group][Orcarella]: me neither
[Group][Orcarella]: so when's good?
[Group][Solace]: I can do whenever
[Group][Orcarella]: how about tomorrow
[Group][Orcarella]: o wait shit
[Group][Orcarella]: got a thing
[Group][Solace]: Wednesday's raid night
[Group][Orcarella]: thurs?
[Group][Solace]: It's a date.
[Group][Orcarella]: cool
```

And it was only later, after they'd said an awkward goodnight and Drew was lying in bed running over the conversation in head, that he tripped over the d-word.

He knew he was probably overthinking, but that didn't stop him from overthinking.

It was probably just a turn of phrase.

But if it wasn't, then that was . . .

. . . good?

CHAPTER

Drew was pretty determined not to get himself into a tizzy over a nondate with an imaginary elf on the internet, but he couldn't really help it. He managed to get on with things, and people didn't seem to notice he was slightly distracted, or if they did, they didn't take the piss. He made decent progress on his project and rolled along to Sanee's birthday thing on Tuesday night. Andy couldn't make it and Tinuviel had shown up with a random philosophy student called Ocean, which, Drew was depressed to realise, left him as the only one without a date. Well, there were a bunch of people from the course there too, some of whom were probably single, but they didn't count.

It was a pretty good evening, though. It basically went the same way as it had last year. Steff had baked a cake with *The cake is a lie* piped delicately over the top in bright-green icing, and Sanee got into a really bitter fight about *The Stanley Parable* with a random guy. Sometimes Drew thought Sanee liked arguing about video games more than he liked playing them. Eventually people drifted off and the survivors found themselves trying to play Twilight Imperium, drunk, at three in the morning.

Drew passed out sometime around his third turn and woke up just in time for lab, with several plastic spaceships embedded in his face. He survived the day but was kind of out of it for the raid that evening. It was all a bit of a blur, and he got through it on Pepsi Max and muscle memory. Despite having a tank on his way down from a cheap-wine-and-board-games bender, the guild took the next three bosses down relatively easily. They wiped a few times but Drew was pretty sure none of them were his fault.

He left the guild celebrating, face-planted into his pillow, and woke up the next morning weirdly missing Solace. They hadn't talked much during the raid, and he'd got strangely used to hanging out on a rock in Alarion.

That afternoon, when he should have been shading a chair, he caught himself freestyling with the drawing pad, and his doodles grew into the outline of an elf and orc sitting next to each other by the ocean.

Sanee leaned over from his terminal. "Dude. Are you drawing fanart?"

"Fuck off."

"Looks good."

"Thanks." He said, *Thanks*. He meant, *Die in a fire*. There was no way Sanee was going to let this slide. He tried to head him off anyway. "It's just my *HoL* character and a guildie."

"I don't think the world's ready for girl-on-girl, orc-on-elf action."

"We're just friends."

Sanee gave him a look. "Yeah right, because I always sketch pictures of my friend's video game characters."

"Dude, I've been trying to make a chair that doesn't look crap for an hour. It's this, or Bejewelled."

"Oh man, step away from the PopCap. But, seriously, you should totally send this to her. Chicks really go for this stuff."

Drew eyed his screen dubiously. It'd actually come out pretty well in a fanarty kind of way. "Wouldn't that be creepy as hell?"

"It'd be creepy if they were naked."

"Thanks, that's really helpful."

"Stop being a wuss, and go for it."

It was probably a bad idea, but Drew opened the guild forum and PMed the picture to Solace. He tried to come up with a nonweird message, failed miserably, so he sent it without comment.

"You do realise," said Sanee slowly, "you probably just sent a cute picture to another dude."

The thought had crossed Drew's mind. Rule One of the Internet: assume everyone is middle-aged, male, and a serial killer. "I told you, we're mates."

"Then I'm sure you're not going to be remotely disappointed when she turns out to be a burly Yorkshireman."

"Maybe I'm into that."

"That would explain why you've never had a girlfriend. And I'm not counting that crazy chick you hooked up with last year."

Drew gave him the finger. "I have had a girlfriend. We broke up when I came to uni because we couldn't do long distance."

Sanee launched into an enthusiastic rendition of "My Girlfriend Who Lives in Canada."

Drew pulled on his headphones and went back to his chair.

About halfway through the afternoon, he got a PM back from Solace. *This came when I was stuck in a super dull solid state lecture, and made my day. Thank you so much. I love it. I'm looking forward to seeing you tonight. I rolled a diabolist. She's called Aconite. S.*

That evening, Drew sat down at his computer and looked at the *Heroes of Legend* character creation screen for the first time in two years. He clicked on the Medusa icon and the system generated him a ridiculously stacked, bright-blue dude with a pornstache made of snakes. He winced and clicked the Female icon. Pornstache vanished, and was replaced by an implausibly curvy young lady with a python Mohawk. After a good twenty minutes of fiddling around with hairstyles, faces, and skin tones, Drew had managed to put together someone he liked. Someone he thought he'd be okay to stick with for eighty-odd levels, but who didn't scream "I'm a miserable nerd-boy and this is the only way I can get to look at a hot chick."

He hovered over the character classes. He was tempted to go for a myrmidon so he'd know what he was doing and wouldn't look like too much of an idiot in front of Solace, but he'd already got one and he was supposed to be trying something new and outside his comfort zone. On the other hand, his inner pragmatist pointed out that as Solace had rolled a pure DPS class, they really needed someone who could heal and/or tank.

Oh screw it, he clicked Elementalist. They were supposed to be this super adaptable hybrid class, which meant they'd wound up being slightly crappy at tanking, healing, and DPS. They'd basically been unplayable in vanilla, but they'd been buffed to the point that they were now just really hard to play. Viridium, the guys so hard-core they were actually paid to play, had famously had a storm elementalist for their MT since Rise of the Underworld.

Okay, he had a race, a class, and a face he could more or less stand. Now for the hard bit: the name.

He stared at the little black box, his mind completely blank. It was a shame Dave was taken. He briefly considered Davella but that would probably get pretty old, pretty quickly.

He alt-tabbed, fired up Google, and since the medusas were vaguely Greeky, searched for Greek girls' names. He tried a bunch and eventually managed to get Efthalia. It sounded a bit like she had a lisp, but by that stage, he'd kind of given up caring.

Then he settled back in his chair to watch the introductory cutscene, which was all arty splash screens and ponderous voice-overs, explaining how the medusas had once been the proud rulers of a mighty empire, struck down for defying their gods blah blah cursed blah blah stone gaze blah blah snakes for hair. It finished up with a fly-over of the Island of Krytos. Here and there he could see starting-level characters bunny-hopping through the ruins as they collected ten whatevers and killed twenty whatsits. For truly of such deeds are legends made.

The first thing he saw when got control of Efthalia was a pretty little medusa sitting under an olive tree. She jumped up and waved, her long, jewel-coloured snakes wriggling excitedly.

Aconite has invited you to join a group: y/n
Aconite is now group leader.
```
[Group][Aconite]: Hi
[Group][Efthalia]: Hi :)
[Group][Aconite]: Have you checked out the
dance animation yet?
```

Drew */danced* and Efthalia writhed in a circle, hips and snakes swaying provocatively.

```
[Group][Efthalia]: i should probably stop
doing that
[Group][Aconite]: Hee
```

```
[Group][Efthalia]: thought I'd try ele
tanking
[Group][Aconite]: Thought I'd try harnessing
the fell powers of the nether realm to rain
death and destruction upon mine enemies
[Group][Aconite]: I don't often get to DPS
[Group][Aconite]: I'm excited
[Group][Efthalia]: don't get too excited
[Group][Efthalia]: you're going to have like
one spell
```

Aconite began to twist her hands in mystical circles as dark energy gathered between her fingertips. After three long seconds, a burst of shadow tendrils exploded from her fingertips, dealing seven points of damage to a hapless kitten.

```
[Group][Efthalia]: !!!!
[Group][Efthalia]: wow you are pure evil
[Group][Aconite]: Bwhahahaha
[Group][Aconite]: Kittens of the world
tremble before me
[Group][Efthalia]: probably a good thing
youre a healer
[Group][Aconite]: :)
[Group][Efthalia]: we should get a quest
```

There was dominatrixy-looking medusa called Magistrix Venetezia standing conveniently close by, as if she expected a never-ending stream of young medusas to appear before her, ready to undertake any number of menial and arbitrary tasks. Drew clicked on her and a lengthy text box popped up. Normally he skipped this stuff and went straight to whatever it was he was supposed to be killing, but he was pretty sure Solace would want to read the whole thing.

It turned out that the power of the medusas was dwindling because Reasons, and this meant that all the people they'd turned into stone over the centuries were slowly turning back, but had gone crazy on account of having been statues for hundreds of years. Which meant it was the sad duty of all young medusas to seek them out and murder them in the face. For, like, honour and fate and shit. Drew accepted this noble quest and bounced up and down to signal his readiness to Solace.

```
[Group][Aconite]: I think there's another
quest over by the fallen temple
[Group][Aconite]: Might as well get them both
```

The two of them jogged obediently over to the temple where Magistrix Demetria suggested they should practice using the mighty legacy of their once great empire to curtail the damage being done to their fragile homeland by the island's ravenous fauna.

```
[Group][Aconite]: So, you want to murder
innocent prisoners or turn goats into stone?
[Group][Efthalia]: goats are a menace
[Group][Efthalia]: I was on this school trip
once and one nearly ate my DS
[Group][Aconite]: Did you kill it for the XP?
[Group][Efthalia]: I would have done but it
was red for me
[Group][Aconite]: Hee
```

Drew took his questing pretty seriously, so he pulled up the map and plotted the most efficient path between the land of the terrible goats and the lair of the completely nonthreatening prisoners.

```
[Group][Efthalia]: kk follow me
[Group][Aconite]: Sir yes Sir!
[Group][Aconite]: Lt Goatkiller reporting for
duty
[Group][Efthalia]: do have any idea of the
penalty for mocking a superior goat killer?
[Group][Aconite]: Court martial followed by
immediate cessation of chocolate rations?
[Group][Efthalia]: lol
```

Drew was grinning as he led the way through the ruins and up a kind of shallow escarpment to where some goats were peacefully grazing.

```
[Group][Aconite]: Omg, check them out,
destroying the ancestral homeland of our
people.
[Group][Efthalia]: horny bastards
[Group][Aconite]: lol
[Group][Aconite]: So, strat?
```

It took Drew a couple of seconds of eying the goats quite seriously to realise this had probably been a joke.

Then he realised he'd left it too long to just laugh, so he had to pretend he'd been going with it all along.

```
[Group][Efthalia]: kk this is a 2 phase fight
[Group][Efthalia]: in phase 1 we cast the
only spells we've got
[Group][Efthalia]: then in phase 2 one of us
remembers to cast stone gaze
[Group][Aconite]: You actually thought about
that for a second didn't you?
[Group][Efthalia]: :(
[Group][Aconite]: Aww, you're cute
```

Efthalia summoned the elemental forces of fire for 2.5 seconds and lightly singed the goat for three points of damage. It lowered its head, and charged her for five points of damage, which was a significant chunk of health.

```
[Group][Efthalia]: omg nerf goats
```

Shadows engulfed the goat and it flumped sideways with a despairing bleat.

```
[Group][Aconite]: Woot! SB crit for 8!
```

```
[Group][Efthalia]: Wow, it's like playing
with Bjorn
[Group][Efthalia]: also we were supposed to
use stone gaze on it
[Group][Efthalia]: not just keep DPSing like
a noob
[Group][Aconite]: :(
[Group][Aconite]: But that's what DPS do!
[Group][Efthalia]: you mocked the goat strat
[Group][Efthalia]: and now look what's
happened
[Group][Aconite]: You're just jealous of my
imba deeps.
```

Efthalia lobbed another impressive-looking but mechanically underwhelming flamebolt at the next goat, and this time Aconite swooped forward and petrified it. Three seconds later the goat recovered, and so they just killed it dead.

```
[Group][Aconite]: Take that you caprine fiend!
[Group][Efthalia]: you what?
[Group][Aconite]: It means, um, goaty
[Group][Aconite]: Now I think about it, it's
not that insulting
[Group][Efthalia]: lol
```

Five minutes later, they'd petrified and slaughtered the requisite number of goats, and Drew pulled up the map again to see where they needed to go next. He was halfway there when he realised he'd left Solace behind. He wheeled about and saw her standing at the top of the escarpment, looking out to sea. He ran back to join her.

There was a gradual slope down to the golden beach and the turquoise sea and the shell huts of the angry crabmen who Aconite and Efthalia would probably be asked to kill in about three levels' time. In the distance he could just about make out the edge of the next island, and beyond that marble columns of the once great city of Minea. Beyond even that, he almost thought he could see the mainland, although it was almost certainly a skybox.

[Group][Aconite]: I've never been here before
[Group][Efthalia]: You haven't done [World Explorer]?
[Group][Efthalia]: I thought it'd be just your thing
[Group][Aconite]: I'm working on it
[Group][Aconite]: But I didn't want to just zoom over everything on my [Tainted Pegasus].
[Group][Aconite]: It's World Explorer not World Ignorer.
[Group][Aconite]: So I'm kind of doing it on foot.
[Group][Aconite]: And I don't want it to become a chore so I'm spreading it out.
[Group][Efthalia]: wow you've really thought about this
[Group][Aconite]: *blush*
[Group][Efthalia]: no its cool
[Group][Efthalia]: most of my achies are raid stuff and the stuff you get automatically like level x or do main quest y
[Group][Efthalia]: I kind of never saw the point
[Group][Aconite]: I'm not sure either
[Group][Aconite]: Either it's stuff I would have done anyway so I don't see why I need an achi
[Group][Aconite]: Or it's stuff I wouldn't do, and an achi isn't going to make me
[Group][Efthalia]: heh
[Group][Efthalia]: Tinuviel would say that achievements validate nonstandard modes of interaction within the gameworld

[Group][Aconite]: Is that someone from your old guild?
[Group][Efthalia]: no that's a friend off my course
[Group][Efthalia]: it's like her actual name
[Group][Aconite]: I don't know whether to feel pleased for her or sorry for her
[Group][Efthalia]: weirdly it sort of suits her
[Group][Efthalia]: she's got long red hair and sort of looks like an elf anyway
[Group][Aconite]: When you say friend?
[Group][Efthalia]: no seriously just friends
[Group][Efthalia]: I think that's why she hangs out with me
[Group][Efthalia]: It's quite hard being a girl on a game art design course
[Group][Aconite]: I can't imagine there'd be that many of them
[Group][Efthalia]: girls or courses?
[Group][Aconite]: Hee, both.
[Group][Efthalia]: Yeah just us, Teesside, Anglia Ruskin, Southampton Solent, and the UCA I think.
[Group][Aconite]: Who's us?
[Group][Aconite]: Sorry, you don't have to answer that if you don't want to
[Group][Efthalia]: no its cool
[Group][Efthalia]: Leicester
[Group][Aconite]: University of Leicester?
[Group][Efthalia]: lol no I mean de montfort
[Group][Efthalia]: but we always call it leicester
[Group][Efthalia]: cos de montfort university sounds crap
[Group][Efthalia]: and simon de montfort was a total dick

[Group][Efthalia]: he like threw all the jews out of leicester
[Group][Aconite]: :(
[Group][Efthalia]: its like going to the University of Davros
[Group][Aconite]: Omg you just made me lol
[Group][Aconite]: And now I feel really bad
[Group][Efthalia]: sorry
[Group][Aconite]: :)
[Group][Efthalia]: so where do you go?
[Group][Efthalia]: i mean you don't have to say
[Group][Aconite]: It's fine
[Group][Aconite]: I, um, actually go to the University of Leicester
[Group][Efthalia]: omg
[Group][Efthalia]: your totally looking down on me now aren't you?
[Group][Aconite]: No!
[Group][Aconite]: I wouldn't.
[Group][Aconite]: I promise.
[Group][Efthalia]: its honestly the best place that does this course
[Group][Efthalia]: except Glasgow
[Group][Efthalia]: but I didn't want to go to Scotland
[Group][Aconite]: I really don't care what university you go to
[Group][Efthalia]: but Leicester's like a proper university
[Group][Efthalia]: and you do a proper subject
[Group][Efthalia]: you're like way too smart for me
[Group][Aconite]: :(
[Group][Aconite]: Don't say that
[Group][Aconite]: A uni is just a uni

[Group][Aconite]: And you study what you like
and what you're good at
[Group][Aconite]: And you're really good at
what you do
[Group][Aconite]: I loved your drawing.
You're very talented.
[Group][Efthalia]: I don't know what to say now
[Group][Efthalia]: Thanks
[Group][Efthalia]: i just worry about this
stuff
[Group][Efthalia]: my parents are really great
but when I said I wanted to do this they were
all like how does that get you a job
[Group][Aconite]: *hugs*
[Group][Efthalia]: sokay
[Group][Efthalia]: i'm not freaking out or
anything
[Group][Efthalia]: hey I've just thought
[Group][Efthalia]: you're just down the road

Shit. That looked totally stalker. He'd been so desperate to change
the subject from "I think you're way too good for me" that he'd
changed it to "I know where you live."

[Group][Efthalia]: do you wanna go kill some
loonies?
[Group][Aconite]: You mean in the game,
right?
[Group][Aconite]: Because out of context that
sounds really weird.

You're in a hole, Drew, stop digging.

[Group][Efthalia]: um yeah in the game
[Group][Efthalia]: I wasn't inviting you to
like come hang out with me
[Group][Efthalia]: and attack the mentally ill

No, stop digging. Stop.

```
[Group][Aconite]: Honestly, first you tell me
you go to a university named after a famous
anti-Semite
[Group][Aconite]: and then you invite me to
come beat up some disabled people
[Group][Efthalia]: :( :( :(
[Group][Aconite]: Aw, don't make sadface. I
was only teasing. I'm sorry.
[Group][Efthalia]: :)
```

They pressed on to the next area and rained arcane death on their next batch of completely innocent bystanders. By the time they returned to the quest-givers, they'd accumulated enough XP to hit level two, which meant their quests sent them each off to talk to their individual class trainer. Drew got a baseline healing spell called Nourishing Soil, and Solace got Infestation, which turned out to be completely useless at this level because between the two of them, they could kill everything they met before the DoT had a chance to tick.

Over the next few hours they massacred most of the native wildlife, collected the lost personal effects of a thirtieth-level magistrix who should really have been able to deal with this shit herself, and tracked down a highly dangerous mad oracle who, when they met her, turned out to be level four. They also spent more time talking, overanalysing quest text, and looking at scenery than Drew had over the whole of the last three years. It kind of meant that by midnight they were still level ten, even with the XP nerfs that had come in with the last couple of expansions. But Drew honestly didn't care. He was having . . . Oh, what was that word again? Fun.

And the more time he spent with Solace, the harder it was to remember his "don't fall for imaginary elves" rule.

```
[Group][Efthalia]: shit i should probably be
in bed
[Group][Efthalia]: do you ever sleep?
```

[Group][Aconite]: I've got a touch of insomnia

[Group][Aconite]: And I kind of like HoL late at night

[Group][Aconite]: It's all quiet, so the game feels like it's just mine

[Group][Efthalia]: except when orcs come and hang out on your rock

[Group][Aconite]: I like that too

[Group][Efthalia]: :)

[Group][Efthalia]: do you want to do this again sometime?

[Group][Aconite]: Definitely

[Group][Efthalia]: Tomorrow?

[Group][Aconite]: Oh, it's the Masqueraid on Fridays

[Group][Efthalia]: Yeah I saw that on the guild calendar

[Group][Efthalia]: I have no idea what it is

[Group][Aconite]: It used to be our night for farming RP gear

[Group][Aconite]: But it's just sort of evolved into a be slightly drunk, wear a silly costume and do something random night

[Group][Aconite]: It's fun. You should come.

[Group][Efthalia]: Uh

[Group][Aconite]: We're going to do Traitor's Spire.

[Group][Efthalia]: I farmed that to death last expansion

[Group][Aconite]: But did you ever do it in a [Lovely Red Dress].

[Group][Efthalia]: I don't think that's Ella's style

[Group][Aconite]: I can tailor you the tuxedo set

[Group][Aconite]: If you want to be all
Radclyffe Hall about it
[Group][Efthalia]: I don't know what that is
but it sounds like a late vanilla dungeon
[Group][Aconite]: Early 20th century novelist
[Group][Aconite]: Wrote a really depressing
book about how miserable it is being a
lesbian in the 1920s
[Group][Efthalia]: how do you know about this
stuff?
[Group][Aconite]: Well I do go the University
of Leicester :P
[Group][Efthalia]: :P
[Group][Aconite]: Seriously, come to the raid
tomorrow. It'll be good.
[Group][Aconite]: Plus I bet you can do
Maladreth in your sleep
[Group][Efthalia]: All right if you promise
there'll be drinking
[Group][Aconite]: Bjorn might even sing
[Group][Efthalia]: and that's supposed to
tempt me how?
[Group][Efthalia]: wait Bjorn goes?
[Group][Efthalia]: it really doesn't sound
like his thing
[Group][Aconite]: Hanging out with his
friends wouldn't be his thing?
[Group][Aconite]: I know he's a bit of a dick
but that's really harsh
[Group][Efthalia]: i just meant he seems all
super hard-core
[Group][Aconite]: Oh he still gets to show
off
[Group][Aconite]: But honestly it's just how
we hang out on our Fridays
[Group][Aconite]: Like other people go to the
pub

[Group][Efthalia]: I guess I'll sign up then
[Group][Aconite]: Yay! See you tomorrow
[Group][Efthalia]: yeah see you then
[Group][Aconite]: I had a really nice time
tonight
[Group][Efthalia]: Me too
[Group][Efthalia]: nn
[Group][Efthalia]: *hugs*

CHAPTER 5

Drew liked to keep Fridays clear just on the off-chance something came up, which meant, in practice, hanging out in the pub with his course mates because none of them had anything better to do. That said, he was pretty sure Sanee would still rip the piss out of him for going on a raid when he could, theoretically, have been at a trendy nightclub or gate-crashing an Embassy party. In Sanee's estimation, raiding was basically one step up from speed-dating.

But he pushed all that stuff aside, got himself a six-pack, and settled down in front of his keyboard. He'd expected it to be a sort of undermanned, overgeared, half-arsed business, but actually, it seemed really popular. There were even people who weren't on the raid hanging out in Mumble chatting as they levelled or played other video games or, in Caius's case, worked from home. And, to his surprise, Drew found he was having a good time.

Solace had posted him an [Elegant Tuxedo] set, so for the first time since he'd started playing, Drew actually put something in Ella's cosmetic slot. She kind of looked like a really angry butler, but he was glad he'd bothered, because everyone else was in an equally silly costume. Solace, as promised, was wearing a [Lovely Red Dress] from the Valentine's event, Morag had a pumpkin head from Halloween, Ialdir was wearing a set of elven chain Drew suspected had some kind of deep lore significance, and Bjorn had somehow managed to polymorph himself into a mushroom, which Drew was pretty sure was one of the really heavy faction rewards from vanilla.

They made a strange party as they burst through the gates of Traitor's Spire in pursuit of Maladreth the Betrayer, the elf responsible for the schism in the elvish people, who, to be fair, was dressed almost as ludicrously as they were. He was sort of this crazy bishi sorcerer with ankle-length black hair, swirly black robes, massive nineteen eighties shoulder pads, and an enormous pointy helm that had been the subject of many cock jokes down the years.

They scythed in a leisurely manner through what had once been top-tier raiding content, bickering affectionately over which drops looked coolest or stupidest or most like a wang. They were constantly stopping to take screenshots for the guild photo album, look at cool things, and listen to Bjorn and Ialdir trying to out-lore each other. People, including Drew, got steadily drunker and louder as the evening progressed. There was even singing, led by Bjorn, who had a surprisingly impressive baritone.

What there wasn't, was anything from Solace. At least not on Mumble, at least as far as Drew could make out. But then it was hard to tell because there were a lot of people chipping in all over the place. It was something he'd been low-key aware of for a while. Different guilds had very different voice policies, and it was hard to keep track of who was saying what in the middle of a raid anyway, but it was getting to the point that it was A Thing. And he felt bad that it was A Thing. After all, it was pretty normal for some people not to talk in Mumble.

The truth was, Sanee's jokes about chicks on the internet had opened up a whole can of gender-related worms that Drew had been very careful to keep closed.

Then again, maybe he'd been right to. Whatever was going on with Solace, they were just hanging out in a video game. And obviously it was better for Drew to imagine this cute, lonely gamer girl instead of, well, someone like him. But basically whether Solace really looked anything like her avatar was none of his business.

Also, Tinuviel would have pointed out that assuming everyone on the internet was a middle-class white dude was totally sexist. And, now he thought about it, SCDD had a pretty high proportion of actual women. Especially compared to Anni, which was a legendary sausage party.

So, really, there was no reason Solace couldn't be a girl IRL. She was into, y'know, looking pretty and being quirky and having feelings about things. That was girl stuff, right? And thank God Tinuviel couldn't hear him thinking like that. She would have torn him a new one.

Drew went to sleep far too late and woke up completely hungover. When he finally peeled himself out of bed and turned on his computer, his desktop was papered with screenies, most of which were him and Solace. He'd basically never taken a screenshot before that wasn't for his course. He stared at them, feeling weird.

It had become blatantly obvious that the "don't fancy imaginary elves" rule was kaput.

And he had no idea what to do about it.

In a panic, he scrambled into his clothes and ran down the hall to Tinuviel's room. There was usually a message on her door if she had company or didn't want to be bothered, but since there was only a picture of a happy llama, he knocked and stuck his head in.

Tinuviel was the only person Drew knew who actually decorated their college room. He had a couple of posters and a duvet cover that didn't look like he'd nicked it from a hotel but that was about as far as it went. Tinuviel had things like throw pillows and a lamp. She was lying on a pink sheepskin rug, fiddling away on one of those razor-thin MacBooks, the sort Drew wouldn't have been able to afford in a million years.

She waved him in, and he collapsed gratefully into the beanbag chair.

"Ramen?" she offered, bouncing to her feet and heading over to her goodies shelf. "Wagon Wheel? Biltong?"

"Uh. Pass." Drew's stomach churned unhappily. "Fragile."

Tinuviel tore open a packet of noodles, emptied them into a rainbow-patterned bowl, sprinkled a sachet of flavouring over the top, and stuck the kettle on. "Good night?"

"Yeah, I mean, no. I mean, kind of. I mean, that's kind of what I want to talk to you about."

She blinked. "It does sound confusing."

"Don't laugh, okay?"

"Okay."

Strangely, that was one of the things Drew liked about Tinuviel. She had this habit of taking the oddest things completely at face value. "I've kind of met this girl on the internet."

ALEXIS HALL

She poured water onto her noodles and mashed them down. "We do walk amongst you."

One of the things Drew found slightly harder to take about Tinuviel was that he couldn't always tell when she was joking. "I think I really like her, and she goes to Leicester, so she's close, so it's like possible, but . . . I only met her a week ago, and like on the internet, so I feel like a crazy person."

"Why does that make you feel like a crazy person?"

"Well, it's the internet. And I don't really know who she is or if she really exists."

"Do you know if anybody really exists?"

Drew sighed. "That's kind of the opposite of helpful, T."

She curled up on the rug, with her noodles cradled in her lap, like a strange, redheaded Yoda. "Well, I think what you've got to remember is that we all sort of construct ourselves based on the identity we want to present to other people, so, in a very real sense, nobody can ever know anybody."

"Still not helping."

"Okay, let's put it another way. If you'd met this girl in a bar or a nightclub, the *only* thing you'd know about her was what she looked like, and the fact you had no idea what sort of food she liked or what music she listened to or whether she was a serial killer probably wouldn't have been a problem for you. So, really, your problem can't be that you don't know anything about this girl. It must be that you're worried she might be a munter."

"Dude, how shallow do you think I am?"

"Well, if that isn't your concern, I don't see what you're worried about."

Drew thought about it for a moment. "She could be a serial killer."

"Well, so could anybody. So could I. People on the internet aren't more likely to be serial killers than people in general."

"I get the feeling you're not taking me seriously."

Tinuviel pulled a pair of extendable chopsticks out of her top pocket and started on her noodles. "I'm taking this very seriously. I don't understand why you think I'm not."

"If you told me you'd fallen for someone you'd met on the internet, and especially if you'd met them in a video game—not, like, through a dating app—I'd be way more worried."

"Why?" She frowned in a noodle-y kind of way. "The way I see it, when you meet someone in"—she did air quotes—"'real life,' all your initial assumptions about them are based on their physical appearance, but these are extremely likely to be ignorant, prejudiced, and misleading. When you meet somebody online, your initial impressions of them are based on what they say to you. This can't be any more misleading, and it's only social conditioning that makes you accept the validity of relationships initially based on nothing but physical response. Online relationships are based on intellectual and emotional connection. If anything, it's a better way of doing it."

This was all a bit much on a hangover. He worked through it like it was a particularly chewy piece of biltong. "Yeah, but what if what they say isn't true?"

"My mum said she once had sex with a woman because she, the woman, not my mum, thought she, my mum, not the woman, played the alto sax."

Drew was definitely way too hungover for this. "Uh?"

"That was long before the internet. People misrepresent themselves, consciously or otherwise, all the time."

"Can we come back to the bit where your mum tells you stories about her lesbian affairs?"

"You know your parents have had sex right?"

He put his hands over his ears and rocked. "I don't like to think about it."

"It's just sex."

"It's your parents."

"Sometimes you have a very strange attitude to things, Andrew."

"If Sanee was here, he'd understand."

Tinuviel sighed. "Before you went weird, I was trying to point out that the only extra information you have about someone when you meet them in person is what they look like. So, if we're disregarding the munter theory, I don't see what you're so worried about."

"Okay," he tried again. "But the thing is, if we ditch all the prejudice stuff, there are still things you can tell by looking at someone that you can't tell over the internet. Like, if they're twelve or a man."

"I think you're oversimplifying gender identity a bit."

He groaned. "I don't know why I thought I should talk to you about this stuff."

"Well, because Sanee would say you were an idiot. Whereas I've spent the last ten minutes telling you that it's probably fine, and you should see what happens. Which is blatantly what you want to hear."

"Oh."

She looked up and smiled. "Come on, Drew, if you really like this girl, what's the harm? I mean, obviously, meet in a public place and tell someone where you're going, but really, if she turns out to be twelve or a man, then what have you lost?"

Drew thought about it. And, actually, she was sort of right. Either he would meet a great girl who he also fancied, and that would be cool, or he would meet a great girl who he didn't fancy, which might be a bit awkward and make him feel shallow, but at least he'd know. Or none of the above in which case he'd still know, and that would be better than . . . than . . . not.

"Thanks, T."

"Anytime. I hope she's whatever you think you're supposed to expect her to be."

Drew had another medusa date with Solace that night, and told himself very firmly that he was going to take the opportunity to come clean, and ask if she wanted to meet up in real life.

He did not take the opportunity to come clean and ask if she wanted to meet up in real life.

Part of the problem was that there wasn't a good time to do it. He kept trying, but it would have seemed really weird to bring it up of nowhere when they were battling crabmen or uncovering hidden demon cults. But mostly he was just enjoying playing the game and being with Solace so much that he forgot he was supposed to be on a mission.

So, what with one thing and another, both Saturday and Sunday slipped by without him making anything that remotely resembled a move. As they were wishing each other goodnight and he was kicking himself for not saying anything *again*, he realised he was genuinely afraid of messing this up. Because Tinuviel had sort of been wrong. He did have something to lose, and that was the time he spent with Solace now, which was turning into the highlight of his day. And if he asked her on a date and she freaked out, that would spoil everything. And if they met up and it didn't work, then that would spoil everything too. And maybe he didn't want to know if she was really a twelve-year-old French boy because this was good enough that it didn't seem to matter.

While he was finishing off his chair on Monday, with Sanee texting Steff at the next terminal, it occurred to him he actually hadn't had a girlfriend in ages. It had been the best part of a year since he'd broken up with Abby, who'd been his obligatory disastrous first-year fling. Admittedly, he'd kind of been busy with other things, but it had been nice having someone who was sort of there for you, and not just in a knocking-on-your-mate's-door-on-a-Saturday-morning way.

He'd never had the super squidgy twu-wuv-forevah thing that Sanee and Steff had, and he wasn't sure he wanted it. His previous relationships—and, to be fair, there were only a couple—had been basically okay, with no expectations that they'd really wind up going anywhere. But he hoped there was some middle ground between that kind of comfortable default and calling each other Smidge. Of course, he didn't want to be all Tinuviel about it either, and have some crazy intense passionate affair that lasted about thirty seconds like a not very good firework.

Basically he wanted someone who he liked being with about as much as he liked being with Solace and who liked being with him about as much as Solace seemed to. And someone who was into the same stuff he was into—kind of like Solace was. And if they were clever and funny and probably too good for him, then that was a bonus.

A train of thought that could best be summarised as: just ask her out already.

They'd probably hang out together in Alarion after the raid, so he could do it then.

Definitely for real this time.

He nipped out to the pub for the Monday-night special with the usual crowd, but for some reason it was really busy and his food didn't show up for an hour. Which left him minutes to get back to his room, get online, repair his armour, double-check his gems and enchants, and make sure he had plenty of consumables. He was already halfway to CoT when he noticed the message from Morag:

Guild Message of the day: Tiff has a hot date, booyah, so Solace will be leading tonight's jaunt into CoT, with Bjorn on loot master, assistance, and sarcasm. Thanks to Sindarella for stepping in with his storm spec. lol. Good luck, have fun, don't do anything I would do. xxx

```
[Guild][Heurodis]: Get your arse in the
instance and your ears into mumble noob
[Guild][Ialdir]: See this is why you don't
get to raid lead
[Guild][Heurodis]: it's so hard when no one
else lives up to your standards
[Guild][Orcarella]: sorry i'm late
[Guild][Orcarella]: dinner took ages
[Guild][Orcarella]: won't happen again
[Guild][Jargogle]: Don't worry, you're not
technically late
[Guild][Jargogle]: Bjorn's just having one of
his little power trips
[Guild][Jargogle]: Despite having no actual
power
[Guild][Heurodis]: hey don't make me
demonstrate my power by gkicking you
[Guild][Jargogle]: You will never gkick me
Bjorn. My DPS is too good.
```

A raid invite came in, and Drew accepted it. He might not have been technically late, but he was the last one in the group.

Ella, still wearing her tuxedo, charged into the instance like she was late for school, and while he waited for the load screen, Drew alt-tabbed and logged in to Mumble.

"—good ship Same Crit Different Day. In Morag's absence, I'll be your raid leader tonight, because the last time Bjorn did it, three people gquit."

"Ah, they were all scrubs and noobs."

Drew's brain had gone a bit frozen. He'd heard the first voice before, but he hadn't managed to place who it was. It was kind of a nice voice—soft, and calm, and a bit laughing and a bit posh—but what it definitely wasn't, was a girl.

"Prospero and I will be your life force replenishment facilitation subcommittee, as usual."

Ah. Right.

Okay.

Well, that answered that question.

"Dave and Magda will be the ministers in charge of sticking pointy objects into people. Bjorn, Jacob, Ignatius, and Mordant will be the department with general responsibility for fiery death."

"Shadowy death," interrupted Bjorn. "Fiery death is for teenagers who can't play a proper spec."

[Raid][Mordant]: Hey!!

The man-who-was-Solace sighed. "Bjorn, you are why we can't have nice things. Ignore him, Mordant, he's just insecure about having another diabolist on the run. Anyway, as I was saying—unless there's anyone else you want to be rude to, Bjorn—Heurodis, Mordant, Ignatius, and Ialdir will be ranged DPS. Our tanks for this evening will be Orcarella and Sindarella. Obviously, we've only got two melee DPS, and our OT is a storm elementalist, so fasten your seat belts, it might be a bumpy raid. Remember we're a good team and it's a fresh reset so we've got a lot of experience with this content, so let's stay calm, stay focused, and kick some arse."

It was a very Solacey speech, and Drew would have enjoyed it if he hadn't been too busy freaking the hell out.

He shouldn't have been surprised, because he'd thought about this probably actually quite a lot. And, as far as he could remember, she'd . . . he'd never actually said she . . . he was a girl.

Solace hadn't actually lied or led him on. At worst he'd been slightly evasive and let Drew make a bunch of assumptions. So he had no reason to feel betrayed.

Except he did. Utterly.

What he really wanted to do was gquit, turn off his computer, and go hide in a hole forever, but that would have made him a total dick. It wasn't the guild's fault that he'd broken the first rule of the internet because he was trying to challenge sexist stereotypes. And also because he'd . . . really liked someone. Who happened to be a boy IRL.

But it wasn't just about Solace. He'd been getting on really well with the guild. They were good people, and he was having fun with them. He was even enjoying raiding again for the first time in what felt like forever. Except he didn't know how he was supposed to stick around now. Maybe Solace hadn't been deliberately making a fool out of him, but that was basically what he'd done.

The raid . . . well . . . the raid happened. It went about as well as it could have done with only two melee DPS, two diabolists, a storm-specced OT, and a main tank who was really pissed off with the raid leader. Half the time, he couldn't decide whether he wanted to yell or lie down and cry. Everyone else seemed to be having a good time, which basically made everything worse. It wasn't like Drew wanted to ruin everyone's evening, but it would have been comforting to know he had the option. And he couldn't say anything because he'd be the one left looking like a desperate pillock.

On top of all that—to really rub it in— Solace turned out to be a pretty good raid leader. He wasn't like any RL Drew had run with before. Morag was firm but fair, and the officers in Annihilation had been basically merciless, but Solace was just kind of Solace. He was softly-spoken and gentle and unfailingly polite, but somehow you ended up wanting to do better.

Even when you were absolutely hating the guy.

Under different circumstances, it would have been a really positive experience. There was something reassuring about Solace's voice in his headphones, calling alerts and directing strats. He was actually really on the ball, and a couple of times managed to switch strategies midfight, which saved them from screwups Drew was pretty sure would have caused wipes otherwise.

And he healed too.

Drew got sadder and sadder as the evening went on.

```
[Ialdir] whispers: you okay?
[Ialdir] whispers: you seem quiet
To [Ialdir]: just tired
```

They called it before Vilicus, because it was getting late and they weren't entirely sure they had the right raid comp, but people seemed to agree it had gone well. While everyone was saying their good-byes, Drew teleported to the City of Stars, intending to log out immediately and hide under his duvet for the next million years.

```
[Solace] whispers: Um, are you okay?
```

Drew stared blankly at the tell, wondering what on earth he was supposed to say.

```
To [Solace]: not really no
[Solace] whispers: um
[Solace] whispers: you thought I was a girl,
didn't you?
[Solace] whispers: That's why you were so
nice to me
To [Solace]: don't want to talk about this
```

He logged out, turned off his computer, and crawled into bed. Where he lay in a weird nonspace, kind of wanting to cry but not being able to, and kind of wanting to sleep but not being able to. His thoughts had got snarled up and stuck, and he couldn't unsnarl them or unstick them. Because Solace had sort of been right and sort of been wrong. Drew hadn't only spent time with Solace because he thought he was a girl. He genuinely liked the time they'd had together. But, the fact remained, it probably wouldn't have gone that far if there hadn't been at least the possibility that Solace would turn out be this hot geeky chick who, for whatever reason, was totally into him.

And now it felt like he'd lost everything: a friend, the chance of whatever he thought there was a chance of, Solace.

With all that buzzing around in his head, he didn't know what time he got to sleep, but when his phone alarm went off, he silenced it and stuck his head back under the pillow. He really didn't feel like doing anything today. He sort of dozed his way to midday, but then he reached that awkward point of needing the toilet more than he needed to wallow in misery.

So he slid out of bed, pulled on a pair of pyjama bottoms, and shuffled down the corridor to the communal bathrooms.

The effort sapped what remained of his spirit, so he went back to bed. Eventually, though, he got bored of staring at the ceiling and feeling sorry for himself, so he grabbed his copy of *Hawkeye: My Life as a Weapon* and started comfort reading. Lots of pictures and not many words felt like all he could cope with at the moment. Also, he'd always been secretly into Hawkeye because he loved the idea of a superhero whose only power was "I've got a bow." It was less a power, more a lifestyle choice, and the reboot was sort of milking that for all it was worth. Drew liked to think of it as *Hawkeye: My Life as Some Dude*.

About halfway through the storyline where Clint archives his ludicrous collection of gimmicky weapons, Drew caught himself wondering if Solace had read it, and if he liked superheroes and, if so, which.

And that left him sniffling into *The Tape, Part 1*.

There was a knock at the door and, without waiting for a response, Sanee and Tinuviel barged in.

Drew threw *Hawkeye* aside and dived back under the covers, worried he looked exactly how he felt. "This totally isn't the time guys."

Sanee annexed the only chair in the room. "You didn't come to lab, you're not answering your phone, we haven't seen you all day, it's totally the time."

"Are you okay?" asked Tinuviel, curling up on the end of his bed.

"If I said I was fine, would you piss off?"

Sanee shrugged. "Probably not."

"Is this about that girl?" Tinuviel gave her patented curious head-tilt.

"Did she turn out to be a dude?" There was an uncomfortable silence. "Oh fuck." Sanee put his hands over his mouth. "She did." Then he giggled, which really didn't help.

Drew burrowed deeper. "It's not funny."

"It's a bit funny."

"Not for me, it isn't."

He poked his head out from under the duvet in time to see Tinuviel giving Sanee a *shut up* look before she turned back to Drew. "How did you find out? Did you meet him?"

"No, he was leading the Monday raid. And he was definitely a dude."

There was a long silence.

"Man," sighed Sanee. "I know I totally told you this was going to happen, but I'm really sorry for you."

Tinuviel pulled her knees up to her chest and hugged them. "Well, yes and no. I mean, I think what you need to ask yourself is how much this changes things."

Drew gaped at her. "Um, it completely changes things?"

"Why?"

Sanee sat forward on the chair. "T, are you being deliberately dense?"

"That's a very strange question. The way I see it, Drew's met somebody he likes. He's clearly sad at the thought of losing him. So the question is: why should he?"

"How about: because he's not gay."

"Well, neither I am, but I've still had sexual relationships with people who defined as female."

"Yes, but you're a girl."

Tinuviel sighed deeply. "If our friend wasn't in the middle of a crisis, I'd be quite cross with you right now."

"I'm not in a crisis," interrupted Drew. "I'm just bummed."

"Poor choice of words, mate."

"Sanee!" chorused Drew and Tinuviel.

He held up his hands. "Oh come on, you walked into that one."

"Look," snapped Drew, "something mildly upsetting happened to me. I just want to take a day to feel sorry for myself about it. I don't need you making gay jokes, or you telling me that's it not a big deal, because, I'm sorry, we weren't all raised by polyamorous hippies. How am I supposed to tell my mum I've suddenly started dating a boy?"

"You could try, 'Mum, I've started dating a boy,'" suggested Tinuviel. Unhelpfully.

"Or just don't tell her." Sanee stroked his chin thoughtfully. "But, you never know, they might be cool. Steff was convinced her mum would freak out at her dating a South Asian guy, but either she was actually fine about it or she was really, really scared of looking racist."

"So you're basically telling me, I have to hope my parents are really, really scared of looking homophobic?"

"Or," added Tinuviel, "they're just not bigots."

Drew put his head in his hands. Tinuviel leaned over and patted him gently on the shoulder.

"Can I just point out," she said, "that your main issues have been that Sanee has laughed at you, and that your parents might not like it."

"So?"

"Well, this is obviously quite hard for me because, as a pansexual, I really don't understand people whose sense of attraction is informed by gender identity or biological sex. But I think if I was monosexual, my main objection to a relationship with someone who was not of my preferred gender would be that I just wasn't into them. Maybe I'm wrong, but your problem doesn't seem to be that you're *not* interested in this person, but that you still are."

While Drew was sorting through that, Sanee steepled his fingers like a supervillain. "Dude, are you gay?" There was a pause. "Like, it's okay if you are."

Drew glared at him. "I think I'd have noticed."

Tinuviel raised a hand. "I suspect you'll think this is a weird question, but what would you have noticed?"

"Well . . ." Drew hated it when T did this. She'd ask you something to which the answer was so screamingly obvious that you'd immediately start second-guessing yourself. And, right now, that was the last thing he needed. "Fancying guys for a start?"

"Maybe you just haven't met any guys you fancy. I mean, I'm pretty sure you're not attracted to Sanee . . ."

Sanee made a valiant attempt not to look horrified. "You're not, right?"

Drew made no such attempt. "I'm really not."

"Okay," Tinuviel went on. "And you don't fancy me either."

"Jesus, just because I don't fancy every girl I meet, that doesn't make me gay."

She looked smug. "And, by the same argument, not fancying every boy you meet doesn't make you straight."

There was a really long silence.

"Holy shit," gasped Sanee. "That's a really scary thought."

"I can imagine it would be to a lot of people, but actually there's nothing scary about rejecting heteronormative notions of binary sexuality."

"So you're saying," said Drew slowly, "I could be gay and not know it? Because that sort of sounds like bollocks."

Tinuviel pushed her hair out of her eyes. "No, I'm not saying that, Andrew. I'm saying that, for many people, sexuality is more fluid and less clear-cut than they're taught to assume. You might, in fact, be completely straight, but it's also possible that you're not. And, even if you aren't, you might have gone your whole life completely happy and not caring and not knowing. And that's fine. But it seems to me that right now you have an opportunity to have something with somebody, and it might work or it might not, but if your only reason for not trying is that you're scared of the idea of being gay, then that's probably quite silly and a little bit sad."

Drew frowned. "Is this your idea of cheering me up?"

"Dude." Sanee spread his hands in a *beats me* sort of way. "She's got a point. I think. Somewhere in there. If you still like this guy, even though he's a guy, then you should probably at least talk to him. I mean, dude, you drew him fanart. And you've kind of been all happy and annoying for the last week."

"Okay." Drew pulled his duvet back over his head. "This has been very helpful. Now will you please go away? I want to continue freaking out, and I'd like to do it in private."

He felt Tinuviel uncurl. "I'm just down the hall if you want anything."

Sanee slapped him somewhere in the region of his arm. "It's all right, mate. We'll still be friends. Even if you do get a taste for dick."

"Thanks," mumbled Drew.

And then he heard the door swing closed behind them.

Once he was sure they'd gone, he made a futile attempt to get back into *Hawkeye*, but it was no good. He had too much stuff in his brain. The one thing he was pretty sure he didn't want to do was lie here trying to work out if he was gay or not. If that was even possible. So he tried to break the whole mess down into manageable chunks, like he'd do with a design project or a maths problem. Chunk one was "Am I gay or what?" but there was nothing he could do with that on his own. Tinuviel might have been all sexuality is fluid blah, but that didn't really mean anything if he couldn't hold hands with a boy or kiss a boy or fall in love with a boy. Even if the boy was Solace.

Chunk two was being lied to, or if not lied to, then misled. Or whatever it was that made him feel bad about everything. Thinking back, and trying to be as objective as possible given the circumstances, he could sort of see that he hadn't really given Solace a chance. It had been hard enough psyching himself up to ask someone out on the internet. He had no idea how you'd slip, "Hey, you know I'm not a girl, right?" into the conversation. But while some part of Drew understood that side of it, it didn't stop him feeling shitty and hurt.

He wondered briefly how Solace was feeling. If he was sad as well, or angry, or confused. Or maybe he was hurt because he'd thought Drew knew, and he hadn't, and that what he'd said after was right: Drew had only been nice because he thought Solace was a girl. Or maybe Solace didn't understand what all the fuss was about, and was just weirded out that Drew had thrown a wobbly.

Which got him onto chunk three, which was, well, Solace himself. And it occurred to Drew that it was really odd to be thinking so hard about this guy when he didn't even know what his name was.

And he wanted to know. He wanted to know all that stuff.

What he was called, and what he was feeling, and what he was thinking.

Except even that was weird now, because every time Solace came into his head, he'd do a kind of mental stammer and have to switch the *she* for a *he*. And that meant he couldn't tell if it was really Solace he was missing or this imaginary girl who'd never even existed.

And that brought him back to "Am I gay or what?" Which was not where he wanted to be. He wasn't Tinuviel. He couldn't just be straight for nineteen years and then decide that everything was an arbitrary social construct so he might as well date dudes. It would have been different if he'd met a guy and been into him. Well, it would still have been pretty confusing, but at least it would've been clear-cut.

Except wasn't that exactly what *had* happened? He had, in fact, met a guy. And he was, in fact, into him. And, okay, he'd thought the guy was a girl, but he'd also known he might not be. And charged . . . or stumbled . . . ahead regardless. Which either meant he'd been wildly optimistic, or some part of him (even if it wasn't something he'd ever noticed or admitted) hadn't minded.

So maybe he was—as Sanee would surely put it—a gay.

Or at any rate: a bi. Since he was pretty sure he was still into girls. Although maybe he wasn't. Because he hadn't had that many relationships and part of the reason Tinuviel hung out with him and Sanee was that they were basically the only men on the course who hadn't tried to get into her pants. So maybe he'd just been pretending all this time. Maybe getting a girlfriend had been kind of like getting your A levels—just sort of something you were expected to do in your late teens.

He gave a little whimper and stuck his head back under the covers. Right now, he had no idea who he was or what he was or where he was going or what he was doing or what he wanted. Tinuviel would probably tell him placidly that *This is all very fluid and complicated, Andrew*, and that *labels were meaningless*.

But, honestly, this felt like a time in Drew's life when a label would be really comforting. It was one of the things he enjoyed about trad MMOs. Everybody had a role and name and you knew what you were supposed to be doing and how you were supposed to be doing it.

He hid for a bit longer. He really needed to talk to someone. Someone who wasn't going to laugh or express their bewilderment at the way he clung to bourgeois conventions of blah blah blah.

Basically he needed to talk to Solace. And not just because there was no one else, but because he was starting to realise that the only thing he wasn't confused about was that he really missed her. Um. Him.

Drew crawled out of bed, booted up his PC, and signed into the game. He was greeted by a stream of cheery hellos in the guild, but Solace wasn't online.

He stared blankly at the screen. He had nothing in particular to do in-game, but logging in and then logging straight out again would look kind of pissy and odd. Also, having spent the best part of a day thinking in circles to get to this point, it was really frustrating not being able to see it through.

Sod it. He was bloody well going to start that World Explorer achievement.

Whipping out El'ir Reborn, he took to the skies.

He started by filling in the blanks around the City of the Stars and Arandiel's Vale. He wasn't quite up to doing it on foot, but he took his time and watched the scenery unfurling beneath him. He hadn't spent very long in this area at all, because he'd never rolled an elf. It was very sub-Tolkien: all trees and stars and dwindling. He found a narrow path that spiralled to the crest of a hill and under a pretty impressive waterfall. It tumbled between the rocks in silver-crested streams and down into a pool that shimmered, blue and green, with the reflected images of the surrounding forest.

He paused to admire the ray tracing. Obviously, the game was getting on a bit and it wasn't much by modern standards, but someone had clearly put a lot of effort into getting the scene just right. He'd already got credit for exploring Arandiel's Vale, but since there seemed to be a cave behind the waterfall, he thought it'd be nice to poke his head in.

It turned out to be the standard cave model, and it was full of level fifteen bullywugs who were probably some kind of bandits or cultists or something. When you were new to the game and at an appropriate level, this cave was probably a complete nightmare, but Ella was high enough level that the mobs basically ignored her except when she actually ran through them. In the end, Drew dragged a bunch of them into a corner and massacred them wholesale with a single Circle of Corruption. There was a certain base satisfaction in one-shotting a bunch of low-level creatures.

Solace has come online.
[Guild][Morag]: Hey
[Guild][Heurodis]: yo
[Guild][Mordant]: Hi :)

```
[Guild][Solace]: Hello everyone
[Guild][Solace]: How was the date, Tiff?
[Guild][Morag]: Nfc
[Guild][Morag]: I really liked her. She was
hot and wrote poetry.
[Guild][Morag]: But I have literally no idea
if she was into me.
[Guild][Heurodis]: you should have told her
your gearscore
[Guild][Morag]: And this is why you're
single, Bjorn.
[Guild][Heurodis]: I am single because nobody
is awesome enough for me.
[Guild][Jargogle]: Keep telling yourself
that.
To [Solace]: can we like talk
[Solace] whispers: thought you didn't want to
To [Solace]: sorry i was freaked out
To [Solace]: and i really want to talk about
this
To [Solace]: if you still want to
[Solace] whispers: okay
```
Solace has invited you to join a group: y/n
Solace is now group leader.

Shit. Drew suddenly realised there was a massive difference between wanting to talk to someone and having any idea what you were going to say to them. And it seemed really weird to be having this kind of a conversation in a chat window in a video game.

```
[Group][Orcarella]: um can we kind of go
somewhere
[Group][Orcarella]: if that's not weird
[Group][Solace]: I'm in Alarion
[Group][Orcarella]: kk omw
```

The journey had never seemed quite so long, even though he wasn't more than three minutes' flight from the City of Stars. And just like the first time he'd gone to meet Solace, he found himself worrying pointlessly about which mount to use. El'ir seemed wanky suddenly. But he wasn't sure he had a mount that said, *Hi, I'm kind of cross with you, and I don't think I'm gay, but I still kind of fancy you. Maybe. Even though I've never met you.*

Finally, he dug out his bog-standard Orcish Wyvern and flapped gracelessly over to Alarion. Solace was perched on their usual rock, still in full raiding getup, fishing line trailing in the water. Ella landed, dismounted, and hunkered down.

Shit, this was difficult.

```
[Group][Orcarella]: um hi
[Group][Solace]: Hey
[Group][Orcarella]: you know, i don't even
know what your name is
[Group][Solace]: It's Christopher
[Group][Solace]: But everyone calls me Kit
```

Kit. Drew rolled the name around in his head, trying to make it connect with something.

Good healing, Kit.

Me and Kit rolled some medusas to see what the starting area was like.

I really like you, Kit.

```
[Group][Solace]: Look, I'm really sorry
[Group][Solace]: I didn't mean to . . .
[Group][Solace]: Mislead you or anything.
[Group][Solace]: I know I kind of did
[Group][Solace]: And I'm sorry.
[Group][Orcarella]: I get its a weird
situation
[Group][Orcarella]: and i get i made a bunch
of assumptions
[Group][Orcarella]: but I don't understand
why you didn't just tell me
```

There was no typing for a very long time.

```
[Group][Solace]: I made assumptions too.
[Group][Solace]: At first I assumed you knew
or maybe I convinced myself you did
[Group][Solace]: And by the time I was sure
you didn't . . . God, this is going to sound
so pathetic . . . but I kind of liked it.
[Group][Solace]: More than kind of.
[Group][Solace]: I liked the way you were
with me.
[Group][Solace]: Kind, and funny, and
interested. And a bit flirty.
[Group][Solace]: I've never had that before.
[Group][Solace]: And I didn't want to lose it.
```

And now Drew didn't know what to say.
And then he did.

```
[Group][Orcarella]: I don't want to lose it
either.
[Group][Solace]: Even though I'm not a girl?
```

Having sort of committed, Drew felt a bit panicky. What if he was actually completely ungay? What if, after all this, Solace (Kit) turned out to be a munter just like Tinuviel had said? What if this was completely unworkable in every possible way?

```
[Group][Orcarella]: I dont know.
[Group][Orcarella]: I'm sorry i just
[Group][Orcarella]: it's always been girls
before.
[Group][Orcarella]: like only three of them
[Group][Orcarella]: but still
[Group][Solace]: Okay.
[Group][Solace]: Look. It's pretty simple
for me.
```

[Group][Solace]: I've always known I liked boys.
[Group][Solace]: In principle at least.
[Group][Solace]: I'm still looking for one to like in practice :)
[Group][Solace]: And I know I could just go out to a club or something and find one.
[Group][Solace]: But that's not what I'm looking for.
[Group][Solace]: But I don't think it would be good for me if the first boy I had this connection with was just . . . well . . . trying me on.
[Group][Orcarella]: :(
[Group][Orcarella]: i'm not trying you on
[Group][Orcarella]: i just want you to know where i'm coming from
[Group][Orcarella]: i've never thought about this stuff before
[Group][Orcarella]: and i've no idea if i'm gay or bi or straight or what
[Group][Orcarella]: I just know i like
[Group][Orcarella]: you
[Group][Solace]: I like you too. I really like you.
[Group][Solace]: But I can't talk you into being bisexual
[Group][Orcarella]: i'm not asking you to
[Group][Orcarella]: i'm just really messed up right now
[Group][Solace]: Sorry Drew
[Group][Solace]: Is there anything I can do to make this better
[Group][Orcarella]: nfc
[Group][Orcarella]: i guess i just need some time
[Group][Orcarella]: is that okay

```
[Group][Solace]: Of course
[Group][Solace]: I'd still like to hang out
with you
[Group][Solace]: Even if you don't
[Group][Solace]: I mean you know
[Group][Solace]: Just as friends
[Group][Solace]: I mean if you still want to
[Group][Solace]: But I get it if you don't
```

Part of Drew—a big part of Drew—wanted to say, *No way, you made me look like a prick and now I'm having a total crisis and it's all your fault.* Except then he realised it wouldn't be particularly satisfying. And also it wasn't true. Well, he was having a crisis and it was sort of Kit's fault, but none of this would have happened if he hadn't genuinely liked the guy. Or liked Solace. And probably that was the same thing. On the other hand, he didn't want to be all like, *Oh, it's fine, no probs,* because that wasn't true either.

Time was passing and the chat window was empty. And an empty chat window could be one of the scariest things on the internet sometimes. However mixed up he felt about Kit right now, he didn't want to just leave him hanging. If it had been the other way round, he wasn't sure he'd have the balls to put himself out there like that and risk getting shot down by a guy he knew was pissed off at him.

```
[Group][Orcarella]: let me think about it
[Group][Orcarella]: sorry that sounds shit
[Group][Orcarella]: it just
[Group][Orcarella]: i just
[Group][Orcarella]: i think id better go
```

Drew's heart was beating way too fast as he logged off. He couldn't tell whether that had gone fine or terribly. Nor had it miraculously cleared up the "Do I fancy *guys* or *this* guy?" question.

It was late, but he'd spent most of the day in bed, so he didn't really feel like going back there. Normally, this would be when he'd log into *HoL.* Except he'd just logged out of *HoL.*

He booted up Steam and browsed his library listlessly.

Then it occurred to him he could roll an alt, so he logged into *HoL* again. Unfortunately the second name on his character list was the medusa he'd rolled to play with Kit.

He shut the game down in an attack of feels.

Which brought him back to his Steam library. He didn't have masses of spare cash, but there'd been enough flash sales and Humble Bundles that he managed to rack up a collection of just over a hundred games. And he basically didn't want to play any of them.

In the end he settled for X-Com. He'd stalled out on his Ironman Enemy Within playthrough about eighteen months ago. Loading it up, it was incredibly disorientating to realise he'd named his squad after a bunch of his mates from school—people he basically hadn't thought about, bar the occasional Facebook message, for the best part of a year.

It would've been too weird to go back, so he started a new game. He honestly wasn't all that enthusiastic, but he just wanted something to take his mind off . . . everything. It worked for a little while, letting him fall into a comfortable strategy rhythm of move, overwatch, move, flank, shoot.

Then Sergeant Sanee "Hazard" Kumar got jumped on and eaten by a giant killer-insect thing while attempting to the save the life of a civilian during Operation Broken Hymn. Then he came back as an infected alien zombie and had to be put down by his former squad mates. Sanee would have been so pissed the South Asian guy was the first to go. Drew almost felt too guilty to continue.

It didn't, however, stop him relating the story to his course mates the next day.

One of the annoying things about small personal crises was not only did everything carry on in the background, but you didn't even have an excuse not to carry on with it. His project still needed finishing, his UF team still needed him at practice, the guild still needed him to MT raids. It didn't seem fair to say, *Sorry, I can't do all that stuff, I'm a bit sad and confused right now.* Even worse, it wasn't like anything could change or be fixed. Not unless he randomly met a girl who was so overwhelmingly perfect for him that he stopped thinking about Kit completely. And he hadn't stopped thinking about Kit completely.

He hadn't stopped thinking about Kit at all.

Every now and again, he'd vaguely look at guys and try to figure out if he found them attractive. Except most of the dudes he met on a day-to-day basis weren't interacting with him in that sort of way so there was no real context for the exercise. He thought about checking out the LGBT+ society, but wasn't sure what he'd say. *Hi, I'm probably not gay but I just wanted to see if I fancied any of you.*

So life just sort of went on. He put the final touches to his chair. It was a good chair. Sanee and Steff got a copy of Dead of Winter, and they passed several pleasant evenings starving, betraying each other, and getting eaten by zombies.

On Monday, in the light of various changes to the core lineup— including Drew as MT—the guild decided not to press any farther into CoT that week, focusing instead on farming earlier content, gearing up, and, as Bjorn put it, "learning to work together so we do not repeatedly chain shit through the raid like a bunch of little noobs."

This wouldn't have been Drew's preference, but he still enjoyed the atmosphere and the more casual guild members really seemed to appreciate the opportunity to get their hands on a pile of loots that were, to them, still shiny and new. In any case, it was actually more effective than he expected, because the next time they took on CoT, the first bosses went down like Jell-O shots.

Morag had recovered from her attempt to date a performance poet and was back RLing. Drew told himself he wasn't disappointed. He'd been too angry and upset at the time to really deal with it, but he'd liked seeing that side of Kit. Being able to hear him talk.

Drew had honestly assumed that Kit had been staying quiet in Mumble deliberately so he wouldn't catch on. But, actually, it seemed like he was just kind of quiet. He kept his banter in chat and only spoke to direct the healing team in a fight. Now Drew thought back, he was pretty sure Kit *had* spoken in earlier raids. He just hadn't been listening because he'd been too busy doing his own job. And secretly hoping to hear from a pretty elf girl.

It made him feel a little bit better. A bit less of a fool and a bit less betrayed. And that freed his brain up to think about the other stuff. How nice it had been hanging out with Kit. All the sweet things he'd said. The ways he'd tried to be honest about what he'd done and why he'd done it.

Drew was doing his postraid faff in the City of Stars, crafting up a stack of [Notorious Cataclysmic Emeralds] for the guild bank, when he saw Solace's little wings flutter past on the way to the auction house.

```
To [Solace]: not fishing tonight?
```

There was a really long pause. Enough for ten emeralds to ping into existence in Ella's inventory. It was awful. Maybe the casual approach was the wrong approach.

```
To [Solace]: so I've been thinking
[Solace] whispers: Sorry, I keep typing
things and deleting them
[Solace] whispers: I'm not ignoring you
To [Solace]: look i'm not promising anything
To [Solace]: but i've really missed hanging
out with you
To [Solace]: so do you want to maybe try that
again
To [Solace]: as friends
[Solace] whispers: yes! :) :) :)
[Solace] whispers: yay
[Solace] whispers: are you sure?
[Solace] whispers: Hmm, I guess I should have
said that the other way round
```

Actually, Drew wasn't sure. He was kind of the opposite of sure. Mainly he was terrified.

```
To [Solace]: yes
To [Solace]: maybe we could medusa a bit?
```

```
[Solace] whispers: I'd like that. When would
work for you?
To [Solace]: I'm free tomorrow after lab
To [Solace]: so kind of eveningish
[Solace] whispers: see you then
[Solace] whispers: looking forward to it
To [Solace]: me too
```

And he was.

Still terrified, but looking forward to it.

CHAPTER

D rew had made the terrible mistake of attempting to render water. And consequently had spent the entire day on the verge of beating himself to death with his own keyboard.

"Dude." Sanee leaned over from the next terminal. "I know what you need. You need to shoot a Mall Santa, eat a horse, and die of frostbite in an abandoned school."

Even if he hadn't arranged to meet Kit, Drew was a little bit Dead of Winter'ed out. Every time Sanee and Steff got a new board game, it was basically all they wanted to do for a week, and Sanee's commitment to doing the same thing over and over again was very slightly higher than Drew's. Which left him two options. He could either mildly hurt his friend's feelings by opting out due to tedium, or he could admit that he had a nondate with a boy he met in an MMO. It wasn't really a choice.

He sighed. "I'm kind of seeing Kit tonight."

"Seeing who?"

"You know . . . Solace, the imaginary elf girl."

"You mean," asked Sanee, a delighted gleam creeping into his eyes, "the imaginary elf girl who's really a dude?"

Drew grit his teeth. "Yes, that imaginary elf girl."

"Lol. All of the lols." And then, in response to Drew's look, "So what are you doing?"

This was getting worse by the second. "We're playing *HoL*. We've rolled some new characters, we're playing the low levels together, and so far I've really enjoyed it. So please shut up."

"Come on mate, I'm only having a laugh."

"Yeah, at me."

"But it is a bit funny."

Drew couldn't tell if he was in a bad mood because of watergate or if Sanee had genuinely crossed a threshold of dickishness. Of course, Sanee could be kind of a dick, especially when he got an idea into his head, but it felt different this time. Maybe because it seemed to be directly about Drew instead of about . . . *things*. Like people who played *Call of Duty*. It didn't help that Drew wasn't used to having these sorts of conversations. Especially not with Sanee.

"I think," he said slowly, trying to wrap his head round it, "that what's bothering me is that I don't think you'd be taking the piss half as much if you just knew I was gay."

Sanee's eyes widened. "Of course I wouldn't. I'm not a homophobe. The thing is, you're, like . . . you."

"So, it's not funny that some guys like other guys in general. It's funny that I might like another guy in particular?"

"Well—" Sanee thought about it for a moment "—yeah. Also the fact you met him in *HoL* makes it about a million times more hilarious. What are you going to tell your adopted grandkids?"

"That when I was at university I met exactly one bloke who wasn't a complete tosser." Drew got up jerkily, and started stuffing his things into his bag. "And now I'm going to get ready for my clearly ridiculous online not-a-date thing that I *was* actually really looking forward to."

Sanee pushed off against the table and sent his wheelie chair careening backwards into Drew's path. "Dude, I'm sorry, okay? If you're— No matter what you are, I'm in your corner. I might be laughing, but I'm definitely in it."

Not counting the Steff Fight Crying Incident They Did Not Talk About, this was the closest to a heartfelt conversation he and Sanee'd ever had. So while Drew was still a bit ticked off, he couldn't quite bring himself to storm out. But at the same time, this wasn't the sort of thing he talked about with Sanee, so it was probably best for both of them if he got it over with quickly.

"Thanks, mate, it's just I'm still a bit mixed up about this. So if you could, y'know, lay off on the gay jokes and the internet-dating jokes, that would really help me out."

Sanee held out his fist for bumping purposes. "You got it."

Drew was heading out the door, all jumbled up with this swirly mess of relief and excruciating embarrassment, when Sanee called after him.

"Genuinely not making a joke but I am a bit worried. You haven't even seen this guy in real life yet. It'd be different if you met him on Tinder or Gay Tinder or whatever."

Drew turned reluctantly. "Why?"

"Rule number one: games aren't real life."

He didn't have an answer for that, so he shrugged and left.

The whole awkward interaction with Sanee had bummed him out and made him later than he'd hoped to be, so he was in a bit of a panic as he got himself settled and logged into *HoL*.

He'd left Efthalia parked in the city of Minea, which was supposed to be this ruined shadow of its former glory, but was actually far cooler and more impressive than the generically medieval human capital of Whitepeak. It had this *Clash of the Titans* vibe: all gold and marble and hanging gardens. And an honest-to-God snake-headed colossus standing astride the entrance.

```
[Aconite] whispers: I was beginning to think
you weren't coming
To [Aconite]: omg no
To [Aconite]: just got held up
```

Aconite has invited you to join a group: y/n
Aconite is now group leader.

```
[Group][Aconite]: You okay?
[Group][Efthalia]: honestly not so much
[Group][Aconite]: :(
[Group][Aconite]: It's okay if you don't want
to do this. I get it.
[Group][Efthalia]: it's not that
[Group][Efthalia]: just had this really
stupid argument with Sanee
[Group][Efthalia]: one of my mates
[Group][Aconite]: What about?
```

[Group][Efthalia]: this actually
[Group][Efthalia]: he kept taking the piss
[Group][Aconite]: :(
[Group][Efthalia]: i guess maybe he could deal with the online thing or the boy thing but not both
[Group][Aconite]: I don't think either of those should be things
[Group][Efthalia]: they are though
[Group][Aconite]: To you or to him?
[Group][Efthalia]: right now i can't figure out what's a thing and what isn't
[Group][Efthalia]: i just know I missed you
[Group][Efthalia]: it might not be the same now I know
[Group][Efthalia]: but i'd still like to find out
[Group][Aconite]: So, more ophidian adventures, then?
[Group][Efthalia]: depends what ophidian is
[Group][Aconite]: Of or pertaining to snakes
[Group][Efthalia]: oh
[Group][Aconite]: It wasn't an invitation to the homosexual underworld
[Group][Efthalia]: i'm only level 10
[Group][Efthalia]: i only get [Portal: Homosexual Underworld] at 25
[Group][Aconite]: Hee
[Group][Aconite]: It didn't unlock until 50 in vanilla
[Group][Efthalia]: was there a long attunement
[Group][Aconite]: That would be quite the pick-up line
[Group][Efthalia]: don't tell Bjorn
[Group][Efthalia]: he's probably always telling people to check out his long attunement

[Group][Aconite]: :D
[Group][Aconite]: I really did miss you, Drew

Drew glowed, his argument with Sanee already almost forgotten. He'd expected hanging out with Kit to feel different now, but truthfully, it didn't at all. If anything, it was even easier to fall back into their . . . their thing. Whatever *that* was. He felt like there'd been something holding him back but he hadn't known it was there, but it was, and now it wasn't. Or something.

[Group][Efthalia]: so what's the plan?
[Group][Efthalia]: i've only got this crappy quest to unlock the flight path to krytos
[Group][Aconite]: Do you want to try Bubbling Marsh?
[Group][Efthalia]: seriously
[Group][Efthalia]: this our reunion medusa date not date thing thing
[Group][Efthalia]: and you want to pug
[Group][Aconite]: Hey, we first met in a pug
[Group][Aconite]: I was thinking of inviting Burnzurfais
[Group][Efthalia]: lol
[Group][Aconite]: Seriously though, I reckon we could 2-man it
[Group][Efthalia]: at lvl 10?
[Group][Aconite]: Well, it was balanced for 12 at release and Bjorn swears it's been nerfed since
[Group][Efthalia]: lololol
[Group][Efthalia]: i'm just imagining them at Tempest HQ being like nerf BM it's messing up endgame
[Group][Aconite]: Hee hee
[Group][Aconite]: But look. You also get access to a lot more stuff at level 10 now. I think it's probably doable

```
[Group][Efthalia]: i guess it'll be a
challenge
[Group][Aconite]: See, I knew that would get
you excited
[Group][Efthalia]: you know me too well
[Group][Aconite]: :)
```

Normally, they would have hopped in the Group Finder, which would have transported them straight to the instance, but then they'd have had to run with randoms. Instead they trekked up there on foot, which neither of them had ever done. They bickered for a little while over the best route and eventually agreed to do the quest that unlocked the flight paths and then take a Pegasus to the City of Ash since Kit, out of loyalty to his dark elf main, was still refusing to have anything to do with "high elf scum."

Unfortunately, when they finished the quest, they realised they couldn't fly to the mainland unless they'd already been to the other cities to open the Pegasus towers there. Which they couldn't do until they got to the mainland.

```
[Group][Efthalia]: wtf
[Group][Aconite]: I think I've spotted a flaw
in our plan
[Group][Efthalia]: wtf
[Group][Efthalia]: are we trapped
[Group][Efthalia]: this is terrible game
design
[Group][Aconite]: I think normally we'd be
following a quest chain which would take us
to the mainland
[Group][Efthalia]: yeah but if you're
creating an open world game you shouldn't
expect people to follow linear paths
[Group][Efthalia]: there's no reason to
restrict players interaction with the
environment like that
```

```
[Group][Efthalia]: what if someone playing
medusa wants to run around with someone
playing an elf
[Group][Efthalia]: >.<
[Group][Aconite]: You're cute when you're
ranting
[Group][Aconite]: I'm sure there's a way. We
just haven't found it yet
[Group][Efthalia]: you're cute when you're
being unhelpfully zen
[Group][Aconite]: I bet Ialdir will know
[Group][Efthalia]: your going to ask the high
elf scum for directions?
[Group][Aconite]: He's my best friend high
elf scum
[Group][Aconite]: I'm going to text him
[Group][Efthalia]: I'll look it up on HoLhead
[Group][Aconite]: Race you :)
```

Drew was competitive enough that he didn't even type "you're on" before alt-tabbing. He soon realised that while the site was an indispensable resource for loot tables, gear lists, and build planners, it was surprisingly low on pages tagged "How to get out of the damn starting areas." There was a page for basically every quest in *HoL*, so if there was a chain that took you from Krytos to the Bone Wastes he'd be able to find it, but then it was a game of "Guess what the low-level quest is called that takes you to the place you want to go." Turned out, this was one of the few games that Drew was legitimately terrible at.

He was about to resort to googling "how to get out of Minea without a flight path" when he realised enough time had passed that he'd probably lost.

```
[Group][Aconite]: Jacob says there's two
boats manned by rival elvish captains in the
NW of the city
[Group][Aconite]: There's also a dude in the
Temple of Serpentis who'll give us a quest to
speak to one of them
```

```
[Group][Aconite]: Drew?
[Group][Aconite]: Are you still there?
[Group][Aconite]: Are you still checking
HoLhead?
[Group][Efthalia]: okay you won
[Group][Aconite]: Ooh, what do I get?
[Group][Efthalia]: A luxury elvish cruise, a
romantic walk through a swamp and this [Musty
Shepherd's Sandal]
[Group][Aconite]: Wow. Thank you.
[Group][Aconite]: I'm a bit worried about
this [Musty Shepherd's Sandal] though.
[Group][Aconite]: Do you think it belonged
to a Musty Shepherd. Or do you think it is
itself musty?
[Group][Efthalia]: Could be both
[Group][Aconite]: Wouldn't that be a Musty
Shepherd's [Musty Sandal]?
[Group][Efthalia]: Or a Musty Shepherd's
[Musty Shepherd's Sandal]
[Group][Efthalia]: Now come on, dude, we'll
miss the boat
```

They nipped over to the Temple of Serpentis and picked up a quest from a priestess who informed them that the once mighty empire of the medusas was being courted by both sides in the on-going conflict between the high and dark elves, and that they were to go immediately to support the side of their choosing.

At the docks, they found two contrastingly dressed elves with question marks above their heads. The high elf dude looked a bit like Ialdir, with long golden braids and a haughty expression. His boat was a silver swan rising delicately out of the water. The dark elvish envoy was a cleavagey pirate chick, her ship covered with an implausible number of spikes.

Needless to say, they went with her.

As soon as Drew had clicked through the dialogue, a loading screen popped up showing two angry-looking elves glaring at one another, and a dodgy medusa being mysterious and shadowy in the middle.

You have discovered Tormenter's Bay.

[Group][Aconite]: Wow, I haven't been back here since Sol was level 14.
[Group][Efthalia]: i've never been here
[Group][Efthalia]: now I think about it i've basically not been on this whole continent except the capitals
[Group][Aconite]: Are you elvist or something?
[Group][Efthalia]: i was just always more about endgame
[Group][Efthalia]: i've only got three alts
[Group][Aconite]: No wonder you're the best geared tank on the server
[Group][Efthalia]: lol
[Group][Aconite]: Well TB is your classic hive of scum and villainy. It's run by dark elf pirates
[Group][Aconite]: It's way cooler than the Glittering Cove, which is where the smelly high elves take you
[Group][Aconite]: There's actually quite a decent quest line where you have to track down this cult that's trying to summon an ancient sea god that totally isn't Cthulhu
[Group][Efthalia]: you can give me the guided tour after we've done BM
[Group][Aconite]: Absolutely. We can have a quiet drink in the Iron Maiden

They made their way north over the blasted heaths surrounding Tormenter's Bay, trying to avoid the level twelve Ash-Touched Bears that lurked close to the port.

You have discovered The Fetid Morass.

[Group][Aconite]: You really know how to show a boy a good time
[Group][Efthalia]: hey this was your idea

As much as Drew appreciated the design effort that went into much of the game, he had to admit that the Fetid Morass was just a bit dull. It was all grey-brown pools of water, grey-brown trees, and the occasional creepily glowing mushroom. He followed Aconite's bobbing snakes to the edge of a vast, dismal lake.

[Group][Aconite]: So you sort of have to swim down to it
[Group][Efthalia]: omg
[Group][Efthalia]: wtf
[Group][Efthalia]: are you seriously telling me that the entry-level group content
[Group][Efthalia]: is hidden at the bottom of the swamp
[Group][Aconite]: That's how they rolled in vanilla
[Group][Aconite]: It was actually pretty exciting the first time I came here
[Group][Aconite]: Jacob brought me on an alt run
[Group][Efthalia]: did he tell you the whole history
[Group][Aconite]: Actually, there's surprisingly little lore on this one
[Group][Aconite]: It sort of ties into the cult thing in TB but that never comes up again
[Group][Aconite]: Basically we swim in, beat up some evil frogmen, and fight an elemental
[Group][Efthalia]: bring it

They plunged into the murky water and, painfully slowly, swam towards the centre of the lake. About halfway through, Drew noticed his health going down quickly.

```
[Group][Efthalia]: wall11lwwaaaa
[Group][Efthalia]: help
```

He frantically swivelled the camera around until he located his attacker: an implausibly large fish that was chewing on Efthalia's defenceless nethers. He attempted to summon the elemental forces of fire to defend himself but the relentless assault of his fishy opponent kept interrupting his spellcasting.

```
[Group][Aconite]: omg
[Group][Aconite]: omw
[Group][Efthalia]: ahhhhhh
```

Efthalia was killed by Irate Turbot: bite (4)
Efthalia has died.

Efthalia's body floated limply in the brownish water.

```
[Group][Aconite]: I will avenge you!
```

There was an explosion of purple shadow.

```
[Group][Aconite]: My name is Aconite. You
killed my . . . the other medusa I hang
around with. Prepare to die!
```

As Drew watched, the evil fish was consumed by tendrils of dark magic and flipped belly up alongside Efthalia.

```
[Group][Efthalia]: rez plox
[Group][Aconite]: Um, this is a pure DPS
class
```

```
[Group][Aconite]: You're the one with the rez
[Group][Efthalia]: ffs
```

Drew clicked Release Spirit and the world faded to shades of grey and blue. His ghost appeared at the nearest graveyard, and he began the undignified jog back to his corpse.

A few minutes later, Efthalia was alive and doing her ridiculous swim animation, as the two medusas continued their descent towards the Bubbling Mire.

You have discovered The Bubbling Mire.

Another loading screen: this one showed a frogman with a spear. It wasn't exactly threatening, but since Drew had just been killed by an angry fish, he was withholding judgement.

Efthalia and Aconite appeared in the mouth of a dripping-wet cave, illuminated by more of the glowy mushrooms he'd seen on the surface. Ahead of them, two frogmen were standing around, ready to be killed.

```
[Group][Efthalia]: tacs
[Group][Aconite]: Um
[Group][Aconite]: Well, I thought we could
tank it with my Doomshadow
[Group][Efthalia]: you want me to heal your
pet.
[Group][Aconite]: Well, it's got more health
than either of us and it's the only one in
the party with an actual taunt.
[Group][Efthalia]: this does not feel like a
pro move
[Group][Aconite]: Welcome to healing
[Group][Aconite]: Dignity is something that
happens to other classes
[Group][Efthalia]: I could try to storm tank it
[Group][Aconite]: And I could keep you alive
with my zero healing spells
```

```
[Group][Efthalia]: . . .
[Group][Aconite]: Honestly. You tanks. You
really do think your health stays up on its
own, don't you?
[Group][Efthalia]: ok ok
[Group][Efthalia]: just let me spend my ONE
talent point
[Group][Efthalia]: and quickbar my TWO
healing spells
```

On some level, Drew was aware he might be taking this too seriously. He set up a couple of targeting macros and rearranged his interface to centralise his party's health bars. Beside him, Aconite jumped up and down, and finally started the longish ritual to summon the blobby demon that would be responsible for keeping them alive and unmolested in the dungeon.

```
[Charnos] says: I have been called
[Aconite] says: Yes. Yes you have.
[Aconite] says: Now, pay close attention,
this is a three-phase fight and your top prio
is keeping the mobs off the healing team.
[Group][Efthalia]: lol
[Group][Aconite]: Right. We're probably going
to die horribly because I've never played a
tanking class or a pet class
[Group][Aconite]: And I'm really not sure
Charnos was paying attention when I told him
the tacs
```

Charnos was, in fact, gazing around distractedly. It was probably just a quirk of the animation, but it wasn't very reassuring. A couple of raid markers popped up over the heads of the patiently waiting frogmen.

```
[Efthalia] says: Dude, focus.
```

```
[Group] [Aconite]: I'll send him against star.
We probably need to give him a couple of
seconds to establish threat
[Group] [Aconite]: Do you have [Incapacitating
Wind]?
[Group] [Efthalia]: yeah but i'm taking
something for it
[Group] [Aconite]: Okay, so you wind dildo
[Group] [Aconite]: Charnos will take star
[Group] [Aconite]: And . . . we'll see if we
live.
```

Efthalia stepped forward and began to gather the elemental forces of the storm. A vortex of swirling wind lifted one of the frogmen into the air and the other one hopped slowly forwards with what might have been a murderous look in its eyes. Except . . . frog.

Charnos drifted out to meet it and there was a dicey moment when Drew really wasn't certain if a level ten summoned creature was able to stand up to a level twelve elite. The demon's health bar wasn't exactly plummeting, but it was going down pretty quickly. Pulse pounding, Drew quickly threw a Life Seed on it and then followed up with a Nourishing Soil.

He was so focused on Charnos's health bar and the two ways he had to maintain it that he had no idea what else was going on. Occasionally he'd see a flurry of shadow from Aconite's direction.

The fight seemed to be lasting forever. But, as it went on, he started to feel more confident. Charnos was taking damage at a steady rate, and he was getting a good feel for when he had to be healing and when he could afford to do other stuff.

With a mournful ribbit, the first bullywug crumpled to the floor and Charnos moved menacingly to the second, who'd just recovered from his attack of Incapacitating Wind. This time Drew was comfortable enough to switch between his two healing spells and his two damage spells, and the frogman fell over substantially faster.

He gave an actual fist pump, exclaiming to his empty room that the frog dudes could, indeed, suck it.

[Group][Aconite]: Yay!
[Group][Aconite]: *hugs Charnos*
[Group][Efthalia]: hey I was here too
[Group][Efthalia]: healing
[Group][Aconite]: *hugs Efthalia*
[Group][Efthalia]: i can't believe we pulled that off
[Group][Aconite]: Don't get too excited
[Group][Aconite]: There's four in the next pack
[Group][Efthalia]: !!!
[Group][Aconite]: But first! The loots!
[Enigmatic Bracers of the Whale] Need/Greed

Drew squinted at the crappy stats on the crappy drop.

[Group][Efthalia]: they are technically an upgrade
[Group][Aconite]: For me too
[Group][Aconite]: My bracers are still grey
[Group][Efthalia]: hey thems healer stats
[Group][Aconite]: You're right. Those 2 points of wisdom will make all the difference to your performance
[Group][Aconite]: You take them
[Group][Efthalia]: i was only joking
[Group][Efthalia]: you have them
[Group][Aconite]: No, you should always take care of the healer first
[Group][Aconite]: You can remember this moment when we go back to our mains
[Group][Aconite]: Besides, I don't think they go with my toga
You have received [Enigmatic Bracers of the Whale].

Drew equipped his shiny new healing gear. It didn't go with his toga either. All the same, Efthalia gave a little /twirl and Aconite /clapped.

Charnos remained unimpressed, stretching his claws in a way that suggested he really wanted to be tearing something's soul from its body right now.

They moved cautiously down the tunnel and into the next cavern. More mushrooms. More bullywugs. Whoever had designed this dungeon had either put no effort into making it interesting or a lot of effort into making it accessible.

And had clearly been a different person to whoever had decided to put it at the bottom of a swamp surrounded by killer fish.

```
[Group][Efthalia]: tacs
[Group][Aconite]: Same again but double, I
guess
[Group][Aconite]: I'll have Charnos take
star and skull. You wind dildo. I'll stick
[Damnable Chains] on circle.
[Group][Efthalia]: sounds like a plan
[Group][Aconite]: Jacob would love this
[Group][Aconite]: We've never 2-manned this
one but I think he'd dig the retro charm
[Group][Efthalia]: you can inv him if you
like
[Group][Aconite]: Do you want me to?
[Group][Efthalia]: only if you want to
[Group][Efthalia]: i mean
[Group][Efthalia]: its up to you
[Group][Aconite]: I like hanging out with
Jacob but we do that all the time
[Group][Aconite]: I kind of like that this is
just us
[Group][Aconite]: If that's okay
```

Drew was in a messy place again. He'd thought Kit wanted Ialdir along, and that had made him feel weird, but it seemed Kit didn't, and that made him feel weirder. He decided it was a happy weird.

```
[Group][Efthalia]: I like it too
[Group][Aconite]: And I brought Charnos
[Group][Aconite]: To chaperone
[Group][Aconite]: Protect your virtue
[Group][Efthalia]: maybe hes my type
[Group][Efthalia]: all big and purple with no
face
[Group][Aconite]: O.O
[Group][Efthalia]: that didn't come out right
[Group][Efthalia]: should we kill these frogs
```

Efthalia and Aconite stepped forward together this time. One of the bullywugs was snatched into the air by Efthalia's wind (someday Drew was going to stop smirking at that) and another was rooted to the ground by chains of living darkness. Charnos floated forward and started making threatening gestures at the other two frog people. With twice the attacks coming in, his health was going down twice as fast and Drew was in a panic.

```
[Group][Aconite]: omg spears
[Group][Aconite]: spears
```

Drew spun the camera to see long wooden staffs piercing Aconite's character model. And then glanced back at the health bars to see that she'd dropped from basically fine to basically dead in about three seconds. His HoT was on cooldown and he managed to get about halfway through a Nourishing Soil before Aconite fell to the ground and Charnos winked out of existence, freeing the two previously incapacitated bullywugs to hop viciously in his direction.

He did what any loyal and courageous Hero of Legend would do. He turned and legged it, straight back up the corridor and out of the portal.

Loading screen again.

```
[Group][Aconite]: omg healer
[Group][Aconite]: y no healz
[Group][Efthalia]: i actually feel really bad
```

```
[Group] [Efthalia]: :(
[Group] [Aconite]: If the DPS die it's their
own damn fault
[Group] [Efthalia]: what happened
[Group] [Aconite]: The frogs at the back had
spears so the one I rooted could still
attack me
[Group] [Aconite]: :(
[Group] [Efthalia]: nerf frogs
[Group] [Aconite]: Nerf spears
```

When Efthalia was close to running out of air and Drew was moderately certain that the frogs had gone back to their stations, he swam back into the dungeon, inched into range of Aconite's corpse, and began to coerce the elemental powers of earth into releasing her spirit from the netherworld.

A second or two later, she popped up next to him and began the ritual to resummon her demonic servant.

```
[Group] [Aconite]: Yay
[Charnos] says: Your will?
[Aconite] says: You noob, Charnos
[Group] [Efthalia]: hey your the one who
pulled threat off the tank
[Group] [Aconite]: Only because my DPS is so
imba
[Group] [Efthalia]: we trying this again
[Group] [Aconite]: Definitely
[Group] [Aconite]: Same strat, I'll just move
the marks so I root the melee
```

This time things went slightly better. They still all died but they managed to take a couple of frogs out with them, which meant they only had two left to deal with on their next run. And they went down fairly easily.

```
[Group] [Efthalia]: wow
```

```
[Group][Efthalia]: this is kind of intense
[Group][Aconite]: Yeah, do you mind we're
desert gorging it?
[Group][Efthalia]: i might if i knew what it
meant
[Group][Aconite]: I picked it up from Jacob
[Group][Aconite]: It basically means winning
by exploiting the fact that you come back
from the dead
[Group][Aconite]: And your opponents don't
[Group][Aconite]: It's from a comic he likes
[Group][Efthalia]: i'm just impressed that
has a name
[Group][Aconite]: But you're okay with this,
right?
[Group][Aconite]: We might die quite a lot
[Group][Efthalia]: my repair bill is like 3
coppers
[Group][Efthalia]: i'm good
```

Drew was actually getting quite into it. There was a sort of . . . cleanness somehow to the challenge it presented: this obstacle is designed to require *x* amount of resources, you have *y* amount of resources, how do you use those creatively to make up the difference. In practice, what it meant was a mix of hit-and-run tactics, kiting, and really intense crowd control. They died a few times, but gradually they developed a kind of military precision and an instinct for what the other person was doing, which meant they often triumphed when they really, really shouldn't have. It was a way of playing the game that Drew would never have thought of, and he was really glad Kit had shared it with him.

Eventually they made it to the final boss, Quagmire the Bog Lord. He was a gigantic tainted water elemental, and apparently he was just sort of hanging out on the off chance a party of adventurers would want to swim to the bottom of a lake, fight their way through a cave full of frogmen, and beat him up.

The poor bastard didn't even have any dialogue.

[Group][Efthalia]: i can't believe we
actually made it
[Group][Aconite]: I know, right?
[Aconite] says: Charnos, when we first met, I
didn't understand the depths of your courage
or the purpleness of your face.
[Aconite] says: But now I understand that you
are a true heroic spirit
[Aconite] says: I couldn't have done it
without you, buddy.
[Aconite] says: You, me, and this other guy
hanging out at the back
[Aconite] says: No idea what he's doing
[Efthalia] says: Hey!
[Group][Efthalia]: any tacs
[Group][Aconite]: Actually, after all that,
he should be pretty straightforward
[Group][Aconite]: I think he's got a tiny
knockback
[Group][Aconite]: And an AoE that will be
meaningless because we've got no melee

It was, as it turned out, as straightforward as Kit had suggested.
Charnos kept Quaqmire busy while Efthalia and Aconite plinked
away at his hit points, with Efthalia throwing out the occasional heal
as needed. A few minutes later, the elemental exploded in a sploosh of
dirty water. It ought to have been anticlimactic, but it felt awesome.

**Achievement unlocked: The Bubbling Mire
[Defeat Quagmire the Bog Lord in The Bubbling
Mire]**

[Group][Aconite]: Yay!!!
[Group][Efthalia]: do you want to get a
coffee some time

Oh shit. Drew'd had no idea he'd been about to type that.
But there it was. And he couldn't take it back now.
And he was pretty sure he didn't want to.

```
[Group][Aconite]: Are you sure?
[Group][Aconite]: Because I can see you might
have been swept up in the moment
[Group][Aconite]: What with the romantic
swamp water
[Group][Aconite]: And Charnos, of course
```

He had been caught up in the moment. But it wasn't really about
the game or—for that matter—Charnos. It was about being with Kit.
Which, he was beginning to realise, he still really liked.
That hadn't changed at all.

```
[Group][Efthalia]: yeah no i'm sure
[Group][Efthalia]: if you want to
[Group][Efthalia]: if it wouldn't be weird
[Group][Aconite]: It might be weird
[Group][Efthalia]: more weird than our swamp
date
[Group][Aconite]: So this was a date then?
[Group][Efthalia]: i guess so
[Group][Aconite]: :)
[Group][Aconite]: I really want to
[Group][Aconite]: But I'm a bit
[Group][Aconite]: You're the first guy I've
been really into
[Group][Aconite]: And you thought I was a
girl
[Group][Aconite]: And we have a really nice
time together
[Group][Aconite]: But I'd rather stick to
that
[Group][Aconite]: Than mess everything up
trying to change it
```

Drew could see where Kit was coming from. *His* worst-case scenario was that they'd meet up and he'd realise he just wasn't into boys, and that would be difficult but basically back to normal. For Kit it would be this massive, unnecessary head-fuck.

```
[Group][Efthalia]: i get that
[Group][Efthalia]: and i can't predict how
it's going to go
[Group][Efthalia]: and if you want to just do
this
[Group][Efthalia]: then we can
[Group][Efthalia]: but i think we might be
missing out
[Group][Efthalia]: i want to see where this
goes
```

There was a slightly fraught silence. Drew's hands were shaking a little against the keyboard. Wow, that was the most serious "we should go out" speech he'd ever given anyone, and he was pretty sure he would never have been able to say it aloud. Not without feeling like an idiot. To be honest, he felt a bit of an idiot now, but it was cushioned by two medusas standing in a puddle around an elemental they'd forgotten to loot.

Still nothing from Kit.

Drew risked putting his fingers back on the keys.

```
[Group][Efthalia]: and look
[Group][Efthalia]: not being funny or
anything
[Group][Efthalia]: but the way i see
[Group][Efthalia]: i've never had a boyfriend
[Group][Efthalia]: and actually you've never
had a boyfriend
[Group][Efthalia]: so we're both pretty new
to this
[Group][Efthalia]: and what have we got to
lose
```

Silence. Silence. Silence.

```
[Group][Aconite]: Okay
```

Drew stared blankly at the screen. He wasn't sure whether to celebrate or hide under the desk.

```
[Group][Efthalia]: seriously?
[Group][Aconite]: Why? Were you hoping I'd
say no?
[Group][Efthalia]: No!
[Group][Efthalia]: i just wasn't sure you
were going to say yes
[Group][Aconite]: After a speech like that,
how could a guy resist?
[Group][Efthalia]: *blush*
[Group][Aconite]: Hee, that's my line.
[Group][Efthalia]: lol
```

It was as close as it was going to get to how it used to be. And Drew was slightly shocked at how happy it made him.

```
[Group][Efthalia]: so . . . like
[Group][Efthalia]: basic internet safety
stuff
[Group][Efthalia]: we should meet somewhere
neutral and public and tell people where
you're going
[Group][Efthalia]: somewhere in town?
[Group][Aconite]: It's not exactly classy but
how about Starbucks?
[Group][Efthalia]: the one in the shopping
centre?
[Group][Aconite]: Yes
[Group][Efthalia]: tomorrow?
[Group][Efthalia]: before the raid
[Group][Efthalia]: 4ish
```

[Group][Aconite]: Yes
[Group][Aconite]: God, I'm terrified.
[Group][Efthalia]: me too
[Group][Aconite]: But I'm looking forward to it :)
[Group][Efthalia]: me too :)
[Group][Efthalia]: shit how will I know who you are
[Group][Aconite]: I'll be dressed as a penguin and reading The Financial Times
[Group][Efthalia]: then I'll be wearing a red carnation and looking through a newspaper with two holes cut in it
[Group][Aconite]: Hee
[Group][Aconite]: Actually, I'm kind of ordinary looking, sort of blondish and I'll be wearing a blue shirt
[Group][Aconite]: Sorry that probably doesn't help
[Group][Aconite]: I'll be reading a secondhand copy of A Canticle for Leibowitz
[Group][Efthalia]: So if I see someone with a brand new copy I've got the wrong dude
[Group][Aconite]: Yeah, he works for the KGB
[Group][Efthalia]: lol
[Group][Aconite]: Are you coming to the raid tonight
[Group][Efthalia]: didn't sign up
[Group][Efthalia]: got a course deadline
[Group][Efthalia]: wasn't sure I'd be free
[Group][Aconite]: See you on Wednesday then :)

And just like that, Drew had a date.

CHAPTER 7

When Wednesday finally came, he told Tinuviel and Sanee just in case Solace turned out to be some kind of serial killer who called himself Kit because he liked to chop people up and assemble new boyfriends out of the pieces.

"You do realise," Sanee said ominously, "that this guy's a geek, which means he's probably going to look like me or, well, you."

"What's wrong with that?"

"Well, would you date you?"

"No. But I *am* me. That would be weird."

Sanee frowned. "I just can't get my head round it. Obviously girls like you. Well, two girls like you, or three if you count that chick at that club that time. I'm not saying you're a minger or anything . . ."

Drew had been feeling relatively good until then. Attractiveness-wise, he'd always thought of himself as being on the right side of average. He washed and shaved and kept in decent shape. He'd been told he had nice eyes, but then he was pretty sure nobody ever said, *Darling, your eyes are really close-set and piggy tonight.*

Some kind of panic must have shown on his face, because Sanee suddenly started talking again. "Sorry, dude. It's just, well, you're a dude, and I'm a dude, and I'm trying to be supportive here, but I'm looking at you now, and I don't fancy you, and I'm having a hard time seeing why anyone would."

"Thanks, mate. Way to build me up before my big date."

Tinuviel glanced up from *Hawkeye.* "I don't fancy Drew either—"

"Should I just kill myself now?"

"—but," she went on, "I can see why somebody else might."

"Wow," said Drew, "see praise comma faint colon damning with."

She blinked at him. "It doesn't matter what we think. It matters what Kit thinks."

"So no pressure, then."

"It'll be fine. Do you mind if I borrow this?" She waved the trade paperback as casually as a geek was capable of treating a comic.

Drew had the feeling his friends weren't taking his concerns seriously. "Yeah, go on, then. You might as well take volume two as well."

While Sanee and Tinuviel were busy with *Hawkeye*, he went over to his wardrobe and peered inside like he was looking for Narnia. He hesitated to ask, but he had trouble picking date clothes at the best of times. "Um, guys, which T-shirt should I wear?"

"Dude." Sanee twisted round. "Maybe you could try wearing an actual shirt like a grown-up."

"Or a schoolkid. Why don't I put on a stripey tie and a blazer as well?"

"Bit kinky for a first date."

Drew gave a long-suffering sigh and reluctantly pulled out his one good shirt. "I feel like I'm going to an interview."

Sanee flipped into lecture mode. "Basically, mate, you are. That's what a date is. It's like a sex interview. So you need to dress up for it. Seriously, you won't regret it. I wore a shirt for my first date with Steff. Chicks love that stuff." There was a pause. "Although . . . that may not be pertinent to this situation."

"I don't care what my date is wearing," offered Tinuviel helpfully, "as long as it reflects their essential self."

Drew shoved his shirt back in the wardrobe. "I'm going with the essential-self plan." He started grabbing T-shirts and holding them up to his chest. *Feelings are boring, kissing is awesome* probably looked a shade desperate, and he was afraid if he wore *I will do science to it*, he'd actually have to know about science, which would be embarrassing since Kit actually did.

"How about this?" He waved *I'm not slacking off, my code's compiling.*

Sanee flinched. "No way, man. The way *xkcd*'s gone recently, he'll think you've got terrible taste in webcomics and it'll all be over."

"So I'm a minger with terrible taste in clothes and webcomics?"

"If it's any consolation, he's probably just as big a loser as you are."

"Well, at least you've stopped being weirded out he's a guy."

Sanee grinned.

Drew disappeared back into his wardrobe and finally emerged. "Okay, I think I've found the perfect one."

They stared at him in polite bemusement.

"I think it works," said Tinuviel, finally. "It's very you."

Sanee seemed less convinced. "So, you're saying that your essential self is 'A wizard has turned you into a whale. Is this awesome? Y/N'?"

Drew shrugged. "I think it'll make him laugh."

An hour later, he was anxiously circling the designated Starbucks, trying to psych himself up to go in.

To be honest, he couldn't figure out what scared him most: the possibility that he wouldn't fancy Kit, or the possibility that he would.

Finally, he pulled himself together and walked through the door. It wasn't particularly crowded in there, and he scanned the tables looking for . . . what? Someone ordinary and blondish and reading a book.

There was only one guy reading. Or, at least, only one guy reading a paper book.

But if Drew'd had to describe him, he wouldn't have gone with ordinary.

He'd been expecting some kind of hopeless geek-boy. But the young man at the table was, well . . . elegant, somehow, his chin propped on one long-fingered hand as he read.

Drew was really beginning to wish he'd worn a shirt.

Kit was wearing a shirt—a dark-blue one with embroidery down the sleeves—and his hair was blondish, as he'd said, but it was a rich, dark gold, slightly curly at the ends, as if he had his own personal stylist hanging out backstage.

Basically, he looked like a catalogue model, or the popular one in a boyband. Kind of slim and lean and clean-cut. The sort of guy you could take home to meet your mum.

He glanced up, saw Drew, and gave him a slightly quizzical, slightly hopeful expression.

And Drew had no choice but to walk over there and pretend he wasn't totally outclassed.

"Solace?" he said. Shit. "I mean, uh, Kit, right?"

The boy nodded and, slowly, a little bit shyly, smiled. It was a good smile. Partially because it was a touch hesitant, like he didn't give it to just anyone. "Hi, Drew."

Drew panicked. "I'm just going to grab myself a coffee. Do you want anything?"

Kit nodded towards the mug already on the table. "I'm fine."

Right. Okay. Stupid question. "Be right back."

There was a longish queue, which was sort a relief and sort of not. It gave him time to freak out at a safe distance while he was pretending to pick a muffin. But he was still close enough that he was very aware of Kit, well, being there. Being a real, physical person, and not just a bundle of internet. And he wasn't sure whether he was supposed to be looking, or not looking, or smiling, or waving, or what.

Things were so much easier on a rock in a cave under a swamp.

He got himself a latte and, since he'd been staring at them, a white chocolate and raspberry muffin, and mooched back to sit down.

"Uh, hi," he said. "Uh, again. Uh, how are you?"

Kit put his book aside. "Honestly? I'm still a bit nervous."

For some reason that really helped. "Shit, me too."

They grinned at each other, kind of awkward, kind of not.

"We missed you at the raid on Monday."

"Sorry. I'm trying to get this water to look right. It's even less interesting than it sounds. Who MTed?"

"Morag, and Bjorn brought his tanking alt. So that was fun."

Kit looked so rueful that Drew had to laugh. "How'd it go?"

"Oh, it was fine, he OTs for us all the time. He's just very Bjorn about it." His voice slipped into a fairly effective imitation of Bjorn's self-satisfied drawl. "Don't worry, this was my main back in vanilla. Did I tell you about the time I soloed Dreadwing after my entire raid died of being noobs?"

Drew grinned. "I dare you to do that in front of him."

"Gosh, no, he'd shard all my loot for a month." He paused for a moment. "Also, I think it might make him genuinely sad. He's quite sensitive really."

"What, Bjorn?" Drew blinked. "Like . . . Bjorn Bjorn?"

"Well, you don't carry on that way if you don't care what people think of you."

"Oh yeah, I've got a mate like that. He's kind of a dick as well, but I guess he gets away with it because he's kind of dick at you, not to you." Remembering Monday, Drew grimaced. "At least, most of the time."

"That's a pretty subtle distinction." Kit gave him a slightly teasing look over the rim of his mug, and Drew felt somewhere between flustered and pleased. And had no idea how to look back.

"I mean," he went on, "Sanee's not nasty to anyone. He just kind of is who he is, and sometimes that's a bit annoying. But if you tell him he's being annoying, he'll try to be less annoying." He remembered Monday again. "At least, most of the time."

"Truly, that is the meaning of friendship."

Drew gave him a mock scowl. "Are you taking the piss?"

"Well, yes and no. Mainly yes. But I also think there's something really nice about having people you can be yourself with, but who you can trust to tell you when yourself is being a dick."

"I can't really imagine you being a dick."

"Hey, I could be a dick if I wanted."

It was probably a bad moment to suddenly notice that they were saying the word *dick* a lot, and Drew felt himself blushing for no reason. "So how's the book?"

Kit grinned wickedly at him. "Wow, way to imperceptibly change the subject."

"Sorry, we were just kind of on a dick train and I wasn't sure how to get off."

The grin vanished. "Sorry, was I making you uncomfortable?"

He honestly wasn't sure. He didn't feel exactly cosy, sitting there talking about dicks with the guy he was on a date with, but he couldn't tell if that was just him being weird. It wasn't like he'd be talking about vaginas with a girl he'd fancied.

Tinuviel probably would, but she was a special case.

Also Kit looked really anxious, and that was really sad-making.

"I'm not uncomfortable. Promise. Honest. It's just I got into this spiral in my head, like you know when you're trying not to think of something, so you do."

"Oh man—" Kit made a frustrated gesture "—I just lost The Game."

"Oh thanks, me too."

They stared at each other helplessly, caught on the verge of laughter.

"There's a guy on my course," said Drew, "who refuses to play The Game."

Kit blinked. "What does that even mean?"

"It's kind of weird actually. It just means that every time someone loses The Game he goes into this speech about how he doesn't play The Game because, like, he's like not a follower or something. I think he actually used the word *sheeple* at one point."

Kit flinched, a bit theatrically, but it was cute.

"But the thing is, he's basically playing this boring meta game of his own, which means he spends all his time waiting for people to mention The Game so he can object. It's like he takes it way more seriously than anybody who actually plays it, and has way less fun." Drew paused, and picked thoughtfully at his muffin. "By the way, do you want some?"

Kit nodded, and they sat there companionably, sharing it.

And it didn't feel weird at all. In fact, it was even better than killing frogmen in a swamp.

"Actually," Drew went on, "thinking about it, the funny thing about The Game is that the most hard-core way to play it is the most casual. Like if you actually care about going a long time not thinking about The Game—"

Kit yelped. "We are losing The Game so hard right now."

"Omg, nerf conversations. But, anyway, if you actually care about winning The Game, you're going to lose The Game, whereas if you don't give a crap about The Game at all, you can actually do pretty well at it."

"To be honest, I'd never really thought about it."

"Well, I'm kind of interested in games, and the way they work. Uh, obviously."

Kit was nodding thoughtfully. "I guess it's a social thing as well. Because, as you say, you can't really play The Game seriously. What it really becomes is a sort of signal. Like wearing a *Dinosaur Comics* T-shirt."

"Oh don't." Drew folded his arms self-consciously over the killer whale. "I really wish I'd worn a shirt. You're all smart, and I look like I made no effort."

"No, it's perfect. I've got 'Partying Is Such Sweet Sorrow' at home, but I only wear it for running."

That gave Drew an image he wasn't quite ready for: Kit, tousled and a little bit sweaty, jogging through the trees in Victoria Park or something. In his nerdy T-shirt. "It's probably a good thing you didn't wear it. We'd have looked a right pair of numpties."

"Or the Leicester Chapter of the Ryan North Fan Club."

Drew laughed into his hands, and then sort of panicked because he couldn't think of anything funny to add. "So you like running, huh?" Shit. That was even worse.

"Yeah." Kit nodded. "Well, since I spend all my time gaming or in lectures, it's kind of my bastion against becoming a fat bastard."

Drew dropped his voice a couple of octaves and adopted a faux cowboy accent. "'Kid just rages for a while.'"

Kit stared at him, not unkindly but clearly bemused.

"Sorry, you said 'bastion.'"

"Oh right, I haven't played it. I don't do so much gaming outside of *HoL*."

"It's good. It's basically just an action RPG, but it's got this cool voice-over that kind of gives context to all the pointless shit you normally do in that sort of game, like smashing barrels with a hammer, and stuff."

Kit smiled shyly at him. "I might take a look at it."

"I'd wait for a Steam sale. It's about a tenner most of the time. And the sequel's pretty cool too. It has a killer soundtrack, although I think you're supposed to be in love with your sword, which is a bit weird." He stopped babbling. And then babbled in a different direction.

"I mean, you could come round and try it on my desktop if you want. See if you like it."

"I bet you say that to all the boys."

Drew spluttered, and knew he was blushing, but it wasn't a bad feeling. "I picked up *AssCreed IV* in the last sale as well. I thought it was worth it because you get to be a pirate."

"I kind of lost track of the series. I think I got the first one for my thirteeth birthday."

It was strange being able to watch Kit talk. He was sort of quiet and gentle and seemed to really think about things before he said them. Drew imagined he would be just the same typing.

"All I can remember," Kit was saying, "is having to ride a horse really slowly around twelfth-century Jerusalem because if you dared to gallop everyone would immediately work out you were an assassin."

"Yeah, they kind of got better, then they got worse, and now it's good again. You get, like, a pirate ship and, well, a pirate ship. I mean, seriously, what more do you want."

"Does it come with Johnny Depp?" Kit arched his eyebrows hopefully.

"No, it comes with really OP swivel guns."

Kit laughed. "Well, I'm in, then."

He had a nice laugh, with a slightly uncertain edge to it, which made Drew feel strangely protective. Then he realised he was staring and smiling and probably looking like an idiot. "Shit, sorry, you were talking about running, and I completely derailed you with that stupid Bastion reference."

"Oh, I thought you were trying to invite me back to your room."

They eyed each other nervously, trying to work out how far was too far. Drew thought, *Screw it*, and decided this wasn't it. He was on a date. With a boy. And the boy was flirting with him, and that was okay. "Yeah, I only bring the pirates out on special occasions."

Kit faffed with the wooden pokey thing they'd given him with his mocha. After a moment or two he looked up a bit sheepishly. "Sorry, that's really nice, in a piratey kind of way, and I don't know what to say. I don't think I'm very good at this."

"What, you mean . . ." Drew made a really unhelpful hand gesture.

"I don't know how to say this without making myself sound completely pathetic and desperate, but I've never actually been on a date before. And I think I'm having a good time, but I'm still as nervous as hell."

"If it helps, I'm definitely having a good time."

Kit ran a hand through his hair, making it go all fluffy. "It's easier behind a keyboard. You've got more thinking time so you can sound way cleverer than you are, and you can sort of take more chances."

"Like how?"

"You've got this . . . wriggle room, I guess? I think because it's hard to know exactly what someone means, if something goes wrong, you can pretend it didn't. But now I feel l like I'm sitting here with this big flashing sign over my head saying 'I really like you,' so if I put my foot in it or I say something wrong, then I won't be able to get out of it, and you'll be right there, staring at me, and thinking, 'Wow, this guy is a loser.'"

For a moment, Drew just gazed at him, a little bit stunned. Nobody had ever been quite that open with him before. It struck him as weirdly valiant, and made him feel kind of warm and smooshy and a little bit embarrassed. "Honestly, Kit. I'd never think you were a loser."

The next thing he knew, he'd reached out, and there he was, holding another guy's hand over the table. He looked down, and thought, *Oh*. Because it was fine.

Kit's strong, elegant fingers tightened around his. "So, I'm doing it right, then?"

Drew smiled. "Yeah."

They kept chatting for a while, still holding hands, until Drew got self-conscious and panicked that he'd come across way too intense.

"Um, is this okay? I mean, this is an okay thing to do? With like . . ." He tried to gesture, but since he was already holding Kit's hand all he did was kind of jiggle it like a mouse.

"It's really okay." Kit smiled at him. "If I'm being a bit odd it's because I probably am a bit odd, but also because I'm still a bit scared you'll decide this was a terrible mistake."

"I'm honestly happy we did this, and I'd really like to—" Unfortunately, at that moment, Drew's phone bleeped at him.

He glanced at it in horror. "Shit. On the subject of terrible of mistakes, we're both supposed to be raiding in about fifteen minutes."

Kit's eyes went very wide. Which, Drew couldn't help noticing, made them very pretty, but this really wasn't the time. "Oh my God, we suck."

They both leaped into action, untangling their hands, sweeping up their various belongings, pulling on their coats. They gazed at each other in panic.

Drew flailed. "I want to stay and stuff and I'm pretty sure this isn't how to end a date, but I don't want to let the guild down."

"No, it's fine. See you in Crown of Thorns."

"We'll do this again, right?"

"Absolutely."

They crashed into a hasty, awkward, clumsy approximation of a hug. One of Drew's hands went into Kit's armpit and Kit bashed his shoulder into Drew's chin. But that was sort of where they were so they went with it, and Drew clutched and Kit squeezed—and he couldn't quite tell in the panic, but he was pretty sure Kit's lips brushed against his cheek.

Then they ran for it.

CHAPTER 8

Back in his room, Drew tore off his dating T-shirt and flung on his raiding pyjamas, started boiling the kettle for a Cup-a-Soup and logged onto Ella.

Guild Message of the day: Still do not ask Tiff about her date.
```
[Guild][Solace]: Hi :) :)
[Guild][Heurodis]: Yo
[Guild][Ialdir]: Hey
[Guild][Orcarella]: Hi
```

Normally he made sure he was already in position outside the instance, but Ella was standing around in front of the AH in the City of Stars. Thankfully he was already well stocked with consumables, so he jumped on a randomly selected flying mount and made for CoT.

On the way, he stared at Solace's "Hi" with its two accompanying smileys.

It felt weird and nice at the same time because they'd been on a date, and normally when you went on a date with someone you didn't see them again immediately. He didn't want to make a big thing about it, but he didn't want to act like it hadn't happened either.

```
To [Solace]: Fancy meeting you here
[Solace] whispers: of all the raid instances
in all the MMOs in all the world, you walk
into mine
To [Solace]: here's looking at you kit
```

```
[Solace] whispers: !
[Solace] whispers: I can't believe you went
there
To [Solace]: I can't believe you thought I
wouldn't
[Guild][Heurodis]: okay peons start getting
in mumble and getting to cot
[Solace] whispers: You're getting on that
skyship with Victor where you belong. You're
part of his guild, what keeps him going.
To [Solace]: god you're such a nerd :D
[Solace] whispers: Hey, that's classic cinema
[Solace] whispers: This is some high class
banter you're getting here.
```

Drew's soup water had gone cold, or at least too cold to make soup with, because he'd been too busy flirting and grinning at the screen like an idiot. He flicked the kettle on again and told himself to pay attention this time.

```
To [Solace]: we'll always have Steamworks -
Furnace (Heroic)
[Solace] whispers: Aww, that can be our
dungeon.
To [Solace]: you're making it really hard for
me to hate it
[Solace] whispers: IMPALED!!!
[Guild][Heurodis]: okay we're waiting on two
noobs who aren't in mumble
[Guild][Heurodis]: you know who you are
Heurodis has invited you to join a group: y/n
[Guild][Solace]: Sorry, I was distracted
[Guild][Orcarella]: Me too
[Guild][Ialdir]: Mmmmhmmmmmm
[Guild][Jargogle]: Mmmmhmmmmmm
[Guild][Heurodis]: less distraction more
raiding
```

Drew pulled himself together, alt-tabbed and fired up Mumble, and his headphones crackled with Bjorn.

"—be tanking. Jargogle and Dave will be providing melee DPS. Ialdir and Mordant will be providing ranged DPS. And I will be providing imba DPS. Our healing team are Solace, Ignatius, and Prospero, assuming Solace is not so distracted that he lets everybody die."

"Oh no, Bjorn, just you."

Kit's voice made Drew tingle a bit. He'd spent a good part of the afternoon listening to it, so it was sort of familiar, but he still wasn't used to hearing him on Mumble. And, for the first time, Drew realised he had a sense of Kit at least as strong as his sense of Solace.

A softly-spoken, softly laughing boy, with wary eyes and warm hands.

And shit, everyone was running into the instance.

Since they hadn't downed Vilicus on Monday, they waded through his tormented trash and assembled in the torture chamber. It took them a couple of tries to get into the rhythm of it, but they squeaked through on the third attempt. Drew wasn't sure if he was distracted or focused, but he was very aware of Solace standing at the back with his shiny wings. They'd raided and played together enough now that he was starting to get that syncronicity thing where you kind of knew when the other person was fine, and when they were struggling, and when they needed you to blow all your cooldowns right the hell now. He'd had a fairly good relationship with Hachiman back in Anni, but it hadn't felt like this.

Also, he'd never wanted to date the guy.

When they'd finished celebrating the demise of this week's incarnation of Lady Bloodrose's favourite torturer, it was time to divide the loot.

"Time to see what Uncle Bjorn has in his magic bag."

[Raid][Jargogle]: I am not certain I want to think about Uncle Bjorn's magic bag.

"You love my bag, Magda. And we haaaave . . ." Bjorn paused dramatically ". . . the Inexorable Axe. Again."

```
[Raid][Heurodis]: [The Inexorable Axe]
[Raid][Dave]: lol
```

Drew sighed. "Honestly, you wait months for a tanking axe, and then three come along at once."

"Can you dual wield it?" asked Ialdir.

"No, it's a unique."

Bjorn: "Can anybody use this thing?"

```
[Raid][Morag]: Champions can't use axes
[Raid][Ignatius]: Shame Caius isn't here. He
could take it for his samnite spec.
[Raid][Dave]: do you want me to start a
tanking spec
```

"Just take the fucking axe, David," Bjorn snapped.

```
[Raid][Dave]: naw just shard it
[Raid][Dave]: dps 4 life 4 eva
[Raid][Orcarella]: i cant believe you're
sharding the axe i quit my guild over
[Raid][Solace]: *hugs*
[Raid][Solace]: It's not just enchanting
mats, it's a valuable lesson about life
[Raid][Orcarella]: dude what lesson?
[Raid][Morag]: life's a bitch and then you die
[Raid][Ialdir]: an axe in the hand is worth
two in the loot table
[Raid][Solace]: Axe not what your guild can
do for you, but what you can do for your
guild
[Raid][Ialdir]: *hi five*
[Raid][Solace]: I'm here all raid, try the
veal.
```

"You know what's weird?" Dave's voice came quite slowly over Mumble. "It's like that was really important to you a couple of weeks ago and now it, like, isn't important at all. So I think the moral is, like, sometimes things are important but, like, later they aren't."

There was a long silence.

"The moral of the story is not to interrupt Bjorn when he is trying to divide up the loot. Next we have a nice little healer off-hand: the Tome of Bloody Confessions."

"Oh," exclaimed Kit theatrically, "those *bloody* confessions."

```
[Raid][Heurodis]: [Tome of Bloody
Confessions]
[Raid][Ignatius]: Upgrade for me
[Raid][Ignatius]: Too much wisdom, not good
for an ele
[Raid][Solace]: It's sort of an upgrade for
me but I'm using [The Staff of Worlds' End]
from Mech and I don't have a main hand.
[Raid][Ignatius]: You should roll if it's an
upgrade
[Raid][Solace]: Can you give me two minutes?
I need to crunch the numbers
```

"Okay," said Bjorn. "The healers are taking a math break. Everyone take five."

Drew went to wash out his soup cup and grab himself a Dr Pepper from his fridge. When he pulled his headphones back on, Solace was mid-theorycraft.

"—think it's going to work out. The best main hand I've got is the Hoary Mace from Wall of Ice."

```
[Raid][Dave]: lol
[Raid][Dave]: horey mace!
[Raid][Jargogle]: Didn't you get that out of
your system two patches ago?
```

"Mana's not an issue for me, so what really matters is wisdom and conviction. My staff's got 112 wis, 408 power. The book's 73 wis, 281 power, the mace is only 44 wis and 130 power, so I'd gain, um, a little bit of wisdom and a little bit of power, and swap some crit for some haste, but not enough to be worth it, when it's a flat upgrade for you, Helen."

"Are you sure?"

"Absolutely. Besides, I've never thought of Solace as a big reader."

A Bjorn-ish sigh buzzed over Mumble. "You know, in some guilds, dividing the loot takes less time than killing the bosses."

"I don't believe that for a second." Somehow Drew could hear the smile in Kit's voice.

"But you guys don't even have proper loot drama," growled Bjorn. "You have loot romantic comedy."

```
To [Solace]: you're hot when you're
theorycrafting
[Solace] whispers: *blush*
[Solace] whispers: You like big brains and
you cannot lie?
To [Solace]: lol
To [Solace]: brainzzzzz
To [Solace]: hehe
```

They trooped back out of Vilicus's tower and into the heart of the maze. They took down several packs of mourning ghosts and finally assembled in the Chamber of Tears. It was a sort of clearing, with walls of stone and thorns, and three overgrown statues forming a triangle around the centre of the room. Drew knew from experience they were a bugger for line of sight.

"Okay," said Morag. She still sounded a bit subdued. Whatever had gone on with the poet had clearly taken its toll. "Welcome to the most sexist fight in the game. The Council of Tears are three evil women who used their vaginas to betray the men who cared about them, and now they're minions of the naked sex elf we've come here to kill."

"Hey." That was Ialdir. "Lauriel wasn't evil. She tried to stop Maladreth destroying elvish society."

"Fine. Two evil women and one victim. That's so much better. Anyway, the central mechanic of the fight is called—" she sighed heavily "—Hysteria. At certain points, one of the three women will get a buff called Hysteria, which will increase her damage output by about four hundred percent and last until she takes a certain amount of damage. Which means, when she gets Hysterical, you have to smack her until she calms down. Once one of them is dead, the other two become Hysterical permanently, so we need to get them all down as close together as possible. That means, when I tell you to stop DPSing, you stop DPSing. You seriously stop DPSing."

"That means you, Dave," added Bjorn.

[Raid][Dave]: hey!

"Each of the three Hysterical women have their own Hysterical woman powers. Hecuba the medusa will turn you to stone permanently if she catches you, so she has to be kited by a ranged DPS. Jacob, she's all yours."

[Raid][Ialdir]: kk

"Rest of the ranged, unless I tell you otherwise, prio her because her snakes will spit venom in melee range. She's also got Beauty's Curse, which will make a random raid member who doesn't have high threat walk towards her. If they reach her, they'll be turned to stone, so they need to be dispelled ASAP."

[Raid][Solace]: We've got a rota sorted

"Lauriel, the elf who's worth it, will stand around crying. She and Cressida will both put stacking debuffs on the tank, so the tanks have to swap before they hit ten stacks. Lauriel's debuff is called Burden of Tears, which increases the damage you take. If it gets too high, she'll do Shattered Heart, which will almost certainly one-shot you, unless you're the best-geared tank on the server. She's also got Lamentation, which means she'll stop and cry really loudly for a bit, which will send waves of emo through the room, and you have to line of sight them behind the statues. That just leaves Cressida, who's a dirty, dirty ho. Her debuff is—" she sighed again "—Faithless Touch. This will reduce your threat generation by up to fifty percent and when it reaches maximum, she casts Seduction, which mind controls you for the rest of the fight. She also does Harlot's Strike, which is a high physical damage cleave so DPS stay away from her tits and close to her arse."

A readycheck popped up on Drew's screen.

"Oh wait. Let's not forget, if they get too close together, they get a buff called Sisterhood, which heals them. And if all three of them get within ten feet of each other, they cast Betrayer's Cry, which does massive raid-wide damage, so don't let that happen. Drew, do you want the crying elf or the slutty human?"

Drew was silent a moment. He had no idea how to answer that without it sounding really, really bad. "I'll go with Lauriel."

The readycheck came back and Drew confirmed he was, yet again, ready. He, Morag, and Ialdir jogged between the statues into the centre of the room, which triggered the arrival of the Council of Tears.

```
[Hecuba] says: We are the betrayers
[Lauriel] says: And the betrayed
[Cressida] says: And you will know our
suffering.
```

As Morag charged at Cressida, her shield glowing with righteous golden light, Ella ran up to Lauriel and whacked her in the face with the Inexorable Axe. As Drew began drawing her back behind the statue of her evil husband, so her AoE wouldn't hit too much of the raid, he saw Ialdir somersaulting away from Hecuba, peppering her with arrows.

This was Drew's least favourite fight in the instance. It had a lot of fiddly little things to keep track of, and it was really easy for one mistake to kick the raid into a death spiral, but it was actually pretty dull to tank. He just had to make sure he wasn't letting his debuff stack too high and to stay alert for the switch. Basically, he felt there wasn't a lot he could do to help the fight go smoothly, but if he lost concentration, he'd screw it up abominably.

They wiped three times in quite small, annoying ways, once because Cressida went down too quickly and the other two Hysteria-ed out and killed everyone, once because of a really badly timed Lamentation, and once because they let the bosses get too close on a switch, nuking the raid. And then they wiped again because Bjorn over-aggro-ed Hecuba, got himself stone-gazed, and everyone was too busy laughing and taking screenies to pay attention so everything fell apart.

"Okay." Morag sounded a bit more cheerful. "We're losing focus here. Let's take five."

Bjorn was uncharacteristically silent.

Guild Message of the day is now: Do not ask Bjorn about Council of Tears.
[Raid][Solace]: I know we all hate this fight, but I really like this part of the maze.

Drew mouse-looked round, being careful not to accidentally trigger the fight. It was a bit like the high elf areas, except it was crumbled and corrupted, with the occasional bloody rose forcing its way through the cracks.

[Raid][Orcarella]: dude your just really into wrecked shit
[Raid][Solace]: Hehe
[Raid][Solace]: I guess I am
[Raid][Dave]: emoooooooooooo
[Raid][Solace]: I'm not being emo. Ruins are not just about loss, they're about time
[Raid][Solace]: You've got things that used to be something
[Raid][Solace]: And now they're something else
[Raid][Solace]: I find it kind of hopeful
[Raid][Dave]: http://www.youtube.com/watch?v=xilOgjeEwPg
[Raid][Orcarella]: It's not emo to like stuff.
[Raid][Dave]: lol
[Raid][Ialdir]: I totally get it, Kit.

[Raid][Ialdir]: You get a real sense of
history
[Raid][Mordant]: made up history
[Raid][Ialdir]: In some ways, that's even
cooler.
[Raid][Morag]: Yeah, man, anything can be
real history.
[Raid][Ialdir]: And it's not just about
the lore. I've been playing these games
for nearly twenty years so it's kind of my
history too.
[Raid][Jargogle]: Some of us actually have
history, children.
[Raid][Ialdir]: It was right after Desert
Storm and I was stuck in this crappy army
base in the middle of nowhere, and all I had
was a battered old IBM, and a copy of Legends
I, Pirates Gold, and fucking Myst.
[Raid][Ialdir]: And we were still under Don't
Ask Don't Tell
[Raid][Ialdir]: So basically it was the most
miserable time I've had in my entire life
[Raid][Dave]: soz man
[Raid][Solace]: *hugs*
[Raid][Ialdir]: Anthariel was one of the
major quest givers in L1 and she used to hang
out in this rose garden with her own theme
tune.
[Raid][Ialdir]: I hadn't seen roses in a year
[Raid][Ialdir]: And Raziel's sort of falling
in love with her
[Raid][Ialdir]: I'd never seen something like
that in a game before
[Raid][Ialdir]: And it reminded me that there
was more to life than being shot at in a
desert.

```
[Raid][Ialdir]: This garden we're in now is
that garden.
[Raid][Ialdir]: So that's important to me.
```

"That's a lovely story, Jacob," said Bjorn. "But perhaps we can do the fight now."

```
[Raid][Jargogle]: I am Bjorn's complete lack
of sensitivity.
[Raid][Ialdir]: I'm good, let's raid.
```

Things finally came together and the Council of Tears went down.

"Okay—" Bjorn crackled over Mumble "—and first up is the Bewailing Breeches."

```
[Raid][Heurodis]: [Bewailing Breeches]
```

Drew let the looting go on around him. He manoeuvred Ella to go stand next to Solace. Their shoulder pads clipped through each other, which was probably the closest you could get to holding hands in an MMO. Solace bounced up and down on the spot. That made Drew smile.

```
[Solace] whispers: Hey you
To [Solace]: hey you back
[Solace] whispers: <3
To [Solace]: :)
```

Next up was Lady Bloodrose. She was a pretty familiar sight to Drew these days—one of Tempest's many not-quite-naked-enough-to-get-the-game-an-R-rating women, wrapped in a few strategically placed climbing roses as she hovered over a dark pit in the middle of the final chamber.

High Theurist Venric had somehow managed to get ahead of them and was standing there, waiting politely for the party to give him permission to have an angsty conversation with his ex-girlfriend.

Heurodis sprinted over and got him started while the rest of the party renewed their buffs and sat down to eat their fish.

```
[Raid][Heurodis]: starting HTV off now
because this speech is really fricking long
[Raid][Morag]: Do you want to do the tacs for
this one, Bjorn?
[Raid][Heurodis]: a rare display of
intelligence undoubtedly fleeting
[Raid][Ialdir]: you know Dave wasn't born
when that game came out
[Raid][Jargoggle]: Stop giving Bjorn
responsibility. It goes to his head.
[High Theurgist Venric] says: Anthariel! It
is not too late. I have forgiven you for your
betrayal, as I have forgiven Raziel for his.
Turn back to the Light, and you yet may be
redeemed.
[Raid][Morag]: Oh man, High Theurgist Venric
got friend-zoned.
[Lady Bloodrose] says: I have been lost in
the dark so long. Come, my love, that I may
look upon your face again.
[Raid][Mordant]: ITS A TRAP!!!
[Raid][Dave]: wait what game
```

"Anyway," interrupted Bjorn, "while High Theurgist Venric, who presumably holds a position of authority in Whitepeak, walks slowly to his doom like a total noob-basket, we should run down the tacs for this fight."

```
[High Theurgist Venric] says: Anthariel . . .
[Raid][Dave]: hey what game
```

"So like all good boss fights, Lady Bloodrose is in three phases. In the first phase, she will hover over the pit and send her briars to tear the raid to pieces. The briars come in four kinds, Thorned, Barbed,

Entrancing, and Entangling. Thorned Briars are large and hit heavily in melee, so they need to be tanked or killed by ranged. Barbed are smaller and faster, but stack Heartsblood on you. Various things in this fight will hit you with Heartsblood, and if it reaches a hundred stacks, you become some kind of slave zombie thing under the control of Lady Bloodrose. If you let this happen, you are a noob and a scrub, and you will need to feel very bad about yourself."

Bjorn sounded like he was really enjoying himself. He reminded Drew a lot of Anni in some ways, but in other ways he really, really didn't. It was like he used all the same words, but they didn't mean the same things.

"The Barbed Briars should be prio-ed by ranged, always. Entrancing Briars will have little white flowers on them, and they will randomly mind-control people. You will stay MCed until the briar is killed. Melee can attack Entrancing Briars safely. Please do so. Finally, Entangling Briars will wander around and grab people. When somebody gets grabbed, DPS them out of it. Also spawning in phase one are the Veiled Attendants. These are the spooky cultist people who come out of the doors in the northeast, northwest, southeast, and southwest of the chamber. They will make a beeline for the nearest pillar, where they will activate its special power."

```
[Raid][Jargogle]: Tell us about the special
powers, Uncle Bjorn
[Raid][Dave]: seriously what game came out
before I was born
```

"Any game worth playing, David." Bjorn took a deep breath. "So these powers—thank you, Magda—include massively increasing the spawn rate of briars, massively reducing the healing output of the party, massively increasingly the damage dealt by everything, and sticking Heartsblood on the whole raid every few seconds until we all die. If an attendant starts channelling, it must be interrupted and then the tanks should pick them up and pull them away from the pillars. During this phase, ranged DPS will be expected to switch between Lady Bloodrose, the briars, and whatever else needs killing. The phase will end when her health drops to seventy percent. There is a lot that can go wrong in this phase, but I get very depressed when we don't make it out of it."

```
[High Theurgist Venric] says: Aaaaagh!
[Lady Bloodrose] says: So trusting, Venric. A
pity to come all this way and then to fall so
easily.
[Raid][Ialdir]: Baldur's Gate 1
[High Theurgist Venric] says: You . . . are . . .
no . . . longer . . . Anthariel.
[Lady Bloodrose] says: Not for many years,
but do not worry, my love, I will not let you
die . . . yet.
[Raid][Ialdir]: There's an enhanced edition
out. You should definitely play it.
[High Theurgist Venric] says: Strike now my
friends, while I still have strength to aid
you!
[Raid][Ialdir]: In a minute, dude, we're
still doing the tacs.
[Raid][Morag]: That's what you get for
pulling without the tank.
```

"In phase two," Bjorn went on, "Lady Bloodrose will come down from the ceiling and start to activate the pillars herself. There is nothing we can do about that except DPS her to make her switch. We want her travelling for as much of the fight as possible. There will still be briars, but if we have not cocked everything up, the Veiled Attendants should all be dead. Instead she will open Nether Portals—"

There was a snigger across Mumble.

"David, I am doing the tacs. You can laugh at the word *nether* in your own time. The Nether Portals will spit out adds, and expand until they fill the entire room and kill everybody. Our portal team, consisting of Magda, Morag, Prospero, and Dave—"

"Woo. Nether Duty."

"—will dive through the portal and destroy the Realm Heart. The rest of us will be dealing with the adds and DPSing our hearts out.

At thirty percent she will go into the final phase, where she explodes into this enormous plant-monster thing and sits in the middle of the room. Then we burn her down really, really fast before we get completely overwhelmed by the buffs from the pillars, which will all be active at this point. Remember, if you are having trouble controlling your Heartsblood stacks, stand near the high theurgist when he puts golden light on the ground, and it will reduce your debuff by 20. Of course, this will also lose you precious DPS time, so it is better to just do things right to begin with."

A readycheck popped up, and when the signal was given, Ella ran towards the middle of the room, triggering the fight.

```
[Lady Bloodrose] says: Come, pierce yourself
upon me.
```

"Oh man," sighed Dave, "that just sounds so wrong."

"You know what else is wrong," said Bjorn, fifty seconds later, "how quickly we screwed that up."

It had not been a good attempt. There'd been so much going on, and the chamber was sufficiently large and full of particle effects, that the raid just hadn't coordinated properly. Nothing had gone down fast enough and they'd been overwhelmed by briars.

```
[Solace] whispers: You okay?
To [Solace]: yeah that was faster than i
expected
[Solace] whispers: :(
[Solace] whispers: Honestly, we've only
beaten this fight once and that was with a
different comp
To [Solace]: oh
[Solace] whispers: But we didn't have the
best geared tank on the server :)
```

The second run was only marginally better. For Drew, this was where you really saw the difference between a casual guild and a hard-core one. Anni had flailed around like this the first time they'd done the fight, but they'd got over it quickly. It was complicated enough that you never really had it on farm, but they could pretty much guarantee that if they wiped, it was because something specific had gone wrong rather than because nothing had gone right.

```
To [Solace]: ffs
[Solace] whispers: This is really bugging
you, isn't it?
To [Solace]: kinda
To [Solace]: i don't mind wiping but i like
to feel we're making progress
[Solace] whispers: We are. It just takes a
little to see it.
To [Solace]: there you go being zen again
[Solace] whispers: You like that, though
To [Solace]: i guess i do <3
[Solace] whispers: Seriously, we'll get it.
We kind of go through a flailing stage, then a
learning stage, and then it comes together.
To [Solace]: kk
To [Solace]: sorry i didn't mean to be an
elitist dick
[Solace] whispers: No, it's cool. I suppose
you're used to things being different.
```

Kit was right, and pissing on other people's learning curves wasn't going to help anybody. So Drew got himself a second can of Dr Pepper and settled down for a long evening of wiping.

"Okay guys," came Morag's voice. "This isn't really coming together for us. I know it's the end of the night and the final boss, but we need to stay focused and work together, or we're just going to be banging our heads against a brick wall."

Of course, the other difference between SCDD and Anni was they had none of the recriminations and bullshit. After two wipes like this, Anni would have dissolved into finger-pointing and epeening.

"I don't think we're doing anything particularly wrong, I just think we need to be a little bit sharper and a little bit more responsive.

Ranged, I think you're spending too much time on Bloodrose and not enough helping the melee. Melee, I know you've got a lot of running around to do, but you need to keep on your toes and get where you need to be when you need to be there. This is a control fight, not a DPS race, so it's better to do it right than to do it quickly. Let's fish up, and try again."

This time round they got to phase two, but the portal team was slow off the mark, so the area filled up with purple death fire and swarming minions. In Anni, they'd sent a seriously tooled-up assassin into the portals solo, and relied on stuns, invisibility, and smoke clouds to keep the portal guardians at bay while he destroyed the Realm Heart. Drew thought about suggesting it, but while he thought Jargogle knew her stuff, she probably wasn't quite geared enough. It was sort of the weird paradox of hard-core guilds, that you were good enough at the game it allowed you to do things the easy way. Which, in turn, sort of took the fun out of it after a little while. Although, for Anni, first had been more important than fun.

```
[Solace] whispers: You're not hating this too
much, are you?
To [Solace]: i'm honestly good now
[Solace] whispers: Think of it as more time
spent with me :)
To [Solace]: dude i really like raiding but
if i had to pick a way to spend time with you
it wouldn't include bjorn yelling in my ears
[Solace] whispers: <3
[Solace] whispers: Maybe we can talk about
that later :D
```

Attempt four, they lost too many people to Heartsblood, so they didn't have the DPS to get through the final phase. The mood in the raid was better than Drew would have expected it to be. Every try had been better than the last, so there was a real "we'll do it this time" vibe, even though it was getting on for half ten, or half eleven for Ialdir, Magda, and Bjorn.

As they were rebuffing, Bjorn took control of Mumble.

"All right, you noobs, it is time for Uncle Bjorn's Awesome Pep Talk. This will be our last attempt. If we fail because we suck, I will be putting a poll on the forum to see if people want to come back and try this on Friday instead of going to Greyhallow Hall to do the opera event. But by far the best scenario here is that we kick butt now and go to the opera on Friday."

[Raid][Mordant]: is that it?

"Do not question the glory of the pep talk."

Nobody else questioned the glory of the pep talk, so Ella pulled out her axes and charged Lady Bloodrose for the fifth time. Phase one went pretty smoothly. Ella basically spent her time jogging round the central pit, picking up Veiled Attendants before they could activate the ritual pillars. She was occasionally grabbed by an Entangling Briar, but the DPS got her out of them pretty sharpish.

Morag: "Careful, attendant wave in five, don't push her over yet."

[Lady Bloodrose] says: Enough of this. Fall before the legions of the Netherworld.

"Well, crap," sighed Morag. "Next time, less DoTs."

"I'm on it. Slow DPS on the adds please." Drew picked up the first attendant and sprinted back across the chamber towards the Pillar of Death, where the second one was channelling a beam of purple energy that would give every enemy in the room a massive damage boost.

"Portal team in. Rest of you, on the attendants."

"Shit shit shit." That sounded like Bjorn.

They managed to burn the two attendants down fairly quickly, but while Drew was maintaining aggro, Netherworld Minions were swarming out of the still-open portal.

"Adds in the ranged."

Ella scuttled backwards round the pit, throwing a taunt at the armour-plated insect demon thing that was presently chewing on Small Mangy Owl.

"Pet tanking for the win," said Ialdir, as Drew began whaling on the monster with his axes.

[Lady Bloodrose] says: Blood of my blood.

That was bad.

"Pillar of blood up," called Bjorn. "All deeps on the boss. Watch your stacks, and get in the light if you need it."

Drew was doing okay for Heartsblood, and he didn't want to a drag a pile of enemies over to where the raid was stacking to rid itself of the fallen elf's malicious influence.

For most of phase two they were playing catch-up, and Drew was beginning to feel the pressure. Because of the attendants, they'd been slow on the portals, and because they were slow on the portals, there were lots of adds to control, and Bloodrose was looking healthier than she should have at this stage in the fight. The RNG Gods had also decided to screw them, and she kept drifting towards the Pillar of Blood, which was the least dealable-with of the debuffs.

When she hit about thirty-two percent, Mordant succumbed to Heartsblood on his way to the theurgist, turned zombie-mind-slave, and started carving up the raid.

[Lady Bloodrose] says: Mine, mine forever.
[Raid][Mordant]: shit soz

"Put him down," cried Bjorn. "Put him down like a dog."

It was slightly demoralising to have to take out one of your own party members, but Mordant disappeared in a hail of arrows and shadow.

That put them further behind on portals, which meant they had to halt DPS on Bloodrose until they could get the last one closed. Drew quickly scanned his raid frames, and it wasn't good. Only one casualty but everyone was hovering at about fifty percent health, and the healers were looking uncomfortably low on mana.

[Lady Bloodrose] says: Must I do everything myself?

They pushed into phase three, and Lady Bloodrose descended into the pit, thorns and roses spiralling out of her body and filling the chamber. From the tank's perspective, this was kind of the most straightforward part of the fight. He rushed forward to get her attention, and started smacking her with his axes. Morag was going to be running around dealing with the briars, which would be coming thick and fast now that the Pillar of Thorns was permanently active.

"Full burn, full burn, but don't forget the barbs."

It was basically carnage. As Bloodrose's health ticked lower, the debuffs from the pillars stacked higher, and the screen exploded with briars and special effects.

Drew's Heartsblood was getting into the high eighties, so he called to Morag for a tank swap, and she got to him just in time for Ella to reach the theurgist before she went psycho on the raid. Drew's fingers were a little slippery on the mouse as he grabbed the boss back. It was a tricky manoeuvre to coordinate at the best of times, and even Anni occasionally screwed it up.

The raid was looking increasingly unhealthy, particularly with the healing debuff from the Pillar of Life, and Bloodrose had only just dipped below ten percent.

Bjorn: "Entangled."

"On it . . . shit, barbs."

[Lady Bloodrose] says: Mine, mine forever.

Bjorn sighed. "Get me untangled, and then kill Dave."

"It wasn't my fault, I was trying to rescue you."

"Less QQ more pewpew."

While they were butchering Dave, Prospero died from raid damage.

"Shit."

[Lady Bloodrose] says: Violets are blue, roses are red, and as for you, you're utterly dead.
[Raid][Prospero]: I fucking hate that taunt
[Raid][Ignatius]: Covering raid
[Raid][Solace]: kk

There was just too much damage and too many adds. Morag went down, then Ialdir, then Ignatius.

Lady Bloodrose was on two percent.

"We can still do this," said Morag. "Keep Ella up as long as you can."

Solace had hardly any mana left, Heurodis and Jargogle were clinging to life by a thread. Drew blew all his cooldowns and hoped. A rampaging minion flattened Heurodis.

```
[Lady Bloodrose] says: Violets are blue,
roses are red, and as for you, you're utterly
dead.
```

"Oh shut up, you stupid elf. My DoTs are still ticking."

They were so doomed. They were all out of resources, but Drew was kind of proud to be fighting on to the bitter end. Anni would have called it the moment Mordant had been HBed because it was an inefficient use of raid time.

But it was scary and fun and exciting in a futile Helm's Deep sort of way.

They probably weren't going to the opera on Friday, but they were damn well going to make this count.

Drew wondered what Kit was thinking, and if he was happy or stressed or what. He found himself wishing he was there, so he could look at him and see.

Then Ella died.

"Sorry, oom," said Kit quietly over Mumble.

Now Ella was no longer holding her attention, Lady Bloodrose whirled round in a rush of blood and petals to face the kobold who'd been busy stabbing her in the back of the knee.

The kobold who immediately vanished.

So that just left a small, winged elf, who she took down with a single strike.

```
[Lady Bloodrose] says: Violets are blue,
roses are red, and as for you, you're utterly
dead.
```

Jargogle reappeared in a cloud of smoke, leaped across the pit, and chained a sequence of flashing finishers into Lady Bloodrose's spine.

```
[Lady Bloodrose] says: Raziel . . . my lord . . .
I have failed you.
```

"You magnificent kobold," roared Bjorn. "I would kiss you if you weren't such a peculiar small furry animal."

And then Mumble went wild with joy.

```
To [Solace]: nice healing <3
[Solace] whispers: nice tanking <3
```

"By the way, Kit," said Madga, once everybody had calmed down a little. "I'm sorry I aggro-dumped on you. I was just so close to everything being off cooldown, and I thought it was our only chance to salvage the encounter."

"Oh it's fine," he answered. "You made the right call."

High Theurgist Venric was still monologuing and bleeding out in the background, but basically nobody cared. They were too busy rummaging in Lady Bloodrose's chest ("Hurr," said Dave, "Lady Bloodrose's chest.") to see what goodies they could plunder. There was a selection of the usual items, all of which went to good homes.

"And finally," announced Bjorn, "we have . . . that tiny, little baby plant-monster thing, which is a vanity pet and therefore of no interest to me."

```
[Raid][Heurodis]: [Briar Seedling]
```

"But I understand they are popular with some people for some reason."

The raid immediately erupted into a menagerie as everybody pulled out their favourite noncombat companion. Drew wasn't a big collector either, but it was impossible to play the game without getting a pet or two, just for buying expansions, doing some questlines, or getting them as random drops. He summoned a squirrel that he had no memory of acquiring. Solace had an incredibly cute baby hippo. Drew didn't even think there were hippos in the game.

"I see what you are doing," Bjorn went on, "and I am ignoring it. As our loot master, I have two suggestions for how to dispose of this nauseatingly cute little artefact. Either we do a raid roll like normal, or alternatively we give it to Magda as a reward for kicking the crap out of its original owner. I will now initiate a readycheck vote. If you wish to give this seedling to our kobold, please click Ready, if not, click Not."

Drew voted to give it to Jargogle. It seemed fairest to him.

"All right, we have a nine-to-one majority. Jargogle gets the seedling, Friday we go to the opera. Good job, everyone."

After a bit of dancing and gratsing, and admiring Jargogle's new pet, they gradually logged out or teleported away.

```
To [Solace]: Alarion?
[Solace] whispers: Yes :)
```

Drew left the raid, grouped up with Solace, and they made their way together to their usual rock, where he got his usual hit of being slightly nervous.

```
[Group][Orcarella]: good run
[Group][Solace]: Yeah, that was kind of crazy
at the end there.
[Group][Orcarella]: you must be totally sick
of me
[Group][Orcarella]: you were stuck with me
this afternoon and then all evening
[Group][Orcarella]: and half the time i was
whinging about wiping
[Group][Solace]: I'm really not
[Group][Solace]: I kind of miss you actually
[Group][Solace]: Sorry, is that weird?
[Group][Orcarella]: no i miss you too
[Group][Solace]: <3
```

```
[Group][Orcarella]: i totally lost track of
time this afternoon
[Group][Orcarella]: you didn't think I was
too creepy or intense or something
[Group][Orcarella]: i was worried you'd think
i was holding you hostage in starbucks
[Group][Solace]: Me too
[Group][Orcarella]: lol we suck
[Group][Solace]: Maybe we could have a pact or
something. To say if we're getting bored or
want some space.
[Group][Orcarella]: that sounds way too
sensible
[Group][Orcarella]: okay
[Group][Solace]: we can shake on it next time
we meet up
```

Drew took a deep breath.

```
[Group][Orcarella]: so like when do you want
to do that?
[Group][Solace]: Whenever you like
[Group][Solace]: But soon, please :)
[Group][Orcarella]: friday? we could have
dinner.
```

That had just sort of . . . happened. And it was a proper proper date. Not just coffee. Which meant he needed to take Kit somewhere. Somewhere classy.

```
[Group][Orcarella]: we could go to Pizza
Express?
[Group][Solace]: I'd love to, but I've
already signed up for the raid.
[Group][Orcarella]: but its just a fun run
[Group][Solace]: Fun's important too. Can we
go on Saturday?
```

[Group][Orcarella]: sure. I'll meet you there
at 7?
[Group][Solace]: :) :) :)
[Group][Solace]: Are you going to come to the
opera?
[Group][Orcarella]: i'm kind of meant to be
meeting my mates in the pub
[Group][Solace]: but you just asked me to
dinner
[Group][Orcarella]: yeah, but that was a date
[Group][Orcarella]: this is a game

   Kit didn't type anything for a while.

[Group][Solace]: okay, I'll see you on
Saturday
[Group][Orcarella]: <3
[Group][Solace]: :)

CHAPTER 9

Drew had barely sat down in the Slug and Lettuce on Friday evening before his friends were bombarding him with questions about his big date with the guy from the internet.

Sanee opened with, "So, are you, like, an official gay now?"

"Oi—" Steff poked him in the arm "—we talked about this."

Drew just rolled his eyes. "No, I've got to send in four passport-sized photographs first."

"Hey," protested Sanee, "I wasn't being rude. I didn't mean gay like lame, I meant gay like gay."

Tinuviel doubled facepalmed. "Sanee, that's ableist *and* homophobic."

"I'm just asking a question."

"No, a question would be something like 'Did you have a nice time?' or 'Did he like your whale T-shirt?' not 'How can I best put your sexual identity in a box that I find comfortable to think about?'"

Drew realised that if he didn't do something now, this would go on all night. "I had a lovely time," he announced. "He liked my T-shirt, we had coffee, and then went raiding. We downed Lady Bloodrose on the final attempt of the evening."

"Dude," said Andy, "you took a guy raiding on a date?"

"No, we were raiding anyway."

Sanee leaned over the table. "That's how they met. Massively multiplaying online."

"Seriously?" Andy blinked. "You're dating someone you met in a video game."

Now Drew double facepalmed. "Look, yes, I'm dating a guy. Yes, he's a guy I met online. No, he's not a twelve-year-old French boy.

Yes, I'm pretty sure he's not a serial killer. No, he's not a minger. Yes, I really like him. No, he doesn't ask me to dress as an elf."

"What about a hobbit?" asked Sanee.

"He doesn't ask me to dress as anything. And, before you ask, I don't ask him to dress as anything either. I like him just the way he is."

"That's very sweet, Drew." Tinuviel smiled her vague smile. "But there's nothing wrong with a little creative cosplay. I once went to Nine Worlds as Geralt of Rivia."

There was a long silence as everyone processed the image.

Sanee got there first. "Do you still have the outfit?"

"No, I took it apart. This year I'm going as Viserys Targaryen."

There was another long silence as everyone processed *that* image.

"Um, why?" asked Andy eventually.

Tinuviel thought about it. "Well, I had the wig. It was that or Sephiroth, but he seemed a bit dated."

"Did it not occur to you," suggested Drew, "that you could have gone as, say, Daenerys."

"I don't really identify with Daenerys."

"So, what, you identify with her psycho, abusive, petty tyrant brother?"

"I don't identify with him, but I think I understand him better. Daenerys is very admirable, but I find it difficult to relate to admirable people, and I feel Viserys is treated unfairly by the world he lives in because he fails to embody conventional masculine virtues. Also the actor who played him is terribly pretty."

"Don't you ever like to dress as girls?" asked Steff.

"Oh yes. Two years ago I was Dolores Umbridge."

Drew sipped his pint. The nice thing about having a deeply weird, highly opinionated friend was that you never had to be the centre of attention if you didn't want to be. The conversation drifted back towards the latest season of *Game of Thrones*, which Sanee was illegally torrenting for the group and had forbidden anyone to watch until he had the whole thing so they could sit down over a weekend and do a proper Throne-athon. They spent the rest of the evening bickering about spoiler etiquette and deviations from book canon.

Once the pub kicked them out, they headed to Sanee and Steff's for their traditional Friday-night board game-age. They settled into a postmidnight session of Arkham Horror that ended with them heroically beating up Yig with tommy guns, and then feeling faintly short-changed.

"Poor old Yig," said Sanee, as he carefully stacked twenty-five different sets of cards into their proper places in the box. "He's more of a mediocre old one, isn't he?"

Drew was kind of sleepy and a little bit sad. He always enjoyed Arkham while he was playing it, but afterwards it always felt like an anticlimax, whether you won or lost. He blinked the board game haze out of his eyes and looked round at his friends. Andy had actually fallen asleep while trying to close a gate to the Great Halls of Celeano and was now slumped facedown on the coffee table. Steff was curled up in Sanee's lap, handing him loose counters, and Tinuviel was reading the Fantasy Flight brochure that came with the game.

Drew missed Kit.

He tried to imagine him here. He sort of managed and sort of didn't.

He couldn't picture them sitting in each other's laps—not least because Kit was pretty tall, and Drew had played a lot of rugby when he was still at school, so it wasn't really clear whether the taller or the heavier one should go on top or underneath—but maybe they'd hold hands under the table and smile at each other when nobody was looking.

By the time he got back to his room, it was the kind of late that was technically early, and he woke up the next day with the sinking realisation that the sun wasn't going to get any higher. He pulled on his pyjama bottoms and logged onto *HoL*, did his auctions and ran a few dailies with Ialdir and Prospero. And then he had to prepare for his date.

Which was complicated by the fact he was coming to the end of a laundry cycle and he'd already worn his best T-shirt.

He'd hoped that, by this point, he'd have this down, but he ended up dithering all over again about what to wear. A shirt seemed appropriate for dinner, but not appropriate for, well, him. In the end, he decided to compromise by wearing a shirt over his T-shirt, but leaving it unbuttoned. Of course, this left him with a problem because anything with a slogan on it would be hard to read and probably looked kind of cluttered. He was hesitating over his Caffeine Molecule when he remembered he had an Epic Purple Shirt kicking about at the back of a chest of drawers. He hadn't worn it much because he hadn't been sure he could get away with a purple T-shirt for reasons that now seemed pretty stupid.

He took a quick glance in the mirror to make sure he didn't look like a complete knob end, decided he didn't, and headed off to meet Kit.

He'd had the foresight to book a table in advance, which turned out to be a good thing because it was a Saturday night and the place was packed. Kit was waiting just outside, still in blue, still looking like a model, still reading *Canticle for Leibowitz*.

He closed the book and smiled, and Drew grinned back and waved, and then felt like an idiot because waving at someone when they were eight feet away seemed a bit much.

"Hi," he said, wishing he could just do less-than-three, and not have to worry about whether he looked happy enough, or too happy, or if he'd be able to think of anything witty to say.

They trooped in, and Drew gave his name to the waiter. He knew it was just Pizza Express, but having to do the whole ritual of booking and being shown to your table made him feel like he was doing an impression of someone he'd seen on TV.

The waiter led them to a table for two tucked into a little niche. There was even a flower in a blue glass-vase thing.

They got sat down, and Kit vanished behind an enormous menu. Drew stared at an equally enormous but totally incomprehensible wine list.

"So," he asked, trying to sound suave, "shall I order the merlot?"

Kit's eyes appeared over the top of his menu. "Um, do you want to?"

"I don't know . . . I just thought it would be a thing . . . that we could . . . do."

"Well, you can if you want, but I don't actually drink that much wine."

Drew had this horrible image of trying to drink an entire bottle of merlot on his own, and he wasn't even particularly sure what a merlot was, other than the second-cheapest, most pronounceable wine they had. "Me neither. I just panicked. I might have a Coke."

Kit hid his face behind the menu again.

"Are you laughing at me?"

"Maybe a little bit."

Drew didn't really mind. It was sometimes nice to be laughed at. If it was the right person laughing. He tried to redeem himself. "I thought we could have the dough balls doppio to start."

Except that just made Kit giggle again.

"No, it's really good. We had it when I came here with Tinuviel's parents."

"The girl from your course? I thought you were just friends."

"We are. She's got those sort of parents. They're academics. They're really weird."

Kit reappeared, his eyes glinting. "Did they order the merlot as well?"

"No, they had the prosecco, but it's slightly out of my price range."

"Oh." He looked a bit flustered. "Were you going to pay for this?"

Drew wasn't sure he'd actually thought about it, but in his experience, dates were things you paid for. Unless you dated Tinuviel, apparently, because something something patriarchal assumptions something something commodity model of sex something something. "I guess so. I mean, I don't have to. I mean, um."

"Well, how does it usually work?"

"Normally the guy pays, but I'm starting to see the limitations of that model."

Kit thought about it for a moment. "Well, why don't we split it?"

"That doesn't seem very . . . special somehow."

"I don't see how the way you pay for it is what makes it special." He smiled across the table. "But if you like, I could pay for your food and you could pay for my food."

Drew was pretty sure that was a silly idea, but it seemed like the best compromise they had. "Okay," he said. "So shall we start with the dough balls?"

"Do these dough balls have cocaine in them or something?"

"Actually, I think they might. I really like them. Also it's a sharing thing."

Kit's eyebrows quirked mischievously. "Are we going to order a big plate of spaghetti and meatballs for a main?"

"We should. I spent all day sourcing a fat Italian stereotype with an accordion." This won him a laugh. "No, but seriously," he went on, "the pasta's usually a bit crap. They call it Pizza Express for a reason."

They both had pizzas in the end. Drew normally went for the American Hot, but he changed his mind at the last minute because chili and dating didn't really mix, and just had the American. Kit ordered something complicated with chestnut mushrooms, a cheese that didn't sound like cheese, and truffle oil.

Drew'd been managing the enormous menu for so long that he felt a bit naked once it was taken away. Now there was nothing between him and Kit except the table and the flower, and he was worried about staring. The truth was, he liked looking at him, and he was getting used to looking at him, and he was still getting used to liking looking. Kit had this one piece of hair that wouldn't quite stay with the rest, and curled down over his forehead. Drew kind of wanted to brush it back up, just to see it fall down again.

Shit, he was meant to be talking. "Uh, so, how was the masqueraid?"

Kit's eyes brightened. "I love Greyhallow. Have you ever been?"

Drew shook his head.

"Oh, it's amazing. As far as I know, it's got no connection to any plot or anything. It's just Count Greyhallow is a mad wizard who has invited the PCs to his house, and wants to test them to see if they'd make suitable heirs. You can only get in by doing this crazy long quest chain, which gives you five gold pieces and an invitation to Greyhallow Hall."

"Let me guess. Bjorn's the one with the invite."

"A couple of people do but—" Solace smiled "—Bjorn likes to make a big thing about letting everybody in. He's got this speech about how back in the day there used to be instance attunements and you couldn't just wander through the front door with your welfare epics."

Drew smiled back. "And you had to slash-walk to the instance uphill both ways at five frames per second in the snow."

"It's like you were there . . ." Kit glanced up hesitantly from his glass of water " . . . except I missed you."

"I missed you too. We were playing board games."

"What were you playing?

"Arkham Horror. Do you know it?"

"No, I don't have much opportunity for board gaming, except at the guild meets or when I visit Jacob in Germany. Last time we played Carcassonne with his kids."

Drew wasn't sure what to make of that. He'd known Kit wasn't particularly sociable, but he couldn't imagine having so few friends you couldn't make up the numbers for a two-to-six-player board game. "You should join us next time."

"I'd like that."

Well, that had been easier than he'd expected. It was sort of a consensus amongst his friends that they tended to scare people away, but then Kit hadn't met them, so maybe that explained his willingness to spend time with them.

Just then, the dough balls arrived and conversation ebbed for a bit while they tucked in.

"I think you were right," said Kit. "These probably do have cocaine in them."

And Drew smiled, feeling like he'd given good date.

"So how come you were in Germany?" he asked, a little later as the waiter was clearing away the starter. "Was it a gap year thing?"

"Oh, no, I go out there most summers."

He blinked. "Just to see Jacob?"

"He's one of my best friends. It's nice to meet up, and he's got a family, so he can't travel as much."

"Isn't Ialdir like fifty?"

"First off, he's forty-five. Secondly, so what?"

Drew nearly said, *Haven't you got any friends your own age?* but realised at the last minute that it was probably the worst thing he could possibly say. And Kit was already sounding a bit defensive. "Sorry," he tried. "It's just my parents are in their forties, so it feels a bit weird to me."

"Isn't that more about them being your parents than how old they are?"

"I guess." He wasn't sure he did guess, but he wanted to be supportive.

Kit folded his elbows on the table, and leaned forward a bit, looking at Drew intently. "You sort of learn in school that you're only supposed to hang out with people who are exactly the same age as you, but actually, if you're not into the things everyone else is into, you can't really live like that. So I just sort of got used to not. I like Jacob, we have stuff in common, and he's always been really kind to me. He was the first person I met who didn't make me feel weird."

"You're not weird."

"I know I'm not." He smiled a bit. "At least, I think I'm not. But I'm aware that I don't do the things that people think I'm supposed to do."

Drew wasn't sure he completely got it. He hadn't exactly been lying when he said he didn't think Kit was weird, but he did think it was a bit unusual to hang out in Germany with a guy whose kids were closer to your age than he was. On the other hand, it struck him as kind of brave to know people would think that, and to do it anyway. And he'd probably made Kit explain himself enough for one evening. "So, uh, what's with the opera?"

It wasn't exactly a seamless transition, but Kit seemed to go with it. "Greyhallow is full of these scripted fights that are pretty awesome, but also pretty gimmicky. It must have been hell to actually raid, but it's brilliant for tourism, and there's some crazy drops. I got this staff once with a whole octopus on the end. I like to get it out when I'm RLing and the raid isn't behaving."

"I could make a tentacle joke right now, but I'm just too sophisticated."

"Don't worry, Dave's got you covered."

Their waiter emerged, and set a pizza down in front of each of them, before producing an enormous peppermill and brandishing it threateningly until they both insisted they didn't want any.

"Anyway," Kit went on, "the opera is basically one of three random scenarios all based loosely on bits of actual theatre. At least I think they are. They're pretty weird."

"Which one did you get?"

"Koblencrantz and Gildenbold Are Dead. Have you ever done Trollheim?"

"Isn't that the really crappy raid that was all just trolls?"

"Hey, it had a dragon at the end."

"Oh, that's fine then."

Kit laughed. "The third or fourth boss was Gragthar the Slave Master. He had this big swarm of kobold minions who would run around and jump on people and sometimes explode. It's the one with the famous YouTube clip of that champion charging a huge mob of kobolds, shouting his name, and then blowing up the whole raid."

"Wait, is that 'many kobolds handle it'?"

"No, that's the other one. So this event is basically two of that guy's minions wandering through a compressed version of the entire Trollheim raid, constantly missing it. You have to DPS them while they walk, and every so often a boss from another bit of the instance will spawn, and the tanks will have to pick him up, and the raid will have to cope with all those mechanics, while the kobolds walk past."

Drew frowned over his pizza. "And the point of that is?"

"We never worked it out."

It took a while, but Drew eventually stopped worrying about Making Conversation and just let it happen. They talked a lot about *HoL*, and the friends they had in common and a bit about friends they didn't, sometimes about books, sometimes about university, all the time finding little points of similarity, difference, and connection. He learned other things too, like all the blues in Kit's eyes, and the way he sometimes hid his smile behind his hand when he was nervous.

At Drew's suggestion, they split a cheesecake for dessert, and laughing, Kit nudged the last decorative strawberry across the plate with his fork.

"I was going to use my nose," he said, "but I remembered I wasn't a loveable cartoon dog."

There wasn't really a good response to that, so Drew picked up the strawberry by the bit of leaf and held it out.

Kit eyed it apprehensively. "I'm sure this would be great in a movie but I'm probably going to mess it up."

"It's a strawberry. How badly wrong could it go?"

"I could get it stuck in my throat, the nice old lady over there could give me the Heimlich manoeuvre, and I could spit it into your face."

"Wouldn't it be worse if she didn't give you the Heimlich manoeuvre and you just died?"

"If I was dead, I'd be a lot less embarrassed."

"Look." Drew mocked scowled across the table. "If we're talking about being embarrassed, I've been sitting here, holding a strawberry for about five minutes now, while my boyfriend talks about spitting in my face."

Kit gave a little moan. "Oh God, I'm hopeless at this."

"And I have way overhyped a piece of garnish."

Blushing slightly, Kit leaned forward, and took a neat bite of the strawberry. They'd dithered about it for so long, that Drew thought it had become a joke. Except it totally wasn't. There was something weirdly intimate about it, just in offering, and being accepted.

Also it was, honestly, kind of sexy.

Having Kit that little bit closer. Being able to see tiny details like the flicker of his light-gold lashes, and a faint suggestion of shadow following the line of his jaw. How close his lips were to the tips of Drew's fingers.

Flustered, he ate the other half of the strawberry and put the leaf back on the plate.

They were quiet for a moment.

"Boyfriend?" said Kit, who was still a little bit pink.

In the midst of all the excitement, Drew had forgotten about that. "Uh. Is that . . . Was that . . . uh."

"No, it's nice."

And Kit put his hand over his mouth, and smiled.

After they'd awkwardly paid for each other's food, which would have been really faffy if Kit hadn't turned out to be good at mental arithmetic, they tumbled out onto King Street, where they stood about for a bit, shuffling.

Still slightly strawberry dazed, Drew went for it. "So, like, last time we were on a date, neither of us wanted to go home, but then we had to raid, so we kind of had to. There isn't a raid tonight. So . . ."

"So . . ." Kit slid his hands into his sleeves. "Do you want to come back to mine?"

"Yes." Wow, that sounded way too eager, but Drew realised he was, in fact, quite eager. And if they went back to Kit's, then he wouldn't have to invite Kit back to his, because his was a state. He'd left most of his T-shirts (and some of his pants) all over the floor, and Tinuviel tended to wander in without knocking or, in one extreme instance, wearing clothes. And Drew was pretty sure any or all of those things would seriously kill the mood.

They got on a bus, and off again twenty minutes later outside the University of Leicester Botanic Gardens.

"You live in a garden?" asked Drew.

"In a house in a garden with three hundred other students."

"Classy."

Drew hadn't actually been this far out of the city centre like . . . ever. It was a little bit like going home to his parents', because it was quiet and leafy, and it made him feel quite distant from his regular life on campus. But not in a bad way. The sun was just on the cusp of setting, so the light was mellow and the shadows were long and golden. And then Kit took his hand, and they walked together under the trees.

Here and there, they wandered past groups of students lounging on the lawn with plastic cups of beer or playing a late-evening game of Frisbee. If he hadn't been out with Kit or raiding, it was the sort of thing Drew might have been doing with his mates. But it didn't seem like the sort of thing Kit did, and Drew couldn't decide whether he felt bad for him.

"This is a really cool place to live," he said.

Kit nodded. "I really like being so close to the Botanic Gardens. There's this willow tree I like to read under. And sometimes I bring my laptop."

Drew gave his hand a squeeze. "Don't you ever want to hang out with people from your course or anything?"

"I sometimes have lunch with my lab partner, and I go to the occasional party, but I don't really feel I'm missing out."

And now Drew couldn't decide whether he felt bad for himself. "Oh man, I always feel like I'm missing out."

"When I first got here, I had this serious freak-out because I thought I was doing it wrong. I was so convinced it was going to be massively different to school, but it wasn't. I was still the quiet guy who didn't have many friends, and there were still the popular kids who seemed to be having this amazing time that I just couldn't be part of." They'd come to a sun-dappled corner of lawn that nobody seemed interested in. "Do you want to stop for a bit? It seems a shame to miss the sunset."

Drew surveyed the area critically. "Well, there isn't a rock and I've left my fishing rod in a fictional universe."

Kit's laugh seemed louder and brighter under the clear sky.

They got settled on the grass, side by side, Drew's arm and leg gently brushing Kit's.

"Anyway," Kit went on, "I wound up having this really intense Skype conversation with Tiff and Jacob at about three in the morning, and they kind of talked me down, and told me that nearly everyone spends university worried that other people are having more fun or getting more sex or finding the work easier than they are. So the guys playing Frisbee are looking at the guys in the library thinking, 'Crap I wish I was that into my course.' And the guys in the library are looking at the guys in the bar thinking, 'Why can't I fit in like that?' And the guys at the bar are looking at the guys playing Frisbee thinking, 'Why am I wasting my life on beer and boring conversations, when I could be doing activities and having experiences?'"

Drew wasn't sure if that made sense or was complete bollocks. "But what if they *are* having more fun, or getting more sex, or finding the work easier?"

Kit shrugged, and Drew felt it, and that was weirdly comfortable. "So what if they are? There's nothing you can do about it, and it's nuts spending your life feeling miserable because you think you should be doing the things you think other people are doing, just because you think that other people are doing them, whether they're doing them or not."

"I can honestly say I've never thought about it like that before." He turned his head and so did Kit, and suddenly he realised how close they were. They stayed like that. "I really like talking to you," he blurted.

A little tinge of pink crept over Kit's cheeks. "I really like being with you."

They angled their heads, nudging and edging at the distance between them. Drew's attention wavered from Kit's eyes—paler in the fading light—to his mouth, and then back again.

"Um," said Kit, his breath fanning soft and warm and faintly strawberry-scented over Drew's lips, "I really hope you're about to kiss me."

"Good." And he did.

There was a brief moment in which all Drew could think was *kissing a boy*, but then that went away, and it was just kissing, and then kissing Kit.

Who seemed to like it too.

Drew had that nervous *am I doing this right* feeling he sometimes got with girls, but then he half opened an eye and saw Kit's hand was waving about between them like he didn't know what to do with it. He caught it, and their fingers got all muddled, and so they were both sort of holding each other. And Drew stopped worrying, and instead let himself disappear into Kit, and the idea that he was the first person ever to do this with him. To learn the shape of his lips, and the way his mouth tasted, and feel the tickle of his hair and the slight roughness of his jaw.

And that made him worry again. Because you didn't want to mess up something like that.

Then Kit made this sound, shocked and happy and slightly muffled. Which made Drew feel kind of awesome, and next thing he knew, he was pushing Kit down into the grass, and Kit was going with it, and they were tangled together in all the ways.

Still kissing.

Kit was warm under him, sharp in places, not in others, hip bones grazing Drew's, lean runner's legs holding him tight. There was something reassuring—and, honestly, kind of hot—about that strength. About the unexpected ways they fit. And how natural it felt.

In his first term, they'd talked a lot about the way games have grammar. It was about the way games teach you to interact with them so there came a point when you weren't thinking *Press* x *to jump*, you were just jumping.

This was kind of like that.

It felt like the bit in a game when you finally got it. When your character stopped toppling off ledges, missing jumps, and pulling out their binoculars instead of their sniper rifle.

The bit where it felt right.

At some point, Kit rolled him over and straddled him, and Drew gazed hazily up at him. Kit was a little glittery in the fading light. Flushed and smiling and mussed up.

Because of Drew.

Drew pulled him down for another kiss.

"You know," said Kit, some time later, "I'm pretty sure it wasn't dark when we started."

Drew blinked. Kit was right. The sun was long gone, and the stars were out. "Man, it's like playing *Civ*."

"You mean—" Kit grinned "—just . . . one . . . more . . . kiss."

"Yeah, I was two turns away from building a wonder." A pause while that sunk in. "Uh, sorry, that sounded way less dodgy in my head."

Kit pushed the hair back from his eyes. "So . . . do you need to get to get back or do you want to . . .?"

"No, I mean, yes, I mean, sorry, what were the options again?"

"Do you need to go home, or do you want to come up to my room? I've got tap water and PG Tips."

It was late and Drew wasn't sure how long the buses ran, but he really didn't want to leave Kit. "Well, I do like tap water."

They got to their feet, brushed the grass off their clothes, and Kit led the way into one of the old-fashioned buildings in the middle of the park. His room was slightly nicer than Drew's, and significantly tidier. He had a rickety bookcase stuffed with tatty paperbacks and physics textbooks, and a scarily bare desk with just a laptop gleaming in the middle of it. Everything else was standard student-issue furniture. Drew glanced warily between the bed and the only chair and, after weighing the potential for awkward, settled on the chair.

Kit disappeared into the en suite and emerged with a University of Leicester mug full of tap water. He presented it ceremoniously to Drew, and sat down on the edge of the bed.

"This is way classier than my room," said Drew. He glanced at Kit's posters. One of them might have been an actual print. It was one of those old-fashioned, hand-drawn adverts where there wasn't even a slogan, just a picture of a dude with the product, and everybody else staring at him like he was awesome. "I like your . . . uh . . . man picture."

"Thanks, it was the effect I was going for. I went into the shop and said, 'Give me your finest man picture.'"

Drew gave him a look. "No, seriously, the geometries are really interesting. It's sort of sharp and fluid at the same time."

"It's a Leyendecker."

Drew made the *over my head* gesture.

"Sorry, I just find it intriguing. The way everyone is gazing at the man in brown, and how easily he's being gazed at. I keep wanting to make up stories about him, but then I remember he's just trying to sell a shirt."

"What about that one?" Drew pointed at the three-panel poster on the opposite wall.

"It's a film poster for the Back to the Future trilogy."

Drew gave him another look. "I know that. It says so on it. But *how* is it the Back to the Future trilogy. It's just dots and semicircles."

Kit laughed. "Come on, I'll show you."

They assembled underneath the needlessly oblique Back to the Future poster, and Kit took his hand as if drawing stars in the sky. Drew stole a sideways glance at him because this felt weirdly romantic, and Kit's lashes were really long and very gold from this angle.

"So—" Kit drew his finger to the third dot on the top row "—we start in 1985, go back to 1955." They followed the line to the second dot. "Then back to 1985." They closed the circle again. "In the second movie—" they slid to next panel "—we start in 1985, go forward to 2015." Their joined hands moved from the third dot to the fourth. "Then back to alternate 1985." They followed the spiral round to the single dot in the second row. "And finally back to 1955 to stop Biff getting the sports almanac."

"Oh, I get it." Drew pulled Kit over to the second dot on the third panel. "They start in 1955, then go back to . . . shit, like, the Wild West, whenever that was."

"1885," offered Kit, wickedly.

"And then finally—" their fingers traced the spiral to the third dot "—Marty comes back to the present. By which I mean, back before I was born."

Kit turned and pressed his lips to Drew's cheek, swift and a little shy. "Do you know they're making a musical?"

"I really don't do musicals."

"You have to. It's part of the Gay Laws."

"Stop labelling my sexuality."

They kissed again under Kit's no longer confusing Back to the Future poster.

And, afterwards, they both sat on the bed, side by side, with their shoulders nudging, and their backs against the wall.

Drew mimed casting a line into the water, and Kit laughed and did the same.

They fished for a little while.

Suddenly, Drew remembered something. "Shit, I haven't done my dailies."

"You can borrow my computer if you like."

"Like, no. Seriously, no. I'm not going to sit in your room with you doing my dailies on your computer."

"It's cool. I don't mind."

Drew swivelled round, scurfing up the duvet. "I'd rather do something with you."

Kit's eyebrows went up.

"Not in a sex way. Not that I wouldn't in a sex way. I mean. Um. Do you want to play a game or something?"

"I'd love to." Kit slid to his feet, grabbed his laptop, and came back. "I'm not sure I've got much that's two player."

Thinking about it, Drew couldn't remember the last time he'd played a co-op game on one screen. That was what the internet was for. But then he remembered Sanee and Steff, and their weekends playing Total War: Era Number, X-Com, and Europa Universalis. "I've got a couple of mates, I mean I've got mates who are a couple, who play strategy games together. They pause a lot and argue about what they're going to do next. Like, 'No, flank the catapharcts.' Or 'We have to core Granada.'"

"That sounds really nice except, y'know, the arguing. And the only strategy games I've got are *Civ* and *CKII*, and that's only because—"

"—it's secretly an RPG."

Kit beamed. "Aw, you remembered."

"So what are we going to play?"

"I've mainly got RPGs."

"I'm good with anything. We can decide which elf to sleep with and whether the Staff of Whatever is better than the Sword of Thingamy."

"I think you'll find—" Kit gave him an arch look "—that what we'll be doing is engaging with complex moral questions through an interactive medium which will aid us in our task by helpfully highlighting all of the evil options in red."

Drew laughed. "Bring it on."

Kit fired up Steam, and scanned down his library. "The problem is a lot of these are a bit too action-heavy. Weirdly, we might be better off with something turn-based."

"Wait. I draw the line at musicals and JRPGs."

"How do you feel about retro?"

"Isometric retro or ASCII retro?"

"Black Isle retro."

"You mean the guys who turned into the company who are legendarily incapable of finishing games?"

Kit closed down Steam, and opened the GoG launcher. "Jacob's got me hooked on Good Old Games. Um, the site, but also games that are old, and also good. He's kind of convinced that PC games are dwindling into the west like Galadriel, and every game worth playing was made in the late nineties."

"Back when everything came on twenty CDs?"

"Pretty much, but now you can just download them for about five dollars." He double-clicked on a picture of an angry-looking blue man with dodgy dreads, and a tiny little cinematic popped up of an island and a storm. "This is one of his favourites, but I haven't actually got round to trying it yet. It's called *Planescape Torment*. It's about this guy who—"

"Kit, I've heard of *Planescape Torment*. It's like the *Breaking Bad* of RPGs. People who've played it won't shut up until you do."

"We can try something else?"

"No, it's cool. It's like a gamer rite of passage, and I've been meaning to look at it for years."

On the screen, a slightly blurry zombie was pushing a slab with a grey dude on it slowly through some kind of dungeon.

"Wait," said Drew. "Do we start off dead?"

"Only mostly."

"Hang on, what's the pillar. Why are there skulls? Who's that chick, and why is she on fire? Is the guy in the mirror us? Why are we a zombie? Is that the same chick and is she dead now? Is she the ghost as well? Hey, stop laughing."

"Sorry." It wasn't a very convincing apology, especially because Kit was still smiling. "I'd say it was an old-games thing, but to be honest I think it's just a Black Isle/BioWare/Obsidian thing. You just kind of have to go with it."

When Drew next checked his phone, five hours had passed. "Shit, it's nearly two. I'd better be getting back."

Kit pushed his laptop out of the way. "Oh my God, I'm sorry. I lost track of time."

"It's that game, man. It sucks you in and it makes no sense, and the journal system is borked. And where the heck are we supposed to find someone to grow this black barbed seed for us? I mean we took it to the people in the market who specialise in growing weird plants, and they were like, no, sorry, not our bag."

"Yeah, I'm beginning to think the humble quest marker gets a really bad rap."

"I'm never complaining about having to kill fifty harpies again."

Kit laughed, and crawled off the bed. "It's really late, do you want me to walk you home?"

"Dude, if you do that, I'll have to walk you back again, and we'll get stuck in an infinite loop."

"And then we'll have to hard reset the evening."

Drew felt a bit goofy, but he went with it anyway. "I wouldn't mind."

"Neither would I."

They smiled and stared at each other.

"Look, I could . . ." Drew began, at the same time Kit said, "Do you want to . . ." and just in case *that* turned into an infinite loop as well, Drew jumped straight to, "Yes."

He'd shared beds with people before for various reasons, but this was different. They dithered for a while about what exactly was appropriate to keep on and what wasn't, and finally settled on boxers and T-shirts as a safe middle ground. And then Drew hopped into bed, pulled Kit's duvet right up to his chin, and tried not to look like a complete dork.

Kit was equipping a slightly worn blue T-shirt, which meant Drew—who wasn't watching, honestly—got to see the curve of his spine, the shift and drag of muscles under his skin, the freckles on his shoulders. Then Kit flicked off the light and slipped into bed.

It was a single, so there wasn't much room to be coy. Too many limbs to sort out. Soon, they were pressed right up against each other, wriggling and kissing, and trying to find places to put their hands.

"This is nice," said Drew sleepily.

Kit answered with a murmur, drowsy and content. He rolled onto his other side, and Drew very naturally curled up round him. Only slightly self-conscious because kissing and closeness and stuff had sort of . . . well . . . if Kit had ever been worried Drew wasn't into him, he now had, um, concrete evidence he was.

Drew was just dropping off when Kit suddenly twitched in his arms. "What's wrong?"

"I just realised something."

"Huh?" This was kind of worrying.

"We met a guy in the hive called Mourns-For-Trees."

Now Drew twitched. "We should totally check that out. Can you remember where he is?"

"I remember he was wearing green."

"I think I saw someone like that near the Flophouse but that might have been the weird guy who gave us the box we weren't supposed to open."

"It might have been down by the Burning Corpse, or maybe I'm thinking of Amarysse. We can look tomorrow."

"Yeah." Drew was smiling as he tucked his head against Kit's neck. "We can look tomorrow."

CHAPTER 10

Between *HoL*, Frisbee, and coursework, Drew wasn't able to visit Kit in person until Thursday. They'd raided together and hung out in the game a lot, but since Drew had got used to seeing Kit and, well, touching Kit, it wasn't quite the same.

He was just stuffing his toothbrush and a spare pair of boxers into his laptop bag when someone banged on his door, and before he could respond, Sanee barrelled in and settled into the chair like he was camping a spawn point.

"New Mortal Kombat. Tournament. My place. Right now."

Drew stared for a long moment. Then pointed at his bag o' pants. "What?"

"I'm spending the night at Kit's."

Sanee shrugged. "Bring him along. There's no better way to meet a bunch of people than to have them rip your spine out."

Drew was kind of aware he'd been blowing Sanee off for a week, but he was pretty invested in a romantic one-on-one evening with Kit and a retro video game. And replacing it with a violent beat 'em up and an undisclosed number of his mates was just . . . not something he wanted to do. "I'm sorry, but we've got plans."

"But do your plans involve buckets of CGI blood, creepily detailed boob physics, and the opportunity to explode heads as a thunder god in a stupid hat?"

"Well, no," Drew admitted. "It involves getting to see my boyfriend when I haven't since Sunday."

"You saw him on Tuesday. That's why you didn't come to the Late Night Chillathon and Impromptu Curly Fry Pig Out."

"We were in *HoL*. And we were running dungeons with two of his friends from the guild."

Sanee was uncharacteristically quiet for a moment. "Mate, are you saying that you skipped the Late Night Chillathon and Impromptu Curly Fry Pig Out so you could pretend to be an elf in a video game?"

Sanee had a point. It had been fun hanging out in *HoL*, but Drew had been slightly paralysed by the knowledge that other stuff was going on and he wasn't there. Kit might have made peace with missing out, but a tiny part of Drew still thought he should be doing everything, and he could never quite shake the fear that the best experience of his life was happening right now to somebody else. "It was the only time we could do it, and Kit has a regular Tuesday night thing with Morag and Ialdir, so it was really important to him."

"So, you didn't hang out with your real friends because your boyfriend wanted to hang out with his imaginary friends?"

Drew stole a look at the time on his mobile. Sanee was clearly upset and that was stressful, but he had somewhere to be—somewhere he really wanted to be—and that was *also* stressful. Basically this was just stressful. "I'd already agreed, and the Tuesday thing is always a bit up in the air. Like, last week we spent about two hours debating whether to play board games or watch a movie and then didn't do either."

"This is a total mischaracterisation of what happened. We played Munchkin."

"Dude, nobody actually *likes* Munchkin. It's just bland enough that no one can strongly object to playing it."

Sanee gave him a wounded look. "Well, then, object next time. Don't just go along with it, and then throw it in my face a week later."

"Look, I'm sorry. It was a one-off. I'm not one of those people who can't tell the difference between real life and video games. I'm not going to die of exhaustion in a café in South Korea."

"I dunno." Sanee rocked the chair onto its back legs. "I think you might be heading that way. You used to play Mondays and Wednesdays. Then it went up to Monday, Wednesday, Friday. And you were there on Thursday *and* Tuesday. And it sounds like this game is most of what you do with your weekends as well. That's not a hobby, mate, that's an addiction."

Drew let the laptop bag slump to the ground. "Wow, you went there really fast. Especially when I know for a fact you put a hundred and eleven hours into *Skyrim*."

"It's not the same. Like, if you were an alcoholic—"

"There's no way I'm going to be able to put up with the end of that sentence."

"I'm serious, Drew. I'm trying to help you here." The chair crashed onto its front feet, as Sanee leaned forward intently. "Being an addict isn't about how much you do something, it's about feeling you have to do it all the time."

"Have you been on Wikipedia again?"

"You're not even going to think about it, are you? If you didn't know I was right, you wouldn't be acting like this."

"I'm acting like this—" Drew wasn't quite shouting "—because I'm late to see my boyfriend—my real, actual, physical, real-life boyfriend—and you burst in here and called me a junkie." He hoisted up his laptop bag again and stomped out. "Make sure the door locks when you decide you're ready to leave."

He was still pretty shaky by the time he got off the bus at the Botanic Gardens. Because, actually, Sanee had been wrong when he'd accused Drew of brushing off his concerns. Right back when he'd first met Solace, he'd been worried that "she" didn't seem to have anything in her life outside *HoL* and studying. And, honestly, there'd been a part of him that had secretly liked the fantasy of coming into this person's life and drawing them out of their shell and into the real world. But now it looked like the opposite was happening.

Drew had always been quite proud that he was a gamer who wasn't like gamers were supposed to be. He played sports, he was not completely socially awkward, he'd had girlfriends and . . . a boyfriend. He went to the pub with his mates like ordinary people did. Yes, they sometimes talked about video games while they were there, but that just happened to be a common interest. One of the things he'd liked about raiding with Anni was that the game was a means to an end. Every single person in that guild wanted to prove that they could compete at the top level. It wasn't about *HoL*, it was about the challenge. And after he'd left, it had been really nice to hook up with people who appreciated the sunsets and elves part of the game, but part of the problem with appreciating a virtual world was that you began to treat it like a real one.

He passed the spot where he and Kit had first kissed, and that cheered him up a bit. Worrying about his game/life balance suddenly seemed a lot less important than having met someone he really, really liked. Who he was going to see right now. And whose evening he didn't want to wreck by dumping all this crap on him.

He resolved not to think about it. And even managed to forget about it completely when Kit opened the door, smiling and looking sufficiently gorgeous that Drew had a rush of *oh my God, I can't believe I'm dating this guy* so intense it knocked basically everything else out of his head.

"So—" Kit gave a slightly self-conscious flourish "—I've sort of done a . . . sort of picnic. Which it belatedly occurs to me that we could have had outside. But it's all set up now."

He'd laid a tartan blanket (which looked new enough that Drew suspected he'd bought it specially) on the floor, and put out a variety of breads, cheeses, cakes, and fruit. It was probably the most romantic thing that had ever happened to Drew, since most of his dates had followed a very set format and he'd never quite had the confidence to suggest anything more controversial than dinner and a movie.

Kit appeared to be accidentally enacting the */shy* animation. "I hope it's okay. I thought we could eat and talk and play a bit of *Torment* and . . ." He blushed.

Consumed by <3, Drew threw his arms around Kit and kissed him, gentle at first, and then not so much. "This is the best," he said, quite a bit later.

They settled down on the picnic blanket and tucked in.

Kit gave him a mischievous look from behind some walnut bread. "I'm sorry I couldn't get any dough balls."

"Well, that's it. We have to break up."

"I mean, you can get them. It's just I don't have an oven."

"You know I'm not *actually* obsessed with dough balls, right? I do eat other things."

"Like strawberries?" Kit produced a punnet from their place of cunning concealment inside a Tesco's bag.

Now it was Drew's turn to blush. "Yeah."

Kit was kneeling a little primly on the edge of the blanket, the strawberries cradled in his lap. "Given the complexity of this encounter, I was thinking maybe we should ... well ... Practice makes perfect, you know."

"Once you get the mechanics down, it'll be a faceroll." Drew leaned forward, plucked a strawberry from amongst its fellows, and held it out to Kit.

It was probably a combination of knowing each other better, having got more comfortable—a lot more comfortable—with touching, and not being in a Pizza Express full of strangers, but any raid leader would have commended their coordination, situational awareness, and teamwork. They even moved on to the hard-mode version, seeing how much they could tease each other's fingers between bites. And then Drew deliberately dropped one and kissed Kit instead—his mouth as soft and sweet as the strawberries.

Once they were out of fruit and the remains of the picnic had been tidied away, they settled down on Kit's bed, got his laptop, and disappeared into *Torment*, which was still as bewildering and intriguing as it had been on Saturday. Progress remained somewhat oblique, but Drew's competitive spirit had kicked in, and now they were keeping extensive and detailed notes about who people were, what they wanted, and most importantly, where the hell they were standing.

They took it a lot slower than Drew would have if he'd been playing alone, but it was honestly more fun this way. They talked to basically everybody with a name and some people without names because Kit was slightly obsessive about it. They went everywhere and discussed everything, and got far too invested in tiny decisions, like whether they should spend their limited resources buying a pet Lim-Lim (Kit felt very strongly that they should) or whether they should tell random strangers their name was Adahn even though it wasn't (Drew felt very strongly that they shouldn't).

It was like they'd stumbled into a lost wilderness of gaming. Drew couldn't remember the last time he'd played a game where he genuinely hadn't known what he was supposed to do next, what was important, or what the consequences of his choices might be. He honestly couldn't decide whether it was terrible game design that the industry had quite rightly grown out of, or if it was something special that had been lost. Perhaps it was a little bit of both.

In any case, the evening whisked by as they snuggled even closer to each other beneath the laptop, heads together, feet entangled. Annoyingly, the more Drew noticed his own enjoyment, the more worried he got about it.

Which meant he finally blurted out, "Kit, do you think we spend too much time playing games?"

Kit parked their party of randoms in a corner of the Gathering Dust bar, and gave Drew a slightly quizzical look. "Well, no. But I'm confused why you're asking."

"You don't mind we just played a video game all evening?"

"Again, not particularly." Kit's brow wrinkled anxiously. "Do you? Are you not having fun?"

"No, no, I'm having a great time. It's just we spend a lot of time in *HoL* as well."

"That's where my friends hang out. And I like playing it."

Drew felt sort of confused and uneasy. He'd been thinking about this quite clearly on his way down, but now, he couldn't make the ideas stick together right. It didn't help that Kit seemed totally unaware of the possibility there could be a problem here. And that made him wonder if Sanee had thought the same thing about him. "But you have to have other things."

"What's this about?" asked Kit gently, closing the laptop and putting it to one side.

That was the point Drew realised he hadn't brought this up as casually as he'd meant to. "I just sort of realised I'm not hanging out with my friends as much as I used to."

"I'd never want to get in the way."

"You're not. Seeing you is really important to me."

Kit smiled. "Same."

"I guess." Drew played his fingers up the side of Kit's wrist, catching the sweet responsive shiver in his skin. "Maybe if we just spent less time in *HoL*. Like the guild is cool and everything, but I'd really like if you wanted to spend time with me and my mates."

Kit's gaze lingered on Drew's hand. He still seemed a bit bothered, but all he said was, "Sure."

Just like when he'd been talking to Sanee, Drew still wasn't quite sure he'd said everything he needed to say or said it right, but he didn't want to make Kit feel like a loser any more than he wanted Sanee to think he didn't care about their friendship. But he also wasn't sure how else the conversation could have played out. Kit had agreed to spend real-world time with him pretty easily, so maybe everything would be fine.

And, in any case, angsting about it now was pointless.

"Um." Kit lay back and stretched out, tucking an arm behind his head. "It's quite late. Are you tired? Or do you want to do something else?"

He looked really good like that—sort of all lean and elegant and inviting. As if he was waiting to be touched. Drew dropped down onto one elbow, his free hand sneaking under the hem of Kit's shirt. "I can't think of anything to say that doesn't sound like the flirt option in a BioWare RPG."

"*Mass Effect* or *Dragon Age*?"

Drew thought about it for a moment. "Do you have a preference?"

"I'm good with you right now."

"That's a relief. Because I left my Commander Shepard costume at home."

Kit's muscles tightened under Drew's palm as he laughed. And Drew rolled over him and kissed him into silence.

"You're really beautiful, you know?" Drew said, a bit awkwardly. It was true, but he wasn't quite sure if you were meant to say it.

"Oh God." Kit went all pink and lifted a hand to stroke Drew's cheek, palm curving beneath his jaw. "I don't know what... Sorry, I'm really bad with compliments." He went, if possible, even pinker, the heat spilling down his throat and disappearing beneath the open V of his shirt. "I'm glad you like me, though."

Drew was suddenly very brave indeed. He kissed his way under Kit's chin. He was a little rough there—this pale stubble he could feel but couldn't see. Kit tipped his head back, no hesitation there, just trust and eagerness, a soft noise, half-sigh, half-moan, slipping from between his lips. It made Drew sit up a moment. Kind of stunned and kind of flustered and excited at how right it all was.

Kit and him. Him and Kit.

He was looking up at Drew, eyes expectant, still bright with memory of laughter. His breath was coming quickly now, matching Drew's.

Well. It seemed as good a time as any. And it seemed kind of unfair to leave all the baring and trusting and scary stuff to Kit. So he whisked off his T-shirt. And was especially glad for the rugby, since he was sort of right there, with nowhere to hide. It wasn't quite what he was used to, but it wasn't as intimidating as he'd expected.

Not when Kit was gazing at him with such pleasure.

It felt pretty powerful actually. And in its own way, kind of hot.

He was starting to think that maybe one of the things about sex was that you put up your own barriers. Worrying about what someone else would think about you. Or what you might accidentally be showing them or telling them.

But if you liked somone—*really* liked someone—then . . . suddenly none of that mattered anymore. And it was no different from anything else you did together.

Talking or sharing a joke or playing a game.

He reached for the first button of Kit's shirt. "Can I?"

"God, yes." A long, hot shudder ran through Kit's body. "Yes, please."

And he caught Drew by the shoulder and pulled him down again.

That Friday, Drew made certain to go to the pub. He probably would have anyway, but he wanted to show his friends that he hadn't forgotten them. Kit, of course, was raiding.

A tiny part of him was worried that Sanee was going to stage an intervention in the Slug and Lettuce, but once they'd all settled down with their drinks and burgers, he instead stood up, tinked on the side of his pint glass with his fork, and proudly announced that he and Steff were hosting the first annual Batstravaganza.

"The original plan," he explained, "was to do *Begins*, *Returns*, and *Rises*, but then we realised that a) we picked up all four 1990s movies for less than a tenner back when HMV closed down, and b) they've done a version of the Adam West movie with Christopher

Nolan–style packaging. So we're going to do all eight Batman films in chronological order this weekend."

"Why?" asked Andy.

"Because he's the Batman," replied Tinuviel in a surprisingly effective Christian Bale impersonation.

Sanee glanced round the table. "So who's with us?"

"Okay." Andy shrugged.

"And my axe." That was Tinuviel.

"Fair warning." Steff looked up from her chips. "At least a quarter of these films will be terrible, but we will have a lot of beer."

"And bring sleeping bags," added Sanee. "Because this is some hard-core movie watching."

Steff waved a sachet of ketchup solemnly. "And honestly, as a medical professional, I recommend being unconscious through *Batman & Robin*."

"Um." Given Sanee's comments yesterday and his conversation with Kit, Drew decided to go for it. He put up his hand. "Can I bring my boyfriend, please?"

"Oh." Tinuviel put her hand up as well. "Can I bring my current romantic partner and/or my current sexual partner?"

Andy squinted across the table. "Are they different people?"

She squinted back. "Is that a real question?"

"Apparently not." Andy gave up gracefully.

"Bring who you like," said Sanee expansively. "We've got plenty of crisps and the nice thing about movies is there's no maximum number of players."

Drew honestly wasn't sure it would be Kit's thing, but he seemed happy enough to be invited. So the next day they met for brunch in this tearoom he liked, detoured back to Drew's room for . . . stuff, because they were getting pretty good at it, and then—only slightly late—legged it to Sanee and Steff's.

Everyone else was already there, so the best beanbags were taken, but they found a corner, and Drew slightly awkwardly introduced Kit to his friends, stalling when he got to Tinuviel's guests because he'd never met either of them before.

Tinuviel gestured left. "This is Tom." Then right. "This is Melissa."

Drew was about to ask which one was romantic and which one was sexual, but realised just in time there was no way it could sound good.

There was a slightly difficult silence.

"So," said Sanee, "you're Drew's hot elf babe."

"Dude." Drew facepalmed.

Kit smiled shyly. "It's the ears, isn't it? They're a dead giveaway."

Steff disentangled herself from Sanee, and brought them a couple of beers. "Please forgive this tactless arse I'm somehow engaged to. He was trying very hard not to open with, 'So you're a gay, then.'"

"I was not," Sanee protested.

"The important thing—" Steff scrambled back onto the sofa, and patted his arm "—is that you believe that."

Now that first contact had been established, everyone could settle down, and Batstravaganaza could officially begin.

Sanee whacked a DVD into the PS4. "Ladies and gentleman, I present Adam West and Burt Ward in their 1966 triumph, *Batman: The Movie*. Because it was from the days when you had to say something was a movie in the title, otherwise people would get confused."

As usual, they didn't spend that much time actually watching the entity that identified itself as a movie. Mainly they drank and ate and did commentary. While Bruce and Dick were biffing, powing, and socking their way through the criminal underworld, Drew and Kit lost their self-consciousness about being a couple in public and naturally folded together.

Kit was quiet, but he seemed to be enjoying himself, and Drew was glad he was there.

A hundred and five minutes later, the credits rolled to raucous applause and a shower of popcorn.

"So," Sanee asked, when the noise had died down, "Bats out of ten. I think I'll give it a seven because it wasn't terrible, but it wasn't really what I want from a Batman movie."

Drew lifted his head out of Kit's lap. "Oh come on, man. The nobility of the almost-human porpoise. That's worth at least an eight on its own."

"That's worth minus eight on its own."

"Well, actually," interrupted Tinuviel before they could get into a fight, "I think one of Batman's great strengths is the way he can encompass many identities, and reflect many worlds. The Batman who leaves Ra's al Ghul to die in an exploding monorail—"

"Oi," yelled Andy, "spoilers."

"—loses his impact if he is not set against the Batman who refuses to throw a bomb into a flock of ducklings."

Melissa nudged into the side of Tinuviel's neck. "Who could respect a man who threw a bomb into a flock of ducklings?"

"What did you think, Kit?" asked Steff, since he'd been obviously quieter than everyone else.

"Oh." He thought about it for a moment. "I'd give it eight bats too. Partly for the porpoise, partly for shark-repellent Bat spray, and partly—with my physicist hat on—for the sheer glorious craziness of . . . if you dehydrate someone, and then rehydrate them with heavy water, then the slightest impact will reduce them to antimatter."

"Are you suggesting—" Drew grinned at him "—it doesn't really work like that?"

"Well," said Steff, "let's go back to basics. With my medicine hat on, when you dehydrate someone, they don't turn into blue dust."

Drew shook his fist in the air. "You lied to me, West, you lied to me."

They romped on through Tim Burton's *Batman* and *Batman Returns*, and then ordered pizza to sustain them through the nadir of *Forever*, and *& Robin*. Drew thought he maybe fell asleep somewhere between Jim Carrey in green latex and Uma Thurman in green latex, soothed by Kit's fingers moving gently through his hair. But he definitely woke up about halfway through *Batman Begins*, mainly because everyone in the room was rasping "Do I look like a cop" as loudly as they could while still doing Batman Voice.

They'd all basically rallied by the time Batman was hanging the Joker off a high building *again*, and an emergency injection of very strong coffee courtesy of Tom carried them all the way to the confusing café scene at the end of *Rises*.

It was 6 a.m., they'd probably got twelve hours of sleep between them. All they'd done was watch eight movies, only some of which were actually good, but nevertheless Drew was left with a tremendous feeling of accomplishment.

Sanee rose a little unsteadily to give his closing statement. "Ladies and gentleman, you have just witnessed the entirety of the cinematographic Bat canon. Those still abed will count themselves accursed they were not here."

Andy was wrapped up in his sleeping bag, snoring softly.

Tinuviel stared meditatively into the middle distance. Drew found it difficult to tell whether she was knackered, wasted, or completely normal. "The thing that troubles me the most about Jack Nicholson's Joker, apart from the fact that it's clearly just Jack Nicholson, is that because he's so physically unthreatening, the final confrontation comes down to Batman beating up an unarmed, mentally ill man in his fifties."

"It does make Batman look kind of a dick," agreed Tom.

Steff pulled Sanee back onto the sofa and snuggled into him. "I'm not sure. I think the fact that Batman keeps whaling on him and he just carries on laughing makes him really freaking scary."

"Most Batman villains are nuts anyway." Sanee tugged a blanket over the two of them. "And Batman's not really all there either. I mean, he dresses as a bat, for God's sake. That's hardly normal behaviour. I think the reason the bad guys are so OTT is to distract you from what a total weirdo Bruce Wayne is."

"You know," said Kit softly, "I heard the original brief for Batman was to create a character who was more down-to-earth and relatable than Superman, and somehow the concept they came up with for this everyman hero was a genius billionaire whose parents were killed in a freak opera-attending accident."

Drew was pleased when everyone laughed. It made him feel that Kit had a place among his friends and also secretly proud that he was dating this beautiful, funny, nerdy guy. "The thing that gets me about Batman is the little pointy ears on his helmet. They're so adorable I don't know how anyone can take him seriously."

Tinuviel shut her eyes for a moment. "I suspect—" she put her fingers to her temples "—that if he did not have the little pointy ears he would look like a butt plug."

"Argh." Sanee yanked the blanket over his head. "You have ruined Batman forever."

"No, Jim Carrey ruined *Batman Forever.*"

Sanee groaned. "Oh, I see what you did there."

By unspoken consensus, people began to find themselves comfortable passing-out nooks. Drew and Kit aligned their sleeping bags and drifted off, holding hands.

It was afternoon by the time everyone was awake again, and they were finishing off the last of the snacks and wondering what to do with the rest of the day. Drew was used to this kind of space. They'd sit around for a while, just chilling, and chatting, and occasionally fiddling on their phones. Eventually someone would suggest playing a game, and eventually they'd play one. It was a nice, low-pressure way to spend Sunday.

At around two, just as they were debating whether it was worth trying to find a board game that would take eight players, or if they should split into groups, or maybe just go for food or something, Kit stood up and said he should be going.

Drew was a bit startled. He thought he'd been having a good time, and he didn't want him to go. "You don't have to. I'm sure we can find something for eight players, or we can do teams."

"It's not that." Kit packed up his sleeping bag. "It's just I think I want to go home now."

Drew wasn't sure if he was supposed to offer to go with him or not, and came down on the side of *not* in case he looked intense, creepy, and codependent. "Um. Okay, well, I'll catch you later."

Kit bent down, kissed him good-bye, and started picking his way between the sleeping bags and the empty snack bowls.

"Dude," said Sanee, "why are you running out on us?"

Kit froze by the doorway. "Um, I'm going to catch up with some friends in *HoL.*"

"Wow, and I thought I was a nerd."

Awkward.

Kit had gone kind of red. "Yeah, see you later."

He hurried out.

Steff whacked Sanee in the arm. "Why are you being such a dick?"

"I wasn't being a dick. I was inviting him to stay. I like the guy."

"Squidge, it's not a personal insult when someone wants to leave your house."

Drew wasn't sure where to look or what to feel. Obviously Kit had a right to go home when he wanted to, but he was still weirdly hurt. It wasn't like Kit had anything else on, so it just felt uncomfortably like being rejected.

They sort of hung until about four, and then Sanee suggested they crack open Cards Against Humanity. Which, after two rounds of play, Tinuviel actively hated.

"I think my fundamental problem," she explained, "is that it bills itself as a card game for horrible people but feels more like a card game for people who want to try very hard to prove how horrible they are."

So they played Dixit instead.

And Drew tried not to miss Kit. And worried he was being needy, and worried that Kit didn't like his friends, or that his friends felt insulted, or that Sanee was right and Kit had needed to run away for his MMO fix. Basically he just worried.

He got home late, and logged in to *HoL* to do his dailies.

```
[Guild][Ialdir]: Yo
[Guild][Morag]: Hey
[Guild][Heurodis]: cant talk must pewpew
[Guild][Solace]: Hi Drew :)
[Guild][Mordant]: Hi
[Guild][Orcarella]: Hi
[Solace] whispers: Sorry for bailing earlier
To [Solace]: it's fine. are you okay?
[Solace] whispers: Yes, I'm good
To [Solace]: so why'd you leave?
[Solace] whispers: Like I said, I just wanted
to be at home
[Solace] whispers: Also I hadn't logged in to
HoL in a while
[Solace] whispers: So I wanted to say hi to
everyone
To [Solace]: You blew off my friends to play
HoL
```

It was a long few seconds before any new messages popped up.

```
[Solace] whispers: Drew, I didn't blow anyone
off
[Solace] whispers: I left your friends who
we'd been hanging out with for more than 24
hours
[Solace] whispers: To come and hang out with
my friends
[Solace] whispers: Who I hadn't seen for a
while
```

Drew stared at the screen.

```
To [Solace]: did you not like my friends?
[Solace] whispers: I like your friends. I had
a good time
[Solace] whispers: But I wanted to go and do
something else
To [Solace]: I could have come with you
[Solace] whispers: You could have, but you
seemed happy with your friends
To [Solace]: i dont want to choose between my
friends and my boyfriend
[Solace] whispers: I'm not asking you to
To [Solace]: but you sort of did
[Solace] whispers: I didn't mean to
[Solace] whispers: But you can't make me
choose between you and my friends either
To [Solace]: dude this is a video game
To [Solace]: i know HoL has been a big part
of your life
To [Solace]: but these are just people you
know on the internet
To [Solace]: half of them are twice your age
To [Solace]: half of them don't live in this
country
```

```
[Solace] whispers: Drew
[Solace] whispers: i really dont know what to
say
[Guild][Ialdir]: Hey Drew, Solace said you
two started playing Torment
[Solace] whispers: or why you're saying this
[Solace] whispers: is this what you really
think of me
```

Drew stared at his screen in horror. He was in the middle of something he was pretty sure was an argument with his boyfriend—an argument he wasn't sure how he'd started, or what it was really about. Trying to have a conversation about classic video games in guild chat at the same time was slightly beyond him.

```
[Guild][Orcarella]: y
[Guild][Ialdir]: How are you finding it?
To [Solace]: i didn't mean it like that
[Guild][Orcarella]: they don't make them like
that any more
[Guild][Ialdir]: Yeah, it's tragic isn't it?
[Solace] whispers: So how did you mean it?
[Guild][Orcarella]: it takes some getting
used to
[Guild][Solace]: There's obviously a lot of
love in it
[Guild][Solace]: Like every zombie in the
Mortuary has its own identity
[Guild][Ialdir]: Every time I play it I find
something new
To [Solace]: i'm just worried about you
[Guild][Ialdir]: You're really lucky you can
discover it together
[Guild][Ialdir]: I tried to get Stefan into
it back when we were first going out
[Solace] whispers: Because I only wanted to
spend 24 straight hours hanging out with your
friends? And not 36?
```

[Guild][Ialdir]: Disaster
To [Solace]: they'll think you don't like
them
[Guild][Ialdir]: I turned into this total
jerky control freak
[Guild][Ialdir]: I was like no, you have to
have wisdom 18
[Guild][Ialdir]: And we should solve this
quest exactly like this
[Solace] whispers: So you think your friends
will be insulted because an adult human
eventually chose to leave their company
[Guild][Ialdir]: And we've got to go to
ragpicker's square as soon as possible
[Guild][Orcarella]: wait what's so important
about ragpicker's square?
[Solace] whispers: And *I'm* the one you
think you have to worry about?
[Guild][Heurodis]: SPOILERS MAN SPOILERS
[Guild][Orcarella]: Seriously, what's in
ragpicker's square?
[Guild][Ialdir]: Oh my god, I am the worst
person ever
[Guild][Solace]: Also I'm pretty sure we
skimped on wisdom
To [Solace]: but you'll spend whole weekends
in HoL
[Guild][Solace]: You can't even play a cleric
[Guild][Ialdir]: la la la I can't hear you
[Guild][Heurodis]: dont worry everyone starts
off as a noob
[Guild][Heurodis]: youll really understand
the game on your third or fourth playthrough
[Guild][Morag]: Sometimes I think life is
just too short for Bjorn.
[Solace] whispers: Yes, Drew. Funnily enough,
I find it easier to spend a long time doing
something I like and have chosen to do

```
[Solace] whispers: with people I've known a
long time
[Solace] whispers: than something somebody
else chose to do
[Solace] whispers: with a group of people
I've only just met
[Guild][Heurodis]: Sadly, Morag, nothing can
change the nature of a man
[Guild][Ialdir]: Wow, you really missed the
point of that game, didn't you?
To [Solace]: you can't build your whole life
around a video game
[Guild][Morag]: I thought the point of that
game was Annah
[Guild][Morag]: Maybe because I played it at
an impressionable age
[Guild][Morag]: But I blame Torment for my
lifelong thing for feisty redheads
Solace has gone offline.
```

Whoa. That had gone super badly wrong. And Drew wasn't sure what to do or even why it had happened. He had a cold, creeping sense it might have been his fault, but then he usually did when he fought with people he cared about.

He sat there for a little while, feeling increasingly terrible. And then sent Kit a quick text: *We okay?* After a moment, he got back: *Just need some space.*

Drew stared at his phone. What did that even mean? Was it a polite way of dumping him? Did it mean they were on a break? Was everything basically fine, and Drew was overreacting? He really wanted to reply and ask for clarification, but he was pretty certain that the one thing it didn't mean was, *Please text me back immediately.*

Between the all-nighter, the argument, and the Batmen, Drew's brain was basically soup. The part of him that was upset and panicky wanted to Do Something Right Now, but the part of him that was operating on eighty minutes' sleep made deciding what the Something should be, or indeed standing upright, borderline impossible.

He reeled away from *HoL* and fell facedown onto his bed. He was conscious just long enough to notice how spacious and empty it felt.

CHAPTER 11

Kit had pulled out of the Monday raid, which meant Morag had to go healz at the last minute, leaving Drew with the dubious pleasure of MT-ing opposite Bjorn's alarmingly well-geared tanking alt. They started a fresh run, still buoyed up by last week's victory over Bloodrose, but progress was a little shaky because they were prioritising alts and people who hadn't done the content yet. They downed Arachnia after a couple of wipes and called it before Vilicus.

It was still fun—surprisingly fun considering how often Drew had done this by now—but Kit's absence made a difference, and not just to Drew. Morale seemed to flag a bit more quickly, Bjorn's irritability seemed less entertaining, and both Morag and Ialdir were less focused than usual.

Once the raid broke up, Drew bamfed back to the City of Stars. He was just checking his supplies for Wednesday when a message popped up.

Morag has invited you to join a group: y/n
Morag is now group leader.
[Group][Orcarella]: hi?
[Group][Ialdir]: Hey :)
[Group][Morag]: Sorry to grab you
[Group][Morag]: We were just wondering if you knew what was up with Kit

Oh crap. Drew had no idea how to handle this or even how he felt about it. On the one hand, he sort of thought what was going on between him and Kit wasn't these people's business. On the other, he couldn't quite shake the sense that he'd been caught out doing something he shouldn't, as if he'd ninjaed all the shards out the guild bank. There was also a nonzero chance he was about to get /gkicked for pissing off the main healer.

[Group][Morag]: Drew?
[Group][Orcarella]: sorry but this is pretty weird
[Group][Ialdir]: Yeah, I can see that
[Group][Ialdir]: And we know it's none of our business
[Group][Ialdir]: We're just worried about him
[Group][Morag]: He hasn't been online since last night
[Group][Morag]: He said he was fine when I texted but he's basically never missed a raid
[Group][Orcarella]: :(
[Group][Orcarella]: we kind of had a fight
[Group][Orcarella]: he said he needed some space
[Group][Morag]: Whoa. Must've been some fight
[Group][Orcarella]: i don't know. I'm still confused
[Group][Ialdir]: I'm guessing you don't want relationship advice from the old dude
[Group][Ialdir]: But Kit's pretty into you and he's scared of messing it up so he's probably a bit wary
[Group][Ialdir]: Might be reacting to things quite strongly
[Group][Ialdir]: I think you guys will be okay
[Group][Morag]: Also, he just tends to take things to heart
[Group][Ialdir]: That's a bit unfair, Tiff
[Group][Ialdir]: We're not all as tactless as you and Bjorn

```
[Group][Morag]: Omg, you're comparing me to
*Bjorn*
[Group][Orcarella]: okay
[Group][Orcarella]: thanks guys
[Group][Morag]: Just give it a couple of days
and say sorry
[Group][Morag]: Even if you're not sure what
you're saying sorry for
[Group][Ialdir]: Is this why I'm married and
you're single?
[Group][Orcarella]: i'll try
[Group][Orcarella]: nn guys
```

Drew logged out of *HoL*, wondering how much time counted as "space." Morag had told him to give it a couple of days. Did that mean from now? Or could he could backdate it to Sunday?

Then he saw the alert light was flashing on his phone and his heart jumped like an enthusiastic kobold. He snatched it up and was in quick sucession disappointed, then guilty at being disappointed, then annoyed at himself both for being disappointed and guilty at it. The message was from Sanee and read: *Yo – MK Tournament Round II. Our place after labs. Who's up in the air now, beyotch?* A second text had come in shortly afterwards: *You will be after I juggle combo you.*

Actually that did sound pretty fun. And like it would take his mind off Operation Give Kit His Space.

He sent back, *Dude, last time we played you couldn't even find the block button.*

The next morning, he woke up to *Blocking is for pussies.* And spent the rest of the day wrestling with water and Not Texting Kit.

"No elf?" was the the first inevitable question when Drew arrived at Sanee and Steff's.

Drew thought about telling them the whole story, but he didn't want another lecture about game addiction and the evils of leaving parties. "Not tonight."

Sanee scowled. "You realise this means I'm going to have to redo the roster."

"What roster? I thought we were just playing *Mortal Kombat*."

"You think," demanded Sanee, with an outrage that bordered on the genuine, "that I'd invite you to a tournament and not provide a tournament?"

Steff staggered in with a pinboard. It was covered in index cards, sorted into tiered match-ups. "It'll be fine, Squidge. We can remove Kit's name."

Sanee did not look entirely mollified. "It's the principle, and besides, it throws off the whole structure."

"No," said Drew, "what'll throw off the whole structure is me pwning all of your asses."

And, thankfully, that distracted Sanee long enough for them to actually start playing the game.

Drew had spent quite a large part of the morning rote-memorising combos, special moves, and fatalities, which meant he put in a creditable performance. He came out third in the rankings, having bested both Sanee and Steff, narrowly losing to Andy, and having his arse comphrensively handed to him by Tinuviel. Who turned out to be terrifyingly good at fighting games.

After her first couple of matches, they realised that the only way anyone else would stand a chance would be if they gave her some kind of penalty, which started out as banning her from playing Mileena, escalated quickly to requiring her to play a randomly selected character, and culminated in her having to play a charcter of her opponent's choice. Tinuviel accepted all of this with good grace, and still won virtually all of her games.

"I don't admit this often," said Sanee, awarding Tinuviel the grand prize of a red-iced and thus ostensibly blood-themed cupcake that Steff had apparently made specially, "but I am genuinely impressed and slightly afraid."

Tinuviel accepted her award gravely, peeled off the paper, and devoured it in two large bites. "Thank you, Sanee. I attribute my success to my supportive family, the voice talents of Karen Strassman, my repressed violent urges, and the fact that none of you would recognise a cancel or a breaker if you fell over it."

Everyone applauded.

Drew still missed Kit, but the evening had turned out to be exactly what he needed. On the way back to his room, he estimated that "a couple of days" could, if you squinted and tilted your head right, just about be said to have passed. So he took a deep breath and started composing a text. It took way longer than the word count really justified.

In the end, he had: *Sorry if I was a dick. I miss you. Can we talk?*

Kit got back to him the next morning, and they agreed to meet in Kit's favourite tearoom before the raid.

So there they were, in the very frilly tearoom, half-lost behind overloaded cake stands. In his anxiety, Drew had already eaten three triangular cucumber sandwiches and a macaron, and was now feeling awkward and clumsy on top of nervous. Kit, of course, looked like just the sort of boy you'd take to a tea shop—except, to Drew, he seemed a little washed out. Not quite his usual self.

"Um." Drew picked up a piece of Victoria sponge and hastily put it down again. "I am really sorry. I was worried and confused and overreacted."

Kit was silent for a while. Finally, he folded his hands on the tabletop and said, "I think it's the worried that upsets me most."

Drew had always been under the impression that worrying about someone showed you cared. "What? Why?"

"Well, I guess I've got used to people making me feel there's something wrong with how I live my life. But I wasn't expecting it from you. I thought you got me."

"Oh my God, I do get you. We have a thing . . . like, a real proper thing." Drew was starting to realise this was way more serious than he'd thought—and he still didn't entirely know why. "I just want you to spend more time with me than you do hanging out in a video game."

Kit blinked. His eyelashes looked a little damp. "But, Drew, we *met* in that video game."

"Yeah, but that doesn't mean it's okay to spend all our time in it."

"I don't understand where this is coming from. Why are you so obsessed with how much I play *HoL*? You've played it as much as I have."

Drew was trying to be calm and apologetic like Morag had said, but he was really struggling with the way Kit seemed to see him. He wasn't that sort of player and never had been. Yes, he'd taken the game seriously, but it had never been his default activity. He had lots of other stuff going on in his life, and he was a bit narked Kit couldn't recognise that.

"I really haven't, mate. I've got three alts, plus the one I rolled with you. Even when I was raiding hard-core with Anni, I was there to do the content. I've actually spent more time in *HoL* since I met you than I did when I was the MT for the number one raiding guild on the server."

"But didn't being MT for the number one raiding guild on the server make you miserable?" Kit pushed his hair exasperately out of his eyes. "Do you think maybe that the reason you've been spending more time in the game now than when you were with Anni is that you're, y'know, enjoying it more?"

Drew opened his mouth, intending to reply, but then realised he didn't really have one. He felt a little bit cheated, like Kit had put him in a position where he couldn't disagree, because he couldn't explain why he disagreed, and had now got him cornered by being right about something slightly different.

"Look, is this even about me?" Kit carefully moved the cake stand to one side so they could see each properly. "Are you genuinely worried about my gaming habits? Or are you unhappy with your own?"

"I'm really confused," said Drew, slightly plaintively.

Kit reached over and took his hand—and that was such a relief that Drew couldn't remember if he was supposed to be angry right now. "The thing is, Drew, it took me quite a long time to get comfortable with who I am. I spent the beginning of my first year trying to fit in with the university geek societies, but I never did. Whenever I told people I played *HoL*, they'd take the piss, and I kept getting this feeling that the only way they could feel okay with what they liked to do, was by looking down on what I liked to do." His lips turned up ruefully. "Some of them even played the game. It just wasn't socially acceptable to genuinely be into it. And I decided there's no point pretending you don't care about things you . . . do."

Everything Kit had said swirled around in Drew's brain looking for things to connect with.

"I care about you," he blurted. "And I also care about my friends. And I really want you to like them and I really want them to like you and everything's . . . sort of . . . bleurgh and . . . this is really important to me."

Kit's thumb stoked soothingly over the back of Drew's hand. "It's important to me too. But I feel that whatever I do, it could . . . take something away from me. I want to be with you and I want to be part of your life, but I want to be me too. But, then, if being me is the thing that messes us up, then . . . I don't know how to deal with that."

"I don't not want . . . I mean I don't want you not to . . . I like who you are. Can't we meet in the middle here?"

"Where's the middle?" Kit sounded kind of wary again.

"I don't know. Like, maybe could you spend a bit more time with me and my friends. And I won't bug you about the *HoL* thing."

As far as Drew was concerned, this cut right to the heart of the issue, and for a moment, he was a little bit impressed by his own maturity and relationship-fu.

Unfortunately, Kit didn't look much happier than he had before. For what seemed like a long time he didn't say anything, and then he sighed. "Well, um. I guess. Let's give that a go."

It was somehow a little delicate after that, but by the time they'd eaten the rest of the cakes and finished their tea, they were deep in discussion about the mysterious yellow orb they'd found in *Torment*, and things were almost back to normal. Almost, but not quite.

A couple of weeks slid by without further disaster. More by luck than by judgement, Drew seemed to have got his Kit/course/friends/*HoL*/pub balance about right. Which meant in practice that he only rarely felt under-Kitted or under-friended and, when he did, it was to about the same degree. Also Sanee had completely dropped the

Drew Is A Loser Gaming Addict thing and was only intermittently entertained by the fact he was dating a boy now.

Things were going well with *HoL* and the guild. Everyone was pretty excited for the next major content patch, which had just launched on the Public Test Realm. Back when he'd been running with Anni, they would have been over there, trying to get as familiar with the new fights as possible, but at the moment, Drew had too many other things to care about. And actually, it was weirdly fun to sort of wait and anticipate and know that they wouldn't be downing the last boss of the expansion within the first week. And then spending the next three to six months farming it and whinging about it.

They'd never actually discussed it, and Drew wasn't entirely sure it had been what he'd meant, but he and Kit had abandoned their medusas at level thirteen, freeing them up to see more of his friends, and to spend more time doing boyfriend things. They'd taken to wandering around the Botanic Gardens on sunny afternoons and mellow evenings, holding hands and geeking out. Sometimes they sat under Kit's favourite willow playing . . . well . . . it was still *Torment* because, seriously, that game was huge and full of words. At least, when they weren't getting distracted by each other. Which they were. A lot. Requiring a number of hasty retreats to Kit's room.

Drew was vaguely conscious that something had sort of changed. He thought he remembered Kit being . . . It was hard to explain, really. More open, somehow? Happier, almost? But it didn't seem like anything he could pin down, talk about, or fix. And, sometimes, Drew wondered if it was just his imagination.

True to his word, Kit was spending more time with Drew's friends. He was quiet, but quietly funny, and they liked that, and Drew was glad everyone seemed to be getting along. Kit still tended to be the first to leave things, but true to *his* word, Drew didn't make a big thing about it. Even though it still bugged him a bit.

It was fine. Really. It was basically fine.

Until Zombicide.

Maybe Drew was reading too much into stuff, but Sanee seemed to be making much more of an effort to give their regular Tuesday hangouts a clear structure. There'd been the *Mortal Kombat* Tournament and then an *Eye of Argon* Reading and then the Using

This Damn Fondue Pot Steff Won In A Raffle In Sixth Form evening, which had honestly put Drew off both cheese and chocolate, at least for the foreseeable future. He felt like a dick, because this had sort of been his fault, but he was getting structured-activity fatigue. He was starting to miss the days of just sitting around chilling, even if what they'd mostly been doing while they were chilling was trying to work out what structured activity they'd do next.

This time it was Games Night of the Living Dead. The plan was to drag out all of the zombie-themed board games from Sanee and Steff's collection. It turned out there were quite a lot of them, especially if you included every game that had a spurious zombie expansion. Drew wore his Plants Versus Zombies T-shirt for the occasion, which Kit had found sufficiently adorable that he wanted to take it off again, and Drew hadn't really objected, so they'd wound up being kind of late.

Everyone was already settled, helping themselves to Steff's brain-cakes and immersed in a warm-up hand of Munchkin Zombies. Drew felt weirdly heart-warmed that of all the quick, opening games they could have picked to start the evening, they seemed to have deliberatedly chosen the one he'd be least upset at having missed. They moved on to Give Me the Brain, which was a long-standing favourite. Kit took to it immediately—it made him laugh so much he spent nearly the whole game behind his hand, emerging every now and then to declare, in a surprisingly convincing zombie voice, that he required the brain because he had to count the meat.

From there, they got serious and, after a brief debate, chose Zombicide over Dead of Winter as their main game of the evening. It would have been Drew's preference anyway because he was in more of a "kill loads of zombies" mood than "get killed by zombies while looking for petrol in an abandoned school" mood, but as it turned out, Dead of Winter wouldn't have taken six players anyway.

Kit was on his phone while they were unboxing and setting up, which made Drew a bit uncomfortable because it wasn't great board game etiquette. But at the same time, they didn't really need him, so it seemed unfair to say anything. Finally they were good to go. Sanee gave a quick rules recap—which Kit at least paid attention to—and dealt out characters and equipment at random.

Drew was less than thrilled to realise that not only was he playing the boring, beardy survivalist whose only ability was that he was slightly better at searching rooms than the rest of the characters, but that his starting gear consisted of two frying pans that he wasn't even allowed to dual wield. He was trying to be a good sport about it, because there was nothing worse than playing a board game with somebody who'd decided they were screwed from the beginning, but he kind of felt like he was screwed from the beginning. Everybody else would be running around racking up sweet kills with their fire axes and their bonus moves, and he'd be getting further and further behind, desperately searching a toilet for bags of rice.

"Okay, team." Sanee stood up and started pointing at the board, like a general in an old war movie. "Our plucky band of survivors starts *here*. Our objective is to get someone into the bunker *here* and clear it of zombies. Sounds simple enough, but we can't open the door until we've taken the objective *here*, but we can't get to *that* until we've taken the other objective *here*. Obviously zombies will be spawning *here*, *here*, *here*, and *here*. But there's no need to panic. If we just stick together, gear up early, and take it slowly and carefully, we should be fine."

They were not fine.

They had a bad spawn in the first building, and Drew got bitten by a zombie, which cost him one of his frying pans. As predicted, everyone else was getting cool shit and he just ... wasn't. His inventory was filling up with bottled water that was useless in this scenario, extra ammo for the guns he didn't have, and half the components of a Molotov cocktail.

And to top it all off, Kit was still on his phone. He had it on his lap and was doing his best to be discreet, but in a lot of ways that made it worse. Everyone had clearly noticed and was clearly being too polite to say anything. Drew kept having to nudge him when it was his turn and remind him of the rules, like for example not gunning down your allies by accident. Worse still, despite his constant distraction, Kit was having a much better game than Drew was. He'd wound up with a chainsaw in one hand and a scoped sniper rifle in the other, and had personally taken out more zombies than anyone else. He was living the Zombicide dream and didn't even seem to care.

Then, when they weren't even halfway through the scenario, Drew got killed. He'd been desperately ransacking a police car, looking for any weapon better than a crowbar, when he'd found a zombie in the boot. He'd spent his last action trying to kill it, failed, and promptly had his face chewed off.

An awkward silence fell over the table.

"And that," said Sanee finally, "is why you shouldn't search when you're playing last in the round."

Drew sighed. "Dude, I didn't have a weapon, searching is my only skill, and frankly, I was kind of dead weight anyway."

"It's a swingy game. All you need is one shotgun and you're back."

"Yes, which is why I was searching the police car. And why I am now dead."

"Shall we stop?" asked Steff, before the argument could build any further. "It seems a bit unfair for Drew to have to sit out."

He really didn't want that to happen. The only thing more depressing than getting knocked out of a game early was feeling like you'd wrecked everything for everybody. "No, it's fine. You guys carry on."

At that moment, Kit looked from the text message he was blatantly sending. "You can take my character, if you like. I don't mind."

Drew didn't want to be an arsehole, but it kind of happened anyway. "I can tell you don't mind. You've been on your phone for the whole *fucking* game."

Everything went silent.

"I'm sorry." Kit gazed at him, wide-eyed. "Something came up in guild."

There was a dull roaring in Drew's brain. "Fuck the guild. I'm sick of the fucking guild. You're supposed to be out, here, with me and my friends. But if you seriously want to be in an imaginary dungeon full of pretend monsters with randoms off the internet, then, y'know what? Go do that."

Somehow it got even more silent.

Kit got up, tucked his phone into his breast pocket, and left the room. The door closed with a *click* behind him.

For a little while, nobody moved, and then Sanee began packing up Zombicide. There was an almost funereal air about it, as if he was laying to rest a good game, taken from us too soon.

"Are you going to go after him?" asked Steff.

Drew hadn't thought that far ahead. To be honest, he hadn't really known what was going to come out of his mouth. And he was in this confused, stuck space where he felt stupid for having made a massive scene, but was sure he'd feel even more stupid if he backed down now. "He was the one being the antisocial dickhead, not me."

"I'm with you, mate." Sanee glanced up from the reboxing. "You just don't come to a thing, then not be at the thing."

Tinuviel was busy dividing the zombies up by type so they could go into their separate bags. "I think," she said, "that you may be failing to account for the essentially arbitrary and constructed nature of social conventions, and for their variability between seemingly similar groups."

Drew was so not in the mood for this.

"If someone gave me a quid everytime you said *arbitrary*, *convention*, or *constructed*, I would own all the expansions for this game by now, and there are a shitload." Apparently neither was Sanee.

She blinked. "I just meant that maybe he didn't know how rude you'd think he was being."

Steff squeezed behind Sanee's chair and wrapped her arms around him. "He was definitely being a bit weird, but you shouldn't just let him walk out like that. You know the rule, Squidge, never go to bed angry."

There was a thoughtful moment. Then Sanee shamelessly one-eightied.

"She's right." He turned his head and nuzzle-nibbled the inside of Steff's elbow. "That's how we do it, and look at us. If I don't deal with stuff when it comes up, it just bugs me forever."

Steff nodded. "It's true. He got superangry at one *xkcd* strip and then never read it again."

"Fine." Drew pushed away from the table. "I'll go after him. Whatever."

Andy, who had been keeping his head firmly down since zombiegate, risked a comment. "Um, look. I'm not the biggest relationship expert here, but I kind of think 'fine, whatever' isn't the best strategy for making up with someone."

"Okay." Drew made a show of sitting down again. "I'll stay. Just make up your minds."

Tinuviel put away the last of the fast zombies. "Andrew, stop projecting. It's terribly clichéd. Either go after your boyfriend because that's what you want to do. Or stay. Because *that's* what you want to do. But there's no point getting angry with us because we didn't cause the situation and we can't fix it."

Drew opened his mouth and closed it again. Pointless or not, he still felt pretty angry. And he kind of knew it wasn't fair but . . . that wasn't how anger worked. It just happened. And was there. He fumed helplessly for a minute or two. And, very gradually, managed to dig through everything until he realised that he was mostly upset at his friends because he'd been relying on them to tell him what to do. In fact, it wasn't even that. He wanted them to tell him to go after Kit so he could do it without it turning into this big public statement of what a dick he'd been.

Even if Kit had been a dick first.

"So I'm going to, um . . . Sorry." He got up again, grabbed his coat, and went after Kit.

He told himself he wasn't going to run. Honestly, he'd probably missed the guy anyway, so he'd just wind up looking stupid. Sort of like when you ran to catch a bus and it pulled away just as you got to it, leaving you breathless on the kerb with everybody staring.

Aaaaaand he was running.

Shit. Shitshitshit.

He caught up to Kit at the bus stop—where, ironically, there was no bus, pulling away or otherwise. Just Kit. Still on his mobile.

Drew was about thirty-percent mindlessly angry, thirty-percent sorry, and forty-percent really not sure what the hell was going on. Now he was here, now they were both here, he realised he didn't have a clue what to say. In the end he went with, "Uh, hi."

Kit looked up. They might have both been there in practice, but he seemed a million miles away. "I'm kind of in the middle of something here."

And, with that, he went back to texting.

Drew was now seventy-percent mindlessly angry and about two-percent sorry and fuck knew about the rest. "For fuck's sake, Kit.

Do you even want a boyfriend and friends? Or do you want to sit alone in your room playing *HoL* for the rest of your life?"

"Right now, I just want you to leave me alone." Kit's thumbs skimmed ceaselessly across the gently glowing surface of his smartphone. "And I've got friends."

Drew literally threw his hands in the air in frustration. "Holy crap, for the last time, they are not your friends. They are just people you play a video game with. And when you stop playing that game, or if anything happens that they don't want to deal with, you will never hear from them again."

He'd started strong but, for some reason, all his anger was draining. And now he was just sad. Really fucking sad. "I raided with Annihilation three times a week for three years and the moment I stopped being what they needed me to be, that was it. I haven't had so much as a whisper from any of those . . . from any of them."

"I'm sorry that happened to you, and I'm sorry it's made you so upset." Kit didn't sound all that sorry, and as Drew was getting sadder, he seemed to be getting colder. "But you do realise the reason it happened is that everyone in Anni thinks about *HoL* the same way you do? That the game isn't *real*, that the people aren't *real*. That you have no obligations and nothing to offer each other except your DPS and your raid buffs."

"That's . . . I mean . . . I . . ." Nope. Not happening. There were thoughts and feelings and stuff, and Drew had no idea what any of them were.

"And what I really don't get is how you can have gone through that and experienced firsthand how shitty it is and still be so keen for me to do the exact same thing to other people. People, by the way, who have actually been there for me when I've needed them. Been there for me in a way that nobody else ever has."

"Okay but . . ." Drew rallied slightly. He wasn't sure how he'd got quite so swept off course, but he was sure he had genuine grievance. Somewhere. "That's no excuse for blanking our mates when we've gone round their house for the evening."

"Drew, I've known them a month. I like them, but they're *your* mates, not *our* mates. I didn't mean to be rude, but I told you something came up."

"What? What came up that was so important that you had to wreck everybody's evening?"

"You remember that poet Tiff was seeing? They got drunk and hooked up last week and now there's a performance poetry thing she's done all over Facebook, and it's all about Tiff, and it's really horrible, and she's really upset about it, and she needed someone to talk to, and Jacob's got kids, and if I'd found out about it earlier I'd have cancelled, but we were already at Sanee and Steff's, and frankly, you've made me so fucking self-conscious about my friends that I didn't feel I could tell you about it."

Drew hit one-hundred-percent sadness, crushed under this horrible mess of loss and failure. The only thing worse than sucking at something was sucking at something you thought you were okay at. And up until now, he'd thought he was an okay boyfriend. "You know you can tell me anything," he mumbled.

"No, I really can't." Kit drew in a shuddery breath, and Drew realised he was close to tears. "I loved being with you and some of the time you made me feel amazing and cared for and sexy and wanted. But you also made me feel wrong and broken and like I was letting you down."

Drew stared at him in horror. "I don't think that. I've never thought that."

"It doesn't matter. Because you acted like you did. You got so hung up on *HoL*, and it was like you wanted to replace my friends with your friends. Like you were doing me a favour. But you just don't get it. Jacob and Tiff and even Bjorn have been my best friends since I was fifteen. When I met them—even if it was just in a game—I stopped being lonely. I stopped feeling like I didn't fit anywhere. It was when I first realised it was okay to just be me and people would like me for it."

"I like you too," put in Drew pitifully.

"I know, and when I first met you, it was like the final piece of the puzzle. Like there was this great guy who got me and didn't want me to be different. Except then you did." Kit pushed a lock of hair out of his eyes. It glinted gold in the light from the bus stop. "And the worst of it is, I liked you so much that I tried to *be* different."

Drew's sadness had decreased by about ten percent, but only to make way for crippling fear. "I'm sorry, I'm really sorry. I didn't mean . . . like, any of this. Can we talk about or fix it or—"

The bus turned the corner and rumbled to a stop in front of them, all cartoon bright and empty. Drew glared at it as if he could force it away again with the power of his mind.

"Please, Kit?"

He shook his head. "I'm done being with somebody who makes me feel bad about myself." He climbed the steps and swiped his bus pass.

He didn't hesitate. Didn't even look back.

The doors closed, and the bus pulled slowly away.

Drew wasn't sure what to do or where to go or even where to look, but he was pretty sure he'd just been dumped at a bus stop. He started walking and, on a kind of autopilot, found himself back at Sanee and Steff's. After a moment of staring blankly, he rang the bell and Sanee buzzed him up.

The evening had clearly been legit ruined. Andy and Tinuviel had left, Steff had gone to bed, and Sanee was in the middle of washing up when Drew let himself in.

"So, we're thinking of getting T.I.M.E. Stories," said Sanee, scrubbing away at a baking tray. "Except the whole only-play-it-once thing feels like it's taking the piss."

Drew wedged himself into the doorway of the tiny kitchen and burst into tears.

There was something a bit panicked about the rigid set of Sanee's back, but he turned round and clumsily tugged Drew into a soapy hug, thumping him slightly aggressively between the shoulder blades in the universal signal for *I'm hugging you but that doesn't make me gay.* "Aww, mate."

Drew squeezed and sniffed and cried some more. And, after a moment or two, Sanee helped him into a chair, rolled off the Marigolds, and sat down opposite.

"Aww, mate," he tried again.

Drew wiped his eyes. "I really fucked that up."

"Honestly, it could have gone better. But couples fight. It's what they do."

"This was way worse than a fight. I've been a really shitty boyfriend, and now Kit thinks I want him to be someone else."

"That's bollocks. You're obviously totally into him. I mean, dude, you went gay for the guy."

"I didn't go—" Drew put his head in his hands. "Look, that's epically not the point."

"Sorry. I just meant you look like quite a good boyfriend to me."

"Yeah, that was kind of the problem. I was so focused on what you guys would think—about me and him and fucking *HoL*—that I totally ignored what Kit wanted."

"What's *HoL* got to do with anything?"

Drew gave him a genuinely dumbfounded look. "What . . . the . . . actual . . . hell? You've been taking the piss out of me for playing this game since I met you. You told me that you thought we were at risk of getting literally addicted to it. And that Kit's behaviour was abnormal and unacceptable."

"Whoa, whoa." Sanee held up his hands. "Don't put this on me. I was just winding you up. It's what mates do."

"Mates also care about what their mates think. And it didn't sound like you were winding me up. It sounded like you meant every word of it."

"I was just, like, saying stuff. Everybody takes the piss out of *HoL*. Even people who play *HoL* take the piss out of *HoL*."

"Well, maybe we shouldn't. Maybe we should just accept that we like what we like."

"I never said not to like it." Sanee sounded faintly offended. "And if I'd known you were really bothered, I would've left it alone."

"Why would I not be bothered by you constantly ripping the shit out of something I really enjoy doing?"

"Drew, I'm a skinny Asian dude who's had one girlfriend in his entire life. I have all of two friends. You play actual sports. You can talk to girls and, as it turns out, boys. Being a nerd is basically optional for you. So why the hell would you be bothered by anything I say about anything?"

"Because you're my best mate, you colossal douche. Of course I care what you think about stuff."

There was a long, mutually confused silence. Sanee was the first to break it.

"You'd better not be angling for another hug."

Drew was too busy putting his brain back together for the thirteenth time that evening. There were only so many glimpses into other people's worlds a guy could take.

"You do realise," he said slowly, "that while you may technically have only had one girlfriend, you and Steff totally win at the relationship thing. You're blatantly the happiest people I know. And this two-friends thing is crap because none of us would be hanging out together if it wasn't for you. Also you're annoyingly smart and you'll probably be running EA in like five years' time."

"Fuck you, I would never work for EA." Sanee grinned. "Also, you're right. I'm way cooler than you."

Drew gave him a slightly feeble smile.

"So anyway—" Sanee made an awkward gesture "—now we've established which of us is best, and that it's definitely me, what are you going to do about, y'know, Kit and stuff?"

"I dunno. I thought I might just sit here for a bit. And then go sit at home. And then maybe never speak to another human being ever again."

"You could do that. Or we could try to fix it."

"I tried. I said I was sorry, I said I'd do better. And he got on a bus anyway."

Sanee sat forward excitedly in his chair. "No, no, no, dude, you have to understand. Sometimes chicks . . . and, uh, also probably dudes—"

"You know, you could just say *people.*"

"Dispensing wisdom here. Sometimes when you've really upset *a person*, you have to wait a bit so when you say sorry, they'll believe you. Otherwise it's like you're just saying it to get them to calm down and do what you want."

"So let me get this straight. Your plan is do nothing. Then do the same thing again and hope it goes better. Wow, I can't believe I didn't think of that."

Sanee shrugged. "Well, you could go stand outside his window with a boom box if you like, but I'm pretty sure romance has moved on since the eighties."

"So I should stand outside his window streaming Spotify on my phone?"

"Honestly, mate, I think that'd just annoy him."

"No offence, but you are really bad at this."

"Look, all I'm saying is that you need to find a way to apologise to him that will show him you're actually serious. Basically, you should do something that shows him you don't think what he thinks you think. Whatever that is."

To Drew's surprise, for what felt like the first time that evening, something made sense. He didn't quite know exactly what he was going to do, but he knew how to start. "Thanks."

"No problem. Should I make up the futon?"

And Drew nodded, not quite wanting to be alone in his room with his thoughts and his laptop.

CHAPTER 12

The next day he woke up with a slightly bad back from the futon, and a plan he'd thrashed out in the small hours of the morning. He'd been thinking a lot about what Sanee had said and what Kit had said, and his time with Anni and his time with SCDD, and he'd come to the conclusion that he'd spent far too long worrying about stuff that was basically meaningless. He'd thought he left Anni because he didn't want to be the sort of person who got angry about a virtual axe in a video game, but actually he'd left Anni because he'd finally realised that nobody there cared about anybody else.

And he thought he'd been worried that Kit spent so much time in *HoL* because he wasn't happy, when really he'd been worrying about—what exactly? What his mates would say? What his old guildies would have thought? The judgement of an anonymous cloud of strangers he vaguely thought of as "everyone." And wasn't that the stupidest thing of all? He'd been so down on Kit for caring about people he rarely met in person, but Drew'd spent all this time obsessing about the opinions of people he hadn't met at all and who probably didn't even exist.

When you got right down to it, killing imaginary pigs with a bloke who lived on a different continent was no worse or sillier a way to spend your evenings than throwing a piece of plastic around with a bloke who lived down the corridor. The *really* silly thing was that he'd ever believed there was a difference. As long as you cared about what you were doing and who you were doing it with, then it didn't matter if you were in a pub or your living room or on a virtual rock in an imaginary kingdom in a video game.

And now he just had to show Kit he'd finally got it. But he couldn't do that without help. Unfortunately, the people best placed to do that probably had good reason to believe he was an irredeemable prick right now. Nevertheless, he used Sanee's wi-fi to log on to the guild forums and send a PM to Jacob. He would have asked Tiff as well, but given what Kit had told him last night, he really didn't think she needed to be bothered with his problems right now.

Then he folded up the futon, gathered his belongings, and hurried back to his room. He took a quick shower and pulled on his serious gaming tartans, before turning on his computer. Technically, he should have been at a lecture, but frankly he was in no fit state to sit through a long talk on visual design.

This was more important than his degree. This was more important than pretty much anything.

Jacob had already messaged him back with some ideas and promised to catch him before the raid to help with Operation Say Sorry For Being A Dick. Inspired by Jacob's unending enthusiasm for obscure *HoL* trivia and the fact he hadn't said anything about the plan being pointless, terrible, or doomed to fail, Drew logged into *HoL*.

What with it being before lunchtime on a weekday, the guild was basically dead. Mordant seemed to be around doing whatever it was he did when he wasn't raiding, and there were a couple of others Drew didn't really know that well. He said hi for the sake of politeness and hit the auction house, where he picked up a [Delightful Red Bouquet] for slightly more in-game gold than he was really comfortable spending on something he would have been unable to avoid acquiring for free during the Valentine's event. He lost about an hour browsing for other cool stuff Kit might like, but it was all either far too common or far too expensive. He did, however, grab some [Very Romantic Fireworks] and a bottle of [Overpriced Elvish Wine] and stashed them in his inventory along with the [Elegant Tuxedo] Kit had tailored for him.

Then he jumped on an airship and flew between continents to the mighty underground city of Koboldeep. While he was hunched in the prow, waiting for the load screen to pop up, he experienced an unexpected rush of affection for this strange, invented, and occasionally hard to navigate world he shared with so many people he'd never meet.

The long-awaited loading screen appeared and flashed away again and the airship juddered to a halt at the top of a rickety tower outside of the kobold capital.

You have discovered Koboldeep.

Jacob had pointed him at this place. Apparently an obscure quest in one of the game's least popular dungeons would supply him with a vital component for any big romantic gesture. He horsed-up and galloped through the twisty, steampunk-inspired streets of Koboldeep until he found the swirly portal entrance to Koboldeep Deeps. As far as he could tell, the kobolds used to be slaves to the orcs, and they'd worked in this big mine, but they'd used their technological know-how to build giant warbots so they could fight back. And now the robots had gone nuts and they needed level thirty-four to thirty-eight adventurers to sort them out. Being level ninety and the best-geared tank on the server, Orcarella basically flattened in there.

It was still a bit of a pain to navigate because it was from vanilla, when they'd designed dungeons to feel like places that might actually exist instead of places it might actually be fun to visit in a video game. As Ella jogged through the corridors, trailing about thirty malfunctioning death bots, none of them capable of harming her, Drew realised he'd got used to playing in company. Kit would have wanted to stop and look at all the giant wheels and steam vents, and Jacob would probably have known all the lore ever, although Drew suspected the lore for this place wasn't much more than "there were some robots, they went evil."

Following Jacob's instruction, he ducked down an easy-to-miss side tunnel, where he found a small, cowering kobold called Sir Yips-a-Lot, who gave him a quest called I Like Big Bots And I Cannot Lie. It involved fighting an endless conveyer belt of giant warbots, which would have been a massive pain to do at level, but which Ella handled with little more than Circles of Corruption and patience. Eventually Drew had harvested the required number of

[Intact Warbot Crankshafts] and returned to Sir Yips-a-Lot for his reward.

He couldn't be bothered to actually finish Koboldeep Deeps, so he activated his bindstone and bamfed back to the City of Stars. From there, he jogged down to the docks, where he recognised the high elf that his medusa had snubbed. There was another ship farther along, which Drew remembered from back when he first started playing. It was a huge longship crewed by angry-looking teddy bears and it took players to what, a few years ago, had been the brand-new continent of Nifelbard, home of the Asbjorn and the Cult of the World Serpent. He hopped aboard and waited for it to depart.

Unlike the journey from Minea, this one was fully animated, at least for a little while. He had just enough time to grab a Dr Pepper as the old world faded into the far clipping plane. Drew was slightly surprised by how nostalgic he was as he rocked up on the shores of Ursa's Spear. Arriving in that zone after the expansion launched had been the first time he'd felt like he was playing the game everyone else was playing, not ahead of the curve yet, but definitely not behind it either.

It hadn't aged so well, but Drew was weirdly comforted by the rough cliffs, the snow, and the northern (or he supposed technically southern, if he remembered the world map right) lights. He was here for a quest chain that had been legendary back in the day and was only accessible if you'd achieved Exalted reputation with the local population of crazy warrior bears. Drew had only ever done rep grinds that led to gear he needed for raiding, and this happened to have been one of them. He was totally loved by violent teddies, and that meant he could purchase an [Invitaton To The Althing] which took place in the Frostharrow Woods, and eventually, when he had completed several bizarre quests—including digging through bear droppings, disguising himself as a bear, and stealing sandwiches off other bears—culminated in the hard-won reward of an [Enchanted Picnic Basket].

By the time Drew had accomplished this, he was exhausted and had a slight headache, but had dropped into that kind of Zen space of farming and grinding. It was also late enough that Ialdir had come online.

Ialdir has invited you to join a group: y/n
Ialdir is now group leader.
Heurodis has joined the group.
[Group][Heurodis]: whats this about jacob?
[Group][Heurodis]: hello drew
[Group][Orcarella]: hi
[Group][Ialdir]: Much as it pains me to say it
[Group][Ialdir]: Help us Bjorni-Wan-Kenobi
[Group][Ialdir]: You're our only hope
[Group][Heurodis]: what do you need?
[Group][Heurodis]: uncle bjorn is here
[Group][Ialdir]: Do you still have the
[Bejewelled Music Box] for MC?
[Group][Ialdir]: I junked mine years ago
[Group][Ialdir]: Bank space crisis
[Group][Heurodis]: of course i have
[Group][Heurodis]: ive been playing since
vanilla
[Group][Ialdir]: I had no idea
[Group][Ialdir]: You never mention it
[Group][Heurodis]: so why do you want to get
your hands on my box
[Group][Orcarella]: i'm trying to get the
ruby golem thing
[Group][Orcarella]: i want to craft it for
Kit
[Group][Orcarella]: to say sorry for being a
dick
[Group][Heurodis]: you must have been
substantially cocklike drew
[Group][Heurodis]: if you have to go to the
second-worst raid in vanilla
[Group][Heurodis]: to get the recipe for the
most needlessly inaccessible vanity pet in
the entire game
[Group][Orcarella]: yeah kinda :(
[Group][Ialdir]: Say it with [Diminutive Ruby
Golem]s

```
[Group][Heurodis]: okay im in
[Group][Heurodis]: lets make this fast
[Group][Heurodis]: i hoped id never have to
set foot in that place again
```
Your group has been converted to a raid.
```
[Raid][Orcarella]: i thought vanilla raids
were best
[Raid][Orcarella]: i thought they didn't make
them like that any more
[Raid][Heurodis]: are you cheeking your
elders andrew
[Raid][Heurodis]: your elders who are doing
you a favour
[Raid][Heurodis]: also i never said vanilla
raids were better
[Raid][Heurodis]: i just said they were
harder
[Raid][Heurodis]: and that we are better
players because we beat them
[Raid][Heurodis]: you scrubs with your "fun"
[Raid][Heurodis]: and your "interesting
mechanics"
[Raid][Heurodis]: back in my day a raid was
40 people
[Raid][Heurodis]: 32 of whom you did not like
[Raid][Heurodis]: 28 of whom would disconnect
immediately
[Raid][Heurodis]: and 6 of whom would die the
moment they stepped into the instance
[Raid][Heurodis]: b/c they had not farmed a
full set of fire resist gear
[Raid][Heurodis]: as they were told
[Raid][Heurodis]: many times
```

By the time Bjorn had finished ranting, they'd basically arrived. Magmarion's Caverns were located in an abandoned dwarf fortress up in the mountains near the human capital of Whitepeak. Drew had vague memories of questing in the area when his human myrmidon had been around level forty-three. He'd wandered down the wrong tunnel and been instantly splabbered by a level sixty elite dragonspawn. This time he just rolled right over four of them on his way through the instance portal.

Ella appeared between two shattered statues of what Drew guessed were probably dead dwarven kings.

```
[Raid][Ialdir]: Oh come on
[Raid][Ialdir]: This place isn't so bad
[Raid][Ialdir]: If every raid hadn't had a
dragon at the end it might even have been
cool
[Raid][Heurodis]: perhaps
[Raid][Heurodis]: but they did
[Raid][Heurodis]: and theres only so much
stay away from the breath and the tail you
can take
[Raid][Heurodis]: and all the other bosses
are just guys with swords
[Raid][Ialdir]: Yes the encounters are a bit
dull
[Raid][Ialdir]: but the lore is actually
really good
[Raid][Heurodis]: you just like it because
its about a soppy love story
[Raid][Heurodis]: that ends in a bloody
massacre
[Raid][Heurodis]: actually
[Raid][Heurodis]: having put it like that
[Raid][Heurodis]: I agree it is pretty
awesome
```

They carried on bickering as the three of them descended through the ruined halls of what Jacob explained used to be the kingdom of Karad-az-Karaz. There were about twelve bosses in the whole instance, most of which were, in fact, guys with swords or—this being a dwarf-themed dungeon—axes. The closest they got to a highlight was the confrontation with the ghosts of Imhear and Iriel, the doomed lovers who had apparently somehow got this place destroyed by dragons and gone mad with grief and guilt in the intervening centuries. Magmarion himself was basically a pushover. He was a huge red dragon who they found sprawled upon an enormous pile of gemstones and duly pwned.

Heurodis jumped onto the top of the treasure pile and activated the [Bejewelled Music Box] which caused a secret door to slide open at the back of the chamber. Inside was a grumpy dwarf called Cormag the Gemcrafter who summoned large sparkly golems, each of which spread what in the day would have been a devastating raid-wide debuff. As it was, they just obliterated him, and Drew picked through his corpse for [Recipe: Diminutive Ruby Golem].

```
[Raid][Orcarella]: thanks guys
[Raid][Ialdir]: no problem
[Raid][Heurodis]: id say any time but
[Raid][Heurodis]: NEVER BRING ME BACK HERE
AGAIN
[Guild][Morag]: Raid starting in fifteen
[Guild][Morag]: Get your arses where they
should be
[Raid][Ialdir]: Good luck :)
```
The raid has been disbanded.

Drew had been in no state to sign up for that week's jaunt to CoT, and a quick check of the guild calendar showed Kit hadn't either. And, in fact, Solace wasn't even online. Hadn't been for a couple of days. Which made Drew feel sad and slightly achey.

He thought about texting him and suggesting they meet in *HoL*, but that just seemed pushy. And sort of like cheating.

So instead he wandered the corridors of Magmarion's Caverns, picking up the crafting mats he needed. And then, when he'd gathered two [Shard of Living Flame]s, six [Flawless Ruby]s, and a [Vial of Magmarion's Blood], he stood by a bit of crumbled pillar and made a [Diminutive Ruby Golem].

He activated his bindstone, but halfway through the cast, he realised he was actually closer to Alarion here than he would be in the City of Stars. So he walked out of the instance the old-fashioned way, hopped on the closest thing he had to a white steed, which unfortunately turned out to be a [Malodorous Mountain Goat], and rode north.

Kit still hadn't logged in by the time he got to Alarion, so he changed into his tux, swapped [The Inexorable Axe] for a [Delightful Red Bouquet], got back on his goat, and waited.

He waited for three hours.

He drank an unwise amount of Dr Pepper and sent the occasional encouraging message to the raid.

Finally...

Solace has come online.

An elf in a pretty dress and a battered hat faded slowly into existence in front of Ella.

```
To [Solace]: please don't /ignore me
To [Solace]: im really really sorry
[Guild][Ialdir]: hey Kit :)
[Guild][Morag]: hi raiding
[Guild][Prospero]: hi
[Guild][Caius]: hello
[Guild][Solace]: Hi guys :)
[Guild][Solace]: How's CoT?
[Guild][Dave]: were on vilicus
To [Solace]: I get it now
To [Solace]: I honestly get it
[Guild][Dave]: im ded
[Guild][Dave]: nobody stacked on me :(
To [Solace]: I want to be with you
To [Solace]: In HoL
To [Solace]: And in your room
To [Solace]: And in Pizza Express
To [Solace]: And like everywhere
```

Drew was getting kind of desperate, so he opened up his inventory and clicked the quest reward he'd got from Sir Yips-a-Lot. Ella's goat vanished and she lifted an oblong clockwork . . . thing over her head. Tinny, obnoxious music started playing, and two tiny kobolds spawned next to her, twitching and gyrating in time to the beat.

Honestly, it was less romantic than Drew had hoped it would be.

It was more sort of . . . stupid.

```
[Solace] whispers: Is that a [Kobold-Together
Boombox]?
To [Solace]: yeah
To [Solace]: its from a movie or something
To [Solace]: like not the kobolds
To [Solace]: just the i'm really sorry here's
me with a boombox thing
To [Solace]: i've also got
```

Hoping it would be slightly less rubbish, Drew clicked on the [Enchanted Picnic Basket]. A sweet little tartan blanket appeared, with a stripy umbrella, a rainbow over the top, and a bemused-looking bear sitting slightly to one side.

```
[Solace] whispers: Drew this is all really
[Solace] whispers: something
[Solace] whispers: really sweet
[Solace] whispers: But I'm still kind of
messed up
To [Solace]: I know
To [Solace]: I didnt think i'd do all this
and you'd be like
To [Solace]: yes everythings okay now
To [Solace]: i'll totally take you back
To [Solace]: I just really wanted to show you
To [Solace]: that I'm here
To [Solace]: and these are your friends so I
want them to be my friends
To [Solace]: and when this is where you are
```

```
To [Solace]: its where I want to be too
[Solace] whispers: Really?
[Solace] whispers: You really mean that?
To [Solace]: yes
[Solace] whispers: And you're not going to
turn round in two weeks and say you think
I've got a problem
[Solace] whispers: And you need to fix me
To [Solace]: no
To [Solace]: I was the one with the problem
To [Solace]: I promise i'll never make you
feel that way again
To [Solace]: i think your great
To [Solace]: and I love being with you
To [Solace]: and i dont want you to change
anything
To [Solace]: for me or anyone
```

Drew was typing in a frenzy and he had no idea what Kit was thinking at the other end. It was honestly terrifying. But he couldn't stop.

```
To [Solace]: i kind of got you something
```

Slightly awkwardly, he right-clicked Solace's avatar and opened up a trade window. He dragged over the [Diminutive Ruby Golem] and selected "offer." There was a heart-stopping moment when he thought Kit might not accept, but then the trade went through.

You have lost [Diminutive Ruby Golem]
```
[Solace] whispers: Where did you get that?
To [Solace]: made it
To [Solace]: jacob and bjorn took me to MC
for the recipe
[Solace] whispers: Seriously?
[Solace] whispers: You did that for me?
To [Solace]: i remember you said you wanted
one
```

```
[Solace] whispers: I'm having a magnificient
grounds at Pemberley moment
To [Solace]: ???
[Solace] whispers: Just I'll feel totally
mercenary if I forgive you now
To [Solace]: omg give it back then
[Solace] whispers: Can't. Used it :)
```
**Solace has earned the achievement: Heavy
Petting.**
```
[Guild][Ialdir]: Grats
[Guild][Caius]: Yay
[Guild][Morag]: Grats
[Guild][Mordant]: gz
[Guild][Dave]: gz dude
[Guild][Dave]: ded again
```

Something tiny, red, and sparkling had started dancing at Solace's
feet.

```
[Solace] whispers: He's so cute
To [Solace]: So am i forgiven?
[Solace] whispers: For a [Diminutive Ruby
Golem] anything
[Solace] whispers: Well. Sort of.
[Solace] whispers: I mean I've been really
upset
[Solace] whispers: But I've really missed you
[Solace] whispers: And this was super weird
but
[Solace] whispers: I really liked it
[Solace] whispers: You're very sweet
sometimes
To [Solace]: i'm trying to balance out all
the times i was a total dickhead
To [Solace]: i know i'm asking you to keep
trusting me
```

To [Solace]: when you've already had to trust
me like loads
To [Solace]: like us meeting in the game
To [Solace]: when i thought you were a girl
To [Solace]: and then wanting to give it a go
anyway
To [Solace]: even though i've never had a
boyfriend
To [Solace]: and all that stuff
To [Solace]: and you've been great and i've
just sucked
[Solace] whispers: Drew, that's not true
[Solace] whispers: You've never messed me
around about anything else and I could have
been more honest about the . . .
[Solace] whispers: Not a girl thing.
[Solace] whispers: I just really thought that
was going to be the thing
[Solace] whispers: And I was so happy when it
wasn't
[Solace] whispers: And that we just worked
[Solace] whispers: And that you liked me
[Solace] whispers: In, y'know, all the ways
[Solace] whispers: And it wasn't weird
To [Solace]: i do like you
To [Solace]: in all the ways
[Solace] whispers: So I was just really
thrown when suddenly HoL was this massive
thing
[Solace] whispers: And if it had been about
me being a boy I'd have understood because
you can't change that stuff
[Solace] whispers: But it was like you were
suddenly looking down on me for all the
choices I've made about being me
[Solace] whispers: And that was really scary

```
[Solace] whispers: Because if the boy who
really likes me thinks I'm a loser
[Solace] whispers: Then maybe I am
To [Solace]: i don't think you're a loser
To [Solace]: and i'm so so so sorry i made
you feel that way
To [Solace]: i want to make you feel
brilliant
To [Solace]: because you are
To [Solace]: and i was so lucky to be with
you
To [Solace]: and so stupid to mess it up
To [Solace]: and i really want to give it
another go
```

The world's longest pause happened. And kept happening. Drew nearly ate his keyboard.

```
[Solace] whispers: So do I
```

The world's second-longest pause happened. And kept happening. This time because Drew was so unbelievably relieved and happy that he was sure he'd break everything if he said anything.

Then he thought about Kit sitting there and staring at an empty chat window. And typed the first thing that came into his head.

```
To [Solace]: oh god really?
To [Solace]: i swear i'm never going to
listen to Sanee again
To [Solace]: shit that was a joke
To [Solace]: i just mean that i
To [Solace]: its really hard to explain
To [Solace]: but i'm done worrying about what
i think other people think
To [Solace]: about anything
To [Solace]: i care what you think
To [Solace]: and about what makes us happy
```

To [Solace]: can you say something now?
To [Solace]: because this is more than i've
ever typed in my entire life
To [Solace]: including my a levels
[Solace] whispers: I believe you
To [Solace]: are we going to be okay?
[Solace] whispers: I'd like to be
[Solace] whispers: I think we will be
[Solace] whispers: Anyway, I want to try :)
To [Solace]: me too
To [Solace]: starting like right now
To [Solace]: like i think you can buy food
from that random bear person
To [Solace]: so we can have a picnic if you
like
To [Solace]: or we could like get our medusas
or something
[Solace] whispers: Actually
[Solace] whispers: I mean that all sounds
great
[Solace] whispers: But what I'd really like
is for you to come over
[Solace] whispers: I mean if you want
[Solace] whispers: It's just our skull's gone
missing
[Solace] whispers: And my bed is kind of cold
[Solace] whispers: And I've still got some
strawberries
To [Solace]: omw

GLOSSARY

Achi

Abbreviation for *achievement*. Basically, sometimes when you do something in a game, a little text box will pop up telling you that you've just done the thing you just did. This is disproportionately satisfying. And often they have amusing names.

Aggro

The attention of monsters. Traditional MMO gameplay places a high importance on making sure enemies are attacking the right people and are not attacking the wrong people. See also: tank, threat.

Alt

Abbreviation for *alternate* or *alternative character*. A character you play who is not your main. Some people have far, far too many of these, an affliction known as altaholism. See also: main.

AoE

Abbreviation for *area of effect*. These are the cool spells that let you do a thing to lots of things all at the same time. This is disproportionately satisfying.

Buff

Something that makes a character better at something. See also: debuff.

Cooldown

After an ability is used, there is usually a period of time during which it cannot be used. This period of time is called *the cooldown*. It is always longer than you would wish. This is disproportionately frustrating. Somewhat confusingly, the word can also be used to describe the abilities themselves, especially powerful abilities that have long cooldowns. This can often lead to such interesting constructions as "all my cooldowns are on cooldown."

Crit

Abbreviation for *critical hit*. This is a hit that does more damage than usual. For players of DPS characters, these are basically the only reason to get out of bed in the morning. See also: DPS.

Debuff

Something that makes a character worse at something. See also: buff.

Deeps

Abbreviation for *DPS*. More specifically, DPS is quicker to type, being three characters, but deeps is quicker to say. See also: DPS.

DKP

Abbreviation for *dragon kill points*. This is a loot distribution system dating back to the first ever MMOs. Please note, the guild in this book does not actually use it. This does not, however, stop them joking about it.

DoT

Abbreviation for *damage over time*. Something that causes a small amount of damage repeatedly for a set period. The experience of watching your enemies slowly wither away from innumerable tiny injuries appeals to a certain sort of player. See also: HoT.

DPS

Abbreviation for *damage per second*. Confusingly, the term is used both to describe the actual damage done by characters and also characters whose primary role is to deal damage. For example, "The DPS need to do more DPS." It can also be used as a verb. For example, "We need more DPS on the boss, so the DPS need to DPS the boss more."

Farming

The laborious or oddly relaxing and Zen-like (depending on who you talk to) process of collecting resources within the gameworld in order to make cool stuff. Or, more commonly, pointless stuff that you need to make five hundred of before you're allowed to make the cool stuff. See also: grinding.

Gear Check

A fight that is mechanically simple but which can only be beaten if the players have good enough equipment to survive their enemies' attacks and kill them quickly.

Greed

In loot distribution, wanting an item that you cannot use immediately, either because you wish to sell it, give it to an alt, or use it in a different spec. See also: alt, need, spec.

Grinding

Playing the same content over and over again in order to acquire money, experience, or materials with which to make cool stuff. Distinct from farming in that it usually implies content that is actually challenging. See also: farming.

Healer

One who, well, heals. Tanks, healers, and DPS form the "holy trinity" of traditional MMO gameplay. See also: DPS, tank.

HoT

Abbreviation for *heal over time*. Something that causes a small amount of healing repeatedly for a set period. Common design is for one healing class to rely more on heal over time effects than other classes. It is traditional for players of this class to enquire whether their fellow players wish their girlfriends had HoTs like them. See also: DoT.

Imba

Abbreviation for imbalanced. Generally, and counterintuitively, used as a term of approbation. Essentially, since the purpose of the game is to excel in your chosen area, performing in an imbalanced way is desirable, hence imba is good. Confusingly, OP, which has similar connotations, can be either positive or negative. See also: OP.

Instance

A self-contained bit of the game of which a unique copy will be created for each group that enters.

Kiting

Moving away from an enemy such that it cannot reach you. Ideally, either you or your allies should be killing the enemy while this happens, otherwise it is something of a short-term solution.

Line of Sight

Sometimes abbreviated to LoS. As a noun, the parts of the virtual space that a particular creature can see. As a verb, the practice of attacking a ranged weapon-wielding enemy and then moving out of that enemy's line of sight so that it will approach you, allowing you to fight it in more favourable conditions.

Macro

A means by which a complex set of commands can be tied to a single key. This has practical uses such as enabling rapid target switching or the casting of healing spells on characters you have not currently selected. It also has less practical applications such as being able to shout, "I shed the blood of Saxon men!" at a moment's notice.

Main

Your highest level and best-geared character. Strangely, people you meet in MMOs are hardly ever playing their mains, who are always much better geared than the character they are currently playing. Or than you. Or than anyone else on the server.

Mainspec

The spec you primarily play or that you play most often with your guild. See also: offspec, spec.

Mana

A resource used to cast spells. Traditionally blue. Traditionally in short supply.

Mats

Abbreviation for *materials*. Many MMOs contain elaborating crafting mechanics that allow players to manufacture a wide variety of strange and wonderful items, none of which anybody wants or has any use for. Crafting these items requires raw materials ("mats").

Melee

Not an abbreviation for anything and actually quite hard to explain without using the word. Fighting things when you are close to those things using sharp things or heavy things.

Mob

Usually an enemy. For those who are interested in the very specific etymology of video games, the term is actually an abbreviation of *mobile object*.

MT

Abbreviation for *main tank*. Usually your best-geared and most experienced tank, who will demonstrate this experience by letting the boss punch them in the face. See also: OT, tank.

Need

In loot distribution, to have immediate use for an item. That is, to be able to use it on your current character in their current spec. See also: greed, spec.

Nerf

To reduce in power or efficacy. Nerfs in MMOs offer a fine example of cultural relativism in microcosm. Nerfs directed at other people's classes are fair, proportional, and justified. Nerfs directed at your class are nonsensical bullshit and evidence that the game developers have no idea how to do their jobs properly.

Offspec

In games that allow switching between specialisations, your offspec is the specialisation with which you are less familiar and for which you have less gear. See also: mainspec, spec.

Oom

Abbreviation for *out of mana*. An unfortunate condition that afflicts healers everywhere, leads to wipes, and is caused primarily by DPS standing in fire. See also: DPS, mana, wipe.

OP

Abbreviation for *overpowered*. Used with about equal frequency as admonition and approbation. For example, "lightning spear is flat-out OP. They should nerf it" (negative). "Omg, I am loving how OP lightning spear is right now" (positive). See also: imba.

OT

Abbreviation for off-tank. Usually the second best-geared tank in a raid. The OT's job is to get hit in the face by all the things that aren't hitting the MT in the face. See also: MT, tank.

Pb AoE

Abbreviation for *point-blank area of effect*. These are slightly less cool spells that let you do a thing to lots of things all at once but only if they're standing right next to you. See also: AoE.

Proc

For those who care about video game etymology, *proc* is an abbreviation of *spec proc*, which is an abbreviation of *special procedure*. Basically a proc is a thing, usually a cool thing, that happens when something else happens. Sometimes it only sometimes happens when the other thing happens and sometimes it always happens when the other thing happens. For example, "when Unrelenting Darkness procs cast Shadow Weave" (this implies that Unrelenting Darkness only happens sometimes, and when it does happen, you should cast Shadow Weave) versus "cast Kidney Stab to proc Blood Frenzy" (this implies that casting Kidney Stab causes Blood Frenzy to happen).

PuG

Abbreviation for *pickup group*. Randomly assigned players put together by the computer to do group content. Sometimes executing tricky tactical encounters with a collection of strangers you will meet again, some of whom may not speak your language, and all of whom are restricted to communicating entirely in text, is more fun than it sounds. Sometimes it really, really isn't.

Pull

To attract the attention of a group of enemies. For the initiated, a convention of the medium is that packs of monsters will obligingly stand around, minding their own business, until the players are ready to attack them.

Raid

A large group of players, often but not always drawn from within a guild, who work together to defeat difficult group content.

Spec

Abbreviation for *specialisation*. Most classes in MMOs can be played in more than one way. Each way of playing the class is a specialisation. Some classes can spec for multiple roles (DPS, tank, healing), others can spec to do damage of different sorts or in different ways. See also: mainspec, offspec.

Solo

To kill an enemy or group of enemies with no help from other players.

Stack (1)

A number of mechanics in this kind of game are proximity related and many of them require all of the players to move close to a single player, forming a sort of giant pile of particle effects and ridiculous shoulder pads. This is called stacking.

Stack (2)

A number of buffs and debuffs can be applied multiple times, having a cumulative effect. This process is known as stacking and the number of iterations of the buff or debuff that have been applied is referred to as the number of stacks. Although this terminology can lead to confusion with the first sense of stack (see above), it is still far more effective to say, "Wait until you get ten stacks of pyroclasm," than "Wait until the pyroclasm buff has been applied ten times without any of the previous applications expiring, thus resulting in a cumulative effect ten times stronger than the original buff." See also: debuff, buff.

Tacs

Abbreviation for *tactics*.

Tank

In traditional MMO gameplay, enemies will ignore all sensible principles of warfare and strategy to focus their attentions on the least vulnerable and most heavily armoured character in the party. Players will ignore all sensible principles of warfare and strategy by arranging for damage to be concentrated on a single character rather than the burden being spread amongst the group. Somehow this works. The character, in both instances, is said to be the tank. See also: MT, OT.

Tempest

The fictional entertainment company responsible for creating and maintaining the fictional MMO played by the characters in this book. Any similarity between Tempest and the real world organisation to which it is obviously a thinly veiled reference is purely coincidental.

Threat

A game mechanical measure of how much a monster wants to murder your face off. Tank characters are good at generating threat and also good at dealing with the resultant face murdering. DPS characters should be good at mitigating threat but often aren't. They are very bad at the dealing with the resultant face murdering, which is why they should also be nicer to healers. See also: DPS, healer, tank.

Vanilla

The original version of a game before it was ruined by expansions and dumbed down for the noobs.

Wipe

The tragic but ultimately unavoidable death of everybody in a group or raid.

Dear Reader,

Thank you for reading Alexis Hall's *Looking for Group*!

We know your time is precious and you have many, many entertainment options, so it means a lot that you've chosen to spend your time reading. We really hope you enjoyed it.

We'd be honored if you'd consider posting a review—good or bad—on sites like **Amazon, Barnes & Noble, Kobo, Goodreads, Twitter, Facebook, Tumblr,** and your blog or website. We'd also be honored if you told your friends and family about this book. Word of mouth is a book's lifeblood!

For more information on upcoming releases, author interviews, blog tours, contests, giveaways, and more, please sign up for our weekly, spam-free newsletter and visit us around the web:

Newsletter: tinyurl.com/RiptideSignup
Twitter: twitter.com/RiptideBooks
Facebook: facebook.com/RiptidePublishing
Goodreads: tinyurl.com/RiptideOnGoodreads
Tumblr: riptidepublishing.tumblr.com

Thank you so much for Reading the Rainbow!

RiptidePublishing.com

ACKNOWLEDGMENTS

As always, I'd like to thank my editor, my agent, and everyone who has supported me in writing this book, particularly Eddie, Kat, and Santino for casting their nerdy eyes over it. Also, much love and gratitude to the Hassell & Hall Facebook Group for helping me with the cover.

I should also probably thank Blizzard Entertainment for creating the game on which *Heroes of Legend* is transparently based. It's not a rip-off, it's a homage. Honest.

ALSO BY
ALEXIS HALL

Spires series
Glitterland
Glitterland: Aftermath (Free download)
Waiting for the Flood
For Real

Kate Kane, Paranormal Investigator series
Iron & Velvet
Shadows & Dreams

Sand and Ruin and Gold

Prosperity series
Prosperity
There Will Be Phlogiston
Liberty & Other Stories

ABOUT THE AUTHOR

Alexis Hall was born in the early 1980s and still thinks the twenty-first century is the future. To this day, he feels cheated that he lived through a fin de siècle but inexplicably failed to drink a single glass of absinthe, dance with a single courtesan, or stay in a single garret.

He did the Oxbridge thing sometime in the 2000s and failed to learn anything of substance. He has had many jobs, including ice cream maker, fortune-teller, lab technician, and professional gambler. He was fired from most of them.

He can neither cook nor sing, but he can handle a seventeenth-century smallsword, punts from the proper end, and knows how to hotwire a car.

He lives in southeast England, with no cats and no children, and fully intends to keep it that way.

Website: quicunquevult.com
Twitter: @quicunquevult
Goodreads: goodreads.com/alexishall
Newsletter: quicunquevult.com/newsletter
Facebook Group: facebook.com/groups/HassellandHall

Enjoy more stories like *Looking for Group* at RiptidePublishing.com!

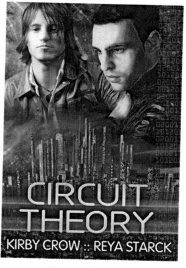

9-16

CPSIA information can be obtained at www.ICGtesting.com
Printed in the USA
LVOW07s1200110916

504132LV00007B/653/P